W9-BRD-723

Death Tidies Up

*Also by Barbara Colley
in Large Print:*

Maid for Murder

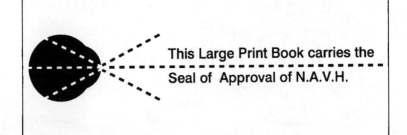

Death Tidies Up

Barbara Colley

Thorndike Press • Waterville, Maine

M
Colley
354—0885

Published in 2003 by arrangement with Kensington Books, an imprint of Kensington Publishing Corp.

Thorndike Press® Large Print Senior Lifestyles Series.

The tree indicium is a trademark of Thorndike Press.

The text of this Large Print edition is unabridged.
Other aspects of the book may vary from the original edition.

Set in 16 pt. Plantin.

Printed in the United States on permanent paper.

Library of Congress Cataloging-in-Publication Data

Colley, Barbara.
    Death tidies up / Barbara Colley.
        p. cm.
    ISBN 0-7862-5223-5 (lg. print : hc : alk. paper)
    1. New Orleans (La.) — Fiction. 2. Women cleaning
personnel — Fiction. 3. Middle aged women — Fiction.
4. House cleaning — Fiction. 5. Large type books. I. Title.
PS3603.O545D43 2003b
    813'.54—dc21   2003045258

To my mother, Doris Logan,
who has always believed in me and my dreams.

As the Founder/CEO of NAVH, the only national health agency solely devoted to those who, although not totally blind, have an eye disease which could lead to serious visual impairment, I am pleased to recognize Thorndike Press as one of the leading publishers in the large print field.

Founded in 1954 in San Francisco to prepare large print textbooks for partially seeing children, NAVH became the pioneer and standard setting agency in the preparation of large type.

Today, those publishers who meet our standards carry the prestigious "Seal of Approval" indicating high quality large print. We are delighted that Thorndike Press is one of the publishers whose titles meet these standards. We are also pleased to recognize the significant contribution Thorndike Press is making in this important and growing field.

Lorraine H. Marchi, L.H.D.
Founder/CEO
NAVH

Acknowledgments

My sincere thanks and appreciation to all who so generously gave me information and advice while I was writing this book: April Colley, my daughter; Lally Brennan and Gerald Aviles at Commander's Palace; John Mcgill and Pamela Arceneaux with the Williams Research Center in New Orleans; Mary Lou Christovich; Cheryl Harrington and her parakeet, Jazz; and my good friends and fellow writers Rexanne Becnel, Jessica Ferguson, and Marie Goodwin.

Last, but never least, my thanks to Evan Marshall, my agent, and John Scognamiglio, my editor. Their support and inspiration have been invaluable.

Any mistakes made or liberties taken in the name of fiction are solely my own.

Chapter One

The cooler, dry air was invigorating, and Charlotte LaRue sighed with pleasure as she stepped onto the front porch of her Victorian double.

The first touch of fall had finally arrived, but not without a battle. Just before midnight she'd been awakened by the clash of thunder and lightning as a cold front fought its way south. Then the rain had begun, torrents of it from the sound it had made beating against her roof. But the rain hadn't lasted long, just long enough to wash away any remnants of the heat and humidity that typically smothered New Orleans.

Of course, by the time the so-called cold front reached the city, it wasn't cold anymore. It was simply cooler. But cooler was good. She'd gladly take what she could get.

Charlotte sighed again. Today would have been the perfect day to raise the windows and air out her stuffy house. Too bad, she thought. Her aging air conditioner could use the rest, and she could use the reprieve from her outrageous electric bill as well.

But duty called. Today she had to go to work, and for the sake of security, she didn't dare leave the windows open without being there. For the first time in a long time, she'd be working through the weekend as well, but Sunday might be a possibility, if she finished up the job on Saturday.

"Probably won't last till Sunday," she muttered. Unlike other parts of the country that had a real, honest-to-goodness fall season, October in New Orleans could be as mercurial as a woman going through menopause.

Charlotte winced at the mental analogy, but she had no illusions about the source. Aging . . . menopause . . . Change of seasons. Change of life. Another year passing. And with another year, yet another birthday.

But not just any birthday. This one was the big one, the one that made her insides shrivel and tighten with dread every time she thought about it.

Turning fifty had been bad enough, a half century bad enough, including menopause and all of the clichéd jokes about being over the hill. But there was just something about even the sound of sixty . . .

Charlotte shuddered. Then, with a determined shake of her head, she lifted her chin and straightened her shoulders. She'd read somewhere that aging was a state of mind, the difference between thinking positive and negative. *You're only as old as you think.* Or maybe that was *feel? You're only as old as you feel.*

"Whichever," she murmured with a shrug. Think . . . feel . . . It didn't really matter. What mattered was concentrating on keeping a good positive attitude instead of dwelling on the negative. She should be grateful for all of the good things about her life, she thought. She had the love of her family and friends, and her health. Her maid service had grown by leaps and bounds, so much so that she'd had to expand and hire help.

Charlotte blinked several times and frowned. Her left eye itched. Though she loved this time of year, unfortunately, her allergies didn't. She reached up to rub her eye. Then, clenching her fist, she quickly lowered her hand.

Rubbing the eyes could cause wrinkles. Yet one more thing to be grateful for, she decided. Thanks to good genes, she didn't

11

have that many wrinkles. Not yet. And the bit of gray in her hair still blended naturally with the dark blond, giving it a highlighted look. Her daily walk and her line of work helped keep her physically fit — her muscles were toned, and she could still wear a size ten petite dress.

Her daily walk . . . Charlotte took a deep breath, savoring the cool air, then let it out in a sigh full of longing. Oh, how she missed her early-morning walks. There was something really special about getting out when everything was still fresh.

Yet another change. Everything changes and nothing stays the same, she reminded herself. It had been five months since she'd begun working for Marian Hebert on Mondays, Wednesdays, and Fridays. Unlike her former clients, the Dubuissons, who had been content with her showing up at nine, Marian wanted her at work by eight. At first she'd set her alarm clock an hour earlier each morning so she could still take her walk. She was not an early riser by nature, though. Getting up earlier had lasted only a week before she'd decided to content herself with walking in the evenings instead.

"Oh, well," she murmured, glancing around for the newspaper. There was no use in worrying about any of it. The only thing to do was learn to roll with the punches.

Worrying about turning sixty wasn't going to change the outcome. Whether she liked it or not, unless she died or the world came to an end, her birthday would come. And worrying about having to change her walking time wouldn't change anything either, not if she wanted to keep her newest client.

Still searching for the newspaper, Charlotte stepped closer to the front of the porch. She spotted it on the second step from the bottom. The paper was enclosed in a clear plastic bag that still held small pockets of water from the rain. She bent down, picked it up, then shook off the excess moisture. Just as she slipped it out of the plastic wrap, she heard the click of the dead bolt on the front door of the other half of her double.

"Oh, no!" she whispered, glaring at the door. Thoughts of making a run for it flitted through her head. The last person she wanted to see and the last person she wanted to see *her* this early in the morning was Louis Thibodeaux.

She still couldn't believe that she'd given in and rented out the other half of her double to him. After the last tenants she'd had, she'd decided against ever renting to anyone again. But Louis was different, and knowing his stay would only be temporary had been the deciding factor.

The house he'd owned Uptown had sold before he'd finished building his retirement home on Lake Maurepas. Once he'd finished his lake house, he would move out.

Charlotte eyed her own front door and calculated her chances. No way would she make it in time, not without breaking her neck on the slippery porch in the process. With a resigned sigh, she faced the door at the other end of the porch as it swung open.

Louis Thibodeaux was a stocky man with gray hair and a receding hairline. Though not pretty-boy handsome, he was an attractive man, in a rugged sort of way. And unlike most men his age, his belly was still nice and flat instead of hanging over his belt.

"Hey, there, Charlotte," he said. "I thought I heard you out here."

Great, she thought, wondering if her hair was sticking up all over the place and wishing she'd at least pulled on a pair of sweats instead of her old ratty housecoat.

In contrast, Louis had already showered,

shaved, and dressed, and every gray hair on his perfectly shaped head was combed and in place.

Charlotte forced a smile and held up the newspaper. "Just getting the paper." She stepped back up onto the porch. Noting that he was wearing jeans and a flannel shirt instead of his usual khaki slacks and dress shirt, she tilted her head and frowned. "You off today?"

"Today *and* tomorrow." He held up crossed fingers. "I'm just hoping that nothing major goes down to interfere."

Charlotte suppressed a shudder. Louis was a New Orleans homicide detective, and to Louis, "major" meant murder and death.

"Since Judith is showing my replacement the ropes," he continued, "I thought this would be a good time to take some vacation days."

Charlotte frowned. "Your replacement? Already? But I thought you weren't retiring until the end of the year."

"I'm not, but the end of the year will be here before you know it."

And so will my birthday. Charlotte immediately shied away from the depressing thought. "How is my niece, by the way?" Better to think about Judith than to think about turning sixty. "I haven't seen or heard from her since last Sunday."

"She's okay." He shrugged. "It's been kinda rough on her, breaking in a new partner, but hey — she's tough, and she'll survive."

Survive! Charlotte didn't like the sound of that, but before she could question Louis about it, he switched subjects on her.

"I'm glad I caught you before I left," he said. "I'll be working out at the camp for the next couple of days, but I'll have my cell phone on, just in case anything comes up. We finally got the roof on last week, so I'm ready to start on the inside. If everything goes as planned, I should be able to move by the end of next month."

Charlotte nodded but gave him a sharp look. "What exactly did you mean by 'survive'?"

His expression abruptly grew tight, and a warning cloud settled on his features. "I didn't mean anything, Charlotte. It's just an expression. The new guy will do just fine. Judith will do just fine," he emphasized. "Besides, he comes highly recommended by the brass."

The last was said with a slight edge in his voice, and that, along with Louis' expression, could mean almost anything.

"Stop it, Charlotte. Get that look off your face and stop it right now."

She narrowed her eyes. "If there's something wrong with Judith or this new partner of hers, I have a right to know, so *you* just stop it. This is my niece we're talking about, a girl I helped raise. And you and I both know that a good partner can mean the difference between life and death for a police officer."

"Judith will be just fine." He separated and emphasized each word as if he were talking to a stubborn two-year-old. "I don't have time for this right now. I've got things to do, and I'd like to get on the road before traffic backs up."

Before Charlotte could protest, he stalked past her, stomped down the steps, and made a beeline for his car.

For long seconds, she stood glued to the spot, fuming, as she watched the detective drive off down the street. Something was going on, something he didn't want to talk about. And just like a man, any time they didn't want to talk about a subject, they either headed for the sanctuary of the bathroom or they simply left the premises.

Finally, with a frustrated shake of her head, she headed inside. But as she passed her desk, she eyed the phone. "I should give Judith a call and find out for myself about this new partner of hers." She glanced up at the birdcage near the front window. "What do you think, Sweety Boy?" she asked. "Should I call her?"

The little parakeet cocked his head to one side, let out a chirp, then began prancing back and forth along the perch inside his cage, squawking out the only word he knew. "Crazy! Crazy!"

"Well, you're no help. And that's enough of that. Why can't you say something nice, something like 'good morning' or even just 'hello'?" For months she'd been trying to teach the silly parakeet to talk, but the one word that he had chosen to say wasn't among the few phrases she'd repeated over and over.

Go figure, she thought as she eyed the phone again. Just about the time she'd made up her mind to dial her niece, the cuckoo clock on the wall over her desk signaled the half hour. Six-thirty.

Charlotte glared at the parakeet, then burst out laughing. "You're right, Sweety. I would be 'crazy' to call this early." Knowing her niece, she probably wasn't even awake yet.

In the kitchen, armed with her first cup

of coffee, Charlotte seated herself at the table. She removed the Lagniappe Arts and Entertainment insert that came with each Friday's paper and set it aside to read later. Though she normally read the paper at the end of the day, she always took time to scan the headlines over her first cup of coffee.

Flattening out the rest of the paper, she began skimming the front page. When her gaze reached the bottom right-hand corner, she froze, her eyes riveted to the caption.

DUBUISSON MURDER TRIAL — JURY SELECTION TO BEGIN.

She'd known it was coming, but the shock of actually seeing it in bold print still stunned her. For long seconds, she stared at the paper, mesmerized. The five months that had passed since the scandalous Dubuisson murder evaporated like rising steam, and she blanked out everything but the horrific events behind the headline.

Like a video on fast-forward, the horrible memories unfolded in her mind in rapid succession. And she saw it all again, beginning with the day she'd first learned that someone in her former client's household had been murdered and ending with her horrifying brush with death that had finally precipitated the arrest of the murderer.

Only recently had her nightmares eased. Only within the last month had she finally stopped reliving her own near-death experience because of her association with the Dubuissons.

Charlotte shivered. When it happened, she'd been lucky that the police kept her name out of the papers. This time, though, she wouldn't be so lucky. First the jury selection, then the trial. And with the trial, the D.A. would subpoena her as a witness for the prosecution. Not only would her name be in the papers, but she'd have to relive it all again, all of it, blow by blow, the whole sordid, ugly affair.

"Wonderful," she muttered, feeling as if the weight of the world had suddenly descended on her shoulders. "Just what I needed this morning." Not only did she have her sixtieth birthday to look forward to, but now this, something else to dread.

Chapter Two

It was the trill of the telephone that finally penetrated Charlotte's morose brooding. With a frown, she shoved away from the table. An early phone call never boded well in her line of business, and usually meant trouble, a problem of some kind.

In the living room, Charlotte picked up the receiver. "Maid-for-a-Day, Charlotte speaking."

"Charlotte, this is Bitsy Duhe."

Charlotte wrinkled her nose in dismay. Why on earth was Bitsy Duhe calling her at this time of the morning? She'd just seen the old lady yesterday.

Usually she cleaned Bitsy's house on Tuesdays, but this week, Bitsy had asked her to work an extra day, so Charlotte had cleaned her house again on Thursday, which was normally her day off. Bitsy's granddaughter was coming into town for the weekend to attend a Tulane alumni class reunion, and she had wanted everything extra spiffy for her granddaughter's visit.

"Have you seen today's headlines?" Bitsy asked.

Charlotte almost groaned out loud. She should have guessed. All Bitsy wanted was to gossip. And this morning, of all mornings, Charlotte was in no mood to put up with her. But typically Bitsy, the old lady launched into a spiel without waiting for any response from Charlotte.

"I heard that Jonas Tipton is going to be the presiding judge at the trial," she said. "How that man is still sitting on the bench is a miracle. Why he's older than I am, and Margo Jones told me he's almost senile. Why, I heard that —"

"Miss Bitsy!" Charlotte sharply interrupted. "You know I would love to talk to you, but the fact is, I can't — not about this or anything else to do with the case. I'm under strict orders from the D.A. not to discuss it with anyone."

Charlotte hesitated only a moment, then, "And my goodness, just look at the time. If I don't get a move on, I'm going to be late. I'll have to call you back later, okay? You take care and enjoy that granddaughter of yours. Bye now."

Without giving Bitsy a chance to reply, Charlotte deliberately hung up the receiver. Even as she prayed that the old lady wouldn't call back, she immediately felt a twinge of guilt for her uncharitable attitude.

Bitsy was simply lonely, an elderly lady with too much time on her hands. But it hadn't always been that way. Bitsy's husband had once been the mayor of New Orleans and the couple had led an active social life, even after he'd retired. Then he'd died a few years back, and all she had left was their son and two granddaughters.

Unfortunately, Bitsy's son and one of the granddaughters lived in California, and the other granddaughter lived in New York. Bitsy, starved for human contact and companionship, had nothing better to do than to spend hours on the phone, calling around and collecting little tidbits of the latest gossip.

When Charlotte returned to the kitchen, she paused by the table and glanced again at the headline. She'd stretched the truth a bit when she'd told Bitsy what the D.A. had said. He'd actually warned her against giving any press interviews about her association with the Dubuissons.

As if she would, she thought, deeply offended by just the thought. One of the first rules she insisted upon when she hired a new employee was complete confidentiality concerning her clients. Gossiping about clients was strictly forbidden and grounds for immediate dismissal. With Charlotte, it was a matter of principle, of pride, and just good business sense that her clientele trust her and her employees.

Charlotte's gaze shifted to the article below the headline. Temptation, like forbidden fruit, beckoned. The D.A. had also cautioned her about letting anything she read or heard in the news influence her in any way. But surely it wouldn't hurt just to read a few lines. . . .

Curiosity killed the cat. Charlotte closed her eyes and groaned. Curiosity, along with disobedience, was also the ruin of Adam and Eve. Before she could change her mind, she snatched up the paper, marched to the pantry, and stuffed it into the trash can.

Besides, she thought as she pulled a box of raisin bran from the pantry shelf, her upcoming birthday was enough to be depressed about. She walked to the cabinet, set the box of cereal on the counter, then took milk and apple juice out of the refrigerator. Dredging up the whole horrible affair connected with the Dubuissons would only make matters worse.

After her bowl of cereal and glass of

juice, Charlotte checked Sweety Boy's supply of water and birdseed.

"My goodness, you've been a thirsty boy," she told him as she removed the water trough. "And hungry," she added, also removing the birdseed container.

Once both were replenished, she ran her forefinger over the little bird's velvety head. "Pretty boy," she crooned. "Say Sweety Boy's a pretty boy."

For an answer, the parakeet ducked her finger and sidled over to the narrow space between her wrist and the cage door. "Oh, no, you don't," she told him as she nudged him away from the door, then quickly eased her hand out of the cage. "I don't have time to let you out this morning." She quickly latched the door. "Tonight," she promised. "I'll let you out for a while tonight."

Having taken care of the little parakeet, Charlotte rushed through her shower, then dressed. At her dressing table, she glared in the mirror at her hair. Just as she'd figured, it *was* sticking out all over her head, and she made a face at the image in the mirror.

Staring at her hair again reminded her of Louis Thibodeaux and what he'd said about Judith. As she switched on the curling iron, her eyes narrowed. It wasn't so much what Louis had said as what he hadn't said. From his tone, he'd given her the impression that he didn't think much of his replacement, but that could mean any number of things.

She'd definitely call Judith, she decided, as she automatically began applying her makeup while waiting for the curling iron to heat. She'd definitely call her today.

Charlotte applied a touch of mascara to her lashes. Another call she needed to make was to the beauty shop. *So write it down now, so you won't forget.*

Removing the pen and small notebook she always kept in her apron pocket, she quickly jotted down a reminder. Slipping the pen and notebook back inside the pocket, she glanced again at her reflection. For now, though, she'd just have to make do.

With a sigh, she began winding strands of her hair around the warm curling iron, and as she attempted to bring some kind of order to her messy hair, she began plotting how she would worm information out of Judith about her new partner. Like Louis, her niece could also be closemouthed and evasive when it suited her.

The short commute to work each

morning was just one of the many advantages of living near the Garden District where most of her clients were located. Normally the drive to Marian Hebert's house took less than ten minutes even with the usual bumper-to-bumper morning traffic on Magazine.

Charlotte was a bit ahead of schedule until she tried to turn onto Sixth Street; there, traffic was at a complete standstill. Craning her head, she could see swirling police lights about a half a block ahead.

She glanced in her rearview mirror, but already a line of vehicles had formed and she was blocked in. With a sigh of impatience, she glanced at the dashboard clock. Being prompt was another of her strict rules, but she still had plenty of time, she decided as she drummed a staccato rhythm with her fingers against the steering wheel.

Finally, after what seemed like an eternity, the traffic began to slowly move once again. When she drove past the source of the blinking lights, her heart sank.

"And another one bites the dust," she muttered, eying the crew of men who were clearing away the debris from a huge oak limb that had split off and fallen into the street.

Between the recent drought conditions in south Louisiana and the Formosan termite invasion, the huge oaks that had shaded the Garden District for almost a century didn't stand a chance. Despite the city's all-out effort to fight the destructive insects, a lot of damage had already been done, and at times, it seemed like a losing battle.

Last night had only been a small storm, and Charlotte shuddered to think what kind of damage a full-blown hurricane might cause. So far, New Orleans had lucked out, though, and contrary to dire predictions from the weather experts, the hurricanes that had formed since June had chosen other paths to wreak their destruction.

Minutes later, Charlotte pulled up alongside the curb in front of Marian's house and parked. Though not as ostentatious as the Dubuissons' home had been, Marian's raised cottage type was just as grand in its own way. Like so many of the homes in the Garden District, it was over a century old and had been lovingly renovated as well as updated to accommodate all of the modern conveniences.

As typical of a raised cottage type, the original floor plan had been simple and consisted of four rooms, evenly arranged and separated by a wide center hall. Raised six to eight feet off the ground, the main living area was on the second level, with a staircase in front leading to the entrance.

Marian and her late husband had remodeled the home to include two large rooms across the back, one a modern kitchen-family room combination, and the other a home office. The bottom level had been turned into a master suite and a huge game room for their two sons.

From the back of her van, Charlotte removed her supply carrier. She let herself in through the front gate then climbed the steps to the porch. Just as she raised her hand to knock, the door swung open.

"Oh, Charlotte, am I glad to see you."

Immediate concern marred Charlotte's face. "Marian, my goodness, what's wrong?"

Not exactly the calm or serene type anyway, Marian looked even more flustered than usual. She was still dressed in her gown and robe, her pale face was devoid of makeup, and her, dark hair looked as if she'd spent a hard night tossing and turning.

Marian backed away from the door so Charlotte could enter. "What's not wrong would be a better question," she answered, wringing her hands. "It's days like this I really miss Bill. At times, I still can't believe he's gone," she added in a whisper.

Charlotte made a sympathetic sound. It had been nine months since Marian's husband had died in a freak accident involving a gas explosion at a house he was listing. Left with two young sons to raise, Marian now owned and operated the real estate company that had belonged to her husband before his death.

The company, according to Bitsy, had been failing miserably before Bill's death, and Bill, according to the gossip mill, had either been outright murdered or had staged an elaborate suicide to look like an accidental death in order for Marian to collect his life insurance.

Charlotte chose to believe that Billy Joe Hebert's death was simply a tragic accident. Nothing more, nothing less. The death of a loved one was hard enough to cope with without adding speculations that could do nothing but hurt the family even more, especially when there were children involved. Each time she thought about how vicious rumors and gossip could be, it left a sour taste in her mouth.

"B.J. did it again," Marian continued in

a quavery voice as she closed the door. A tear slid down her cheek. "What am I going to do about that boy?" she cried.

Chapter Three

Charlotte had only worked for Marian for five months. From the beginning, she'd discovered that the younger woman not only seemed fragile at times, but she often over-reacted to stressful situations. She'd thought Marian's wide mood swings strange at first. But judging by the various vials of antidepressants and antianxiety medications she'd found when cleaning Marian's bathroom one day, she'd decided that her employer was either bipolar or suffered from acute clinical depression.

Usually the medications kept Marian on an even keel. There had been times, though, like now, when Charlotte had smelled liquor on her breath, a definite no-no for someone with her mental problems, and to Charlotte's way of thinking, a definite no-no for anyone at eight o'clock in the morning.

Marian pulled a tissue from her housecoat pocket and dabbed at her eyes. "I'm at the end of my rope with that boy."

"Now, now," Charlotte soothed. "You're

upset right now, and when we're upset, things sometimes seem a lot worse than they really are, especially when it concerns our children."

"Oh, Charlotte, I — I just don't know." Marian shook her head. "You raised a son. Are they all so — so —" Marian threw up her hands.

"Unpredictable?" Charlotte raised her eyebrows as she filled in the blank. With a chuckle, she gave an exaggerated nod. "At times they are, along with aggravating, messy, loud, and just plain ornery, not to mention that they'll eat you out of house and home. All boys go through a rebellious stage when they hit fifteen. And girls too." Charlotte smiled, hoping to reassure the distraught woman. "Being rebellious is part of the requirement for being a teenager."

"Even Hank?"

Charlotte nodded. "Even Dr. Hank LaRue, the great surgeon." She grinned. "But don't tell him I said so. He hates it when I remind him that he's a mere mortal like the rest of us."

A tiny smile pulled at Marian's lips, just the reaction Charlotte had hoped for. Though it was true that Hank had rebelled in his own way during his teenage years, it was also true that he'd never truly caused her the kind of heartache that Marian seemed to be experiencing with B.J.

Charlotte had always considered herself fortunate. Raising a child as a single parent wasn't easy by any stretch of the imagination even under the best of circumstances. But unlike B.J., who'd at least had the benefit of having a father for the first fifteen years of his life, her Hank had never known his father.

Hank's father . . . *Don't even go there,* she told herself as she immediately slammed the mental door on the precious memories of her son's father. Opening that door only made her sad, and she was depressed enough.

"And B.J.'s no different, just a typical teenage boy," she continued. "It's just his way of coping with changing hormones." But even as Charlotte tried to reassure Marian, she was beginning to have her doubts.

"I don't remember having all this trouble before Bill — before he —" Marian swallowed hard and pressed her lips into a tight line.

Charlotte patted her on the arm. "I'm sure that's part of it. B.J. misses his father too. And I'm equally sure that some of his

34

behavior is due to coping with his loss, but he's a good boy and he's going to be okay."

"I wish I could believe that, but —" Marian shook her head. "I just can't, not when things seem to be going from bad to worse. He's failing in school, and just last week he got suspended for smoking. And now — now this!"

"This?"

Marian nodded. "He sneaked out again last night after curfew."

"Again?"

Marian waved her hand. "I caught him sneaking out once before, but this time it was the police who caught him. Did you know the police have a Curfew Center on Rampart?" Without waiting for an answer, Marian shook her head. "Well, I didn't, but I do now. I had to drag poor Aaron out of bed at midnight and go all the way over to Rampart to pick up B.J. — and that's another thing. I'm going to have to cancel and reschedule an important appointment with a new client this morning because Aaron is —"

"Mom! Hurry!"

At the sound of the plaintive cry from Marian's eight-year-old, she groaned, "Oh no, not again." Giving Charlotte a harried look, she rushed down the hallway toward the boy's bedroom. "Some kind of stomach virus," she called over her shoulder. "He's been throwing up off and on all night."

Just seconds after Marian disappeared into the boy's bedroom, Charlotte heard an awful retching sound. Poor little guy, she thought as she headed toward the kitchen. She'd have to remember to use gloves when she stripped Aaron's bed and make sure she used disinfectant when she cleaned his bathroom. The last thing she needed or wanted was to catch a stomach virus.

The moment Charlotte stepped into the kitchen, she froze. From the looks of the room, it was hard to believe that she'd left it spotless on Wednesday, just two days ago. The entire kitchen was a disaster area. The stovetop was splattered with what appeared to be spaghetti sauce and grease, and there were dirty dishes everywhere . . . on the table, strewn along the countertops, piled haphazardly in the sink.

Charlotte frowned. How on earth could just three people use so many dishes? she wondered. Then she glanced at the floor and her frown deepened. She'd swept and mopped on Wednesday and had left it shiny clean. Now the light gray ceramic tile was marred with splotches of some unidentifiable dark liquid that had been spilled in front of the refrigerator, then again near the table. No one had bothered to wipe it up, and the stuff had congealed into a gooey glob.

Only one explanation for the mess made any sense, she decided. In spite of all the medications Marian was taking, her condition was getting worse. And that, along with B.J.'s escalating behavior problems, spelled real trouble.

Wondering how Marian would feel if she suggested that they might all benefit from some family counseling, Charlotte set down her supply carrier, then shoved up her sleeves.

It took almost an hour before Charlotte finally had the kitchen back in order. Giving the room a final inspection and a nod of approval, she turned her attention to the connecting family room.

Separated from the kitchen by a row of cabinets and an island, the large room was messy but not really dirty the way the kitchen had been. After she'd straightened and dusted the room, she made a quick trip to her van to bring in her vacuum cleaner. Years of experience had taught her to use her own equipment, equipment she knew she could rely on to do the job right.

She had just shut off the vacuum cleaner when Aaron wandered in.

"Mom said if it was okay with you, I could watch Cartoon Network."

"That's fine, hon," she told him, unplugging the vacuum. "I'm finished in here anyway."

With his blond hair and blue eyes, the boy reminded her a lot of her nephew, Daniel, when he was Aaron's age. Though not as mischievous as Daniel had been, Aaron was usually rosy-cheeked, full of life, and extremely talkative. Today, though, the eight-year-old was pale and listless as he wandered over to the sofa.

"How are you feeling?"

The boy gave a one-shoulder shrug then mumbled something that sounded like, "Okay."

"Can I get you anything? Something to drink?"

He shook his head. "Mom said I couldn't have anything for a while. She's afraid I'll throw up again." From the sofa table, he picked up the TV clicker and pointed it at the television set. Sounds of Tweety Bird and Sylvester soon filled the room.

Deciding that now was as good a time as ever to clean Aaron's room, Charlotte unplugged the vacuum. Retrieving her supply carrier and dragging the vacuum along behind her, she headed down the hallway.

The little boy's room was a large one, and almost every inch of the floor was covered with either Legos, Hot Wheels, or the DragonballZ and Gundam Wing action figures that had been made famous by Japanese cartoons.

The moment she stepped inside, Charlotte wrinkled her nose against the distinctive sour smell. Since the bed had been stripped down to the mattress, and the sheets and comforter were piled in a corner, it didn't take her long to figure out that Aaron had been sick all over the bed during the night. She figured that the bedding was more than likely the source of the stench.

The pine-scented disinfectant she always used would go a long way in making the room smell better, but a good airing out would help even more, she decided, eying the large window.

The wood-framed window proved to be stubborn, but after tugging on it for several frustrating minutes, she finally got it raised. Almost immediately, a steady breeze filled the room with fresh air.

After pulling on a pair of rubber gloves, Charlotte gathered the pile of soiled bedding and clothes, then carried the bundle to the laundry room, located just behind the kitchen. While the washing machine filled with hot sudsy water, she separated the sheets from the comforter.

A large lump of something was tangled in the corner of the fitted bottom sheet. When Charlotte shook the sheet, a small teddy bear tumbled out, its dark brown furry covering matted and wet.

As Charlotte gingerly picked up the bear, she smiled. Hank had slept with a teddy bear too until he was just about Aaron's age. Her smile widened. Hank had named his bear Company, and she wondered if Aaron had given his bear a name too. She'd once asked her son why he'd named it such an odd name, and he'd simply grinned and told her that he hadn't. Then he'd reminded her that each night when she'd tucked him into bed, she'd always included the bear and told him it would keep him company, so he'd simply assumed that Company was the bear's name.

But Hank was no longer a little boy like

40

Aaron who slept with teddy bears. Nor was he a teenager like B.J. Charlotte's smile faded, and a stab of longing knifed through her. Her Hank was a grown man now, almost forty-two. *And you will be sixty in a few days.*

Charlotte swallowed hard to ease the sudden tightness in her throat as she checked the tag on Aaron's teddy bear to see if it was washable. Once she'd determined that it was, she dropped it into the washing machine with the sheets.

Cleaning Aaron's room was always a challenge. In Charlotte's opinion, the boy had been overindulged since his father's death and had enough toys for ten kids. Yet another sign of Marian's instability, she thought as she separated the Legos from the Hot Wheels and dropped them into brightly colored plastic tubs that had been placed on a low shelf against the wall.

Before Charlotte began on B.J.'s room, she returned to the laundry room and transferred the sheets and bear from the washer to the dryer. When she came out of the laundry room, the sight of Marian standing near the kitchen counter gave her a start.

"Oh, Marian." She placed her hand on her chest above her racing heart. "I didn't hear you come in."

Marian waved at the toaster and loaf of bread. "Aaron says he's hungry, and I thought some dry toast might be better for his stomach than a bowl of Cocoa Puffs. I don't want to even imagine the mess that would make if he threw it up," she added with a shudder as she removed a slice of bread from the loaf and dropped it into the toaster.

"Me either," Charlotte agreed, noting that Marian had finally dressed. An attractive woman in her late thirties, Marian was wearing a lightweight royal blue sweater and matching slacks that flattered her already slim figure.

What a difference a little makeup and the right clothes made, Charlotte thought, noting that the particular shade of blue was a perfect foil for the younger woman's dark hair and flawless, ivory complexion. "How about some oatmeal to go along with the toast?" she suggested.

Marian shook her head as she turned on the toaster. "Thanks, but not yet. Maybe later, after we see if he can keep the toast down. And, Charlotte —" She hesitated, looking decidedly uncomfortable. "I apologize for leaving such a mess in here, but the last couple of days have been pretty hectic. A terrific opportunity came up out of the blue — one of those offers too good to refuse. But I've had to really scramble to finalize the deal."

Charlotte smiled and waved away her apology. "Hey, that's why you hired me, isn't it?"

Marian didn't answer but gazed just past Charlotte to a window. "With Aaron sick, I need to make a call and cancel my luncheon appointment with Jefferson Harper," she said, clearly distracted, as if talking to herself. "Maybe I can reschedule for tonight. B.J. could stay with Aaron . . . maybe have dinner with Jefferson instead of lunch."

The toaster dinged and the slice of bread popped up, all evenly brown and crisp. Marian stared at it as if she had never seen it before. Then she shook her head and groaned. "Too many distractions," she mumbled. "And too much to do." She removed the toast and placed it on a saucer.

"Jefferson Harper," Charlotte murmured. "Hmm, why does that name seem so familiar?" But as soon as she voiced the question out loud, she suddenly remembered where she'd heard the name before. "Isn't he the nephew that inherited the old

Devilier house on St. Charles?"

Marian nodded. "That's the one. Jefferson's mother was Foster Devilier's sister. She and her husband died when Jefferson was just a young boy — a car accident I think — and Foster raised him. Since Foster never had children of his own, he left everything to Jefferson. Then about a year ago, Jefferson decided to renovate the old family home and turn it into luxury apartments. A friend of a friend recommended my firm to handle the leasing of the apartments."

"Such a small world," Charlotte murmured.

Marian frowned. "Excuse me?"

Charlotte waved a hand.

"Sorry, just thinking out loud. One of my employees has been dating the son of the man who did the Devilier renovations, and Maid-for-a-Day won the contract for the cleanup. I've scheduled the cleanup for tomorrow and Sunday. In fact, when I finish here today, I intend to go over to the Devilier house and take one last walk-through."

"No kidding?"

Charlotte grinned. "I kid you not." She stepped closer and took the saucer of toast from Marian's hand. "Now you go ahead and make that call, and I'll see that Aaron gets his toast. And what about a small glass of apple juice to go with it? We don't want him to dehydrate."

Marian nodded. "Thanks, Charlotte. And good idea about the apple juice, which reminds me — Aaron's pediatrician is another call I need to add to the list," she grumbled, clearly distracted once again. "Just to be on the safe side, I'd like for the doctor to check him over," she added, still muttering to herself as she headed toward the door that led to her office. "That's assuming that I can get an appointment."

Charlotte simply shook her head and opened the refrigerator. The poor woman just couldn't seem to get it all together this morning, she thought as she removed the bottle of apple juice.

Taking a glass out of the cabinet, Charlotte poured it full. Just as she put the bottle of juice back into the refrigerator, Marian rushed back in the kitchen.

"Oh, Charlotte," she cried, her face flushed with excitement, her eyes bright. "I just had the most fantastic idea. I've been racking my brain, trying to come up with a gimmick to advertise those apartments. Between you and me, the price Jefferson

45

wants for them is outrageous. So what if —
as an added incentive — I offered the prospective clients free weekly maid service?
That would make them even more exclusive, and the monthly rent could be
padded just a bit to absorb the cost. So
what do you think?"

If the monthly rent was already outrageous, Charlotte wasn't sure that adding
an additional fee, even if it was for maid
service, would be any more appealing. But
Marian's excitement was infectious, and a
slow grin pulled at Charlotte's lips as her
mind raced with the possibilities. As it
stood, her schedule was pretty packed
already. She'd have to hire a couple of
extra employees. But that wouldn't be a
problem, and over the long haul, the added
income might be well worth it.

"I think that's a terrific idea," Charlotte
finally told her. "But only if Maid-for-a-
Day supplied the service. Otherwise, I
think it's a terrible idea," she added with
mock seriousness.

Marian burst out laughing. "Silly
woman. Well, of course Maid-for-a-Day
would supply the service. Now, if I can just
sell the idea to Jefferson Harper — but first
I need to see if he can meet for dinner
tonight instead of lunch."

The more Charlotte thought about Marian's proposition over the next couple of hours as she cleaned, the more excited she became.

When noon rolled around, she chose to take her lunch break out on Marian's front porch. While she ate the smoked turkey sandwich and apple she'd brought along with her and savored the deliciously cool air and sunshine, she mentally weighed the pros and cons of Marian's idea.

Don't count your chickens before they hatch, a tiny, persistent voice of reason warned her. "I'm not," she muttered. "I'm simply thinking ahead." But when she pulled the notebook out of her apron pocket to do a bit of calculating, she saw the reminder she'd written earlier about calling the beauty shop, and she frowned.

She'd fully intended to call early in hopes that her beautician could work her in around the time she finished up at Marian's, but now . . .

Charlotte pulled out her cell phone and quickly punched in the number of the beauty salon.

Her call was answered on the third ring.

"Lagniappe Beauty Salon, Valerie speaking."

"Valerie, this is Charlotte LaRue —"

"Oh, hey, Charlotte. I've been meaning to call *you* — to thank you."

Charlotte frowned. "To thank me — thank me for what?"

"Not what, silly. Who. Why, none other than Mrs. Bitsy Duhe is now a regular customer of mine. She said she'd always admired the way your hair looked, and her regular hairdresser wasn't that dependable."

Charlotte rolled her eyes. Had she ever mentioned Valerie to Bitsy? She didn't remember doing so, but then lately there seemed to be a lot she didn't remember.

"And she wants a standing appointment," Valerie continued. "Every Friday morning. Isn't that terrific?"

Though she wasn't exactly sure why, Charlotte felt a bit funny about Bitsy using the same beautician that she used. But she forced an enthusiasm she didn't feel anyway. After all, it was a free country. "That's great, hon," she told Valerie. "And speaking of appointments, I need one. And I'm afraid I'm in a bind. If at all possible, I desperately need a haircut today."

"Hmm, I'm looking at my afternoon appointments here. I can probably work you in around four."

Charlotte frowned in thought. A haircut and blow-dry shouldn't take more than an hour. If she finished up at Marian's by three forty-five, she should still have enough time to check out the Devilier house before dark. "Four sounds great," Charlotte told her. "See you then."

As she slipped the cell phone back inside her pocket, Charlotte's frown deepened. Was her memory getting worse of late? Should she be concerned? What if she was going senile, or what if, heaven forbid, she was in the beginning stages of Alzheimer's? What if . . .

Stop it, Charlotte. Stop it right now.

With a shake of her head, she ripped the reminder note off the pad, wadded it up, then stuffed it in her pocket. *The new job. Think of the job Marian was talking about earlier.*

All along, even before she'd known for sure she had won the Devilier contract, she'd planned on adding the profits from the job to her retirement account. By doing the job on the weekend, she'd figured she could utilize all of her regular employees without having to hire extra help, thereby ensuring a larger profit margin.

But the Devilier job was a onetime deal.

What Marian was proposing could be a continuous income for several years to come, and would go a long way toward ensuring her financial independence.

She quickly scribbled down some numbers, calculating the amount she would need to charge. A moment later, she looked up from the number figure she'd come up with and stared with unseeing eyes at the passing traffic in front of Marian's house. For months Hank had been pressuring her to retire and let him take care of her. Though she half suspected that her son was just a wee bit embarrassed because his mother still worked as a maid, she knew that deep down, he truly had the best of intentions.

The fact that Hank could well afford to support her wasn't even a consideration. As far as Charlotte was concerned, the whole idea of retirement was simply out of the question. To begin with, she had no plans for retiring any time soon. Retire to what? What on earth would she do with herself all day long, day in and day out? Why, she'd be bored silly. But besides boredom, just the thought of *having* to depend on Hank or anyone else, for that matter, gave her the willies. Doing such a thing, in her opinion, would be the ultimate admission that she truly was getting old.

Since Marian's office was Charlotte's least favorite room to clean, she always saved it for last.

Marian seemed to have a real knack for dealing in real estate, and by all accounts had turned her husband's failing business into a profitable venture. But in Charlotte's opinion, the woman's organizational skills left a lot to be desired.

Since the very first day that Charlotte had worked for Marian, the younger woman had made it clear that nothing was to be moved around in the office, so cleaning the room was a real challenge. And dusting it was a nightmare due to the stacks of papers and mail that were piled on every available surface.

But Charlotte had learned a few tricks over the months. Each stack was dealt with on a one-by-one basis. First she'd carefully move the stack; then, after dusting and waxing the space where it had sat, she placed it in the same position she'd found it to begin with. That way, she could leave the room looking exactly the same, only clean and free of dust.

As usual, Marian was seated at the computer when Charlotte entered the office. By mutual consent, normally neither woman spoke or disturbed the other while working, so it was a complete surprise when Marian turned away from the computer and struck up a conversation.

"So far, so good," she said.

Charlotte frowned. "Pardon?"

"Aaron," Marian qualified. "Since he was able to keep the toast and juice down earlier, I gave him some chicken noodle soup and crackers for lunch, and so far, he hasn't thrown it up yet. Maybe — just maybe, the worst of this awful virus is over."

Charlotte smiled and set down her supply carrier. "We'll certainly hope so for Aaron's sake. Poor little guy."

Marian nodded in agreement. "I'm still taking him to the doctor though, just as a precaution. I was able to get an appointment for this afternoon — Oh, and by the way, I was also able to change my appointment with Jefferson Harper as well.

"Before my meeting, though, I'd like to rework my original proposal to include a rough estimate for the maid service we discussed earlier. Later, we'll draw up an official contract, of course, but what I need right now is an amount — just a ballpark figure — for what you would charge for supplying weekly service for each apartment."

Charlotte stepped closer to the desk. "I understand there are four apartments in the building. Is that correct?"

When Marian nodded, Charlotte pretended to do a quick mental calculation. After all, business was business, as Hank was always reminding her. *These people are your clients, Mother. They're not your friends.* It was a lesson she'd learned the hard way, dealing with her former clients, the Dubuissons. And, in all fairness to her son, she had to agree that it was just plain good business sense not to let a prospective client know how eager she was about a job.

With just four apartments, she'd already figured out that she'd only have to hire one additional full-time employee. She pointed at a pen and pad of paper. "May I?" she asked.

When Marian nodded, Charlotte picked up the pen and proceeded to jot down the figures she'd done earlier. The first figure she came up with was a calculation of the number of hours per week needed to service the four apartments. Then she multiplied the resulting figure by the hourly wage she normally charged a client. Built into that figure was her margin of profit, an allowance for cleaning supplies, and insurance, as well as the employee's hourly wage and benefits. Circling the final figure, she pointed at it with the pen.

"This total per week should be pretty accurate," she told Marian.

Marian stared at the figure for several seconds, then nodded. "Good. At least now I have something to work with."

When the phone jangled, both women jumped at the unexpected intrusion. Just as Marian reached for the receiver, Aaron cried out.

"Mom! I'm sick again!"

With a long-suffering but worried look, Marian shoved away from the computer and stood. "Guess I spoke too soon," she said, casting an irritated glare at the phone as it rang again. "That could be a call I'm expecting."

"Mom! Hurry!"

"I'm coming, Aaron," she yelled. To Charlotte she said, "Could you get that for me?" Then, without waiting for an answer, she rushed toward the door. "Just take a number," she said over her shoulder, "and tell them I'll call them right back."

As Marian disappeared through the door, Charlotte picked up the phone.

"Hebert Real Estate. May I help you?"

There was no response for several seconds, then . . . "Charlotte? Is that you, Charlotte?"

"Ah . . . yes. May I ask —"

"So now Marian has you answering the phone too. Or have you gone into real estate instead of the cleaning business?"

Charlotte frowned, trying to place the familiar female voice. When a mental image of a former client named Katherine Bergeron suddenly clicked into place, her frown turned into a warm smile. "No, Katherine," she answered. "I still run Maid-for-a-Day. I wouldn't know the first thing about selling real estate. But my goodness, what has it been, at least a couple of years since I've seen you? I'm amazed you recognized my voice."

"Process of elimination, Charlotte. Marian probably didn't mention it, but I'm the one who recommended you to her in the first place. We've known each other for years. Why, Bill and Marian grew up with my husband, and we were all the best of friends. Bill even once worked for my father. Then after Daddy died and Drew took over the firm, Bill worked for him as well until he decided to jump ship and form his own company."

Charlotte already knew about Bill Hebert's association with her former client, thanks to Bitsy. Once Bitsy had learned that Charlotte was working for Marian Hebert, she'd been quick to fill Charlotte in on all the gossip concerning Marian's husband. And according to Bitsy, Bill's and Drew Bergeron's parting had been a bitter one, though Bitsy didn't know exactly why.

"But, Charlotte," Katherine continued, "I would have recognized your voice anyway. You know I've never forgiven you for leaving me, especially in my delicate condition."

"Now, Katherine, that's not fair and you know it. There's no way I can work exclusively for anyone, besides which, with you threatening to miscarry and all, you needed specialized help at the time. And speaking of your former delicate condition, how is that baby girl of yours? What is she now? Almost four?"

"She'll turn four in November. And she's not a baby anymore. What she is, though, is a handful. I'm afraid I've spoiled her rotten ever since . . ."

. . . *ever since Drew's death.* . . . Charlotte mentally completed Katherine's sentence. It had been a tragic accident — Drew

Bergeron's small private plane had gone down in a storm over the Gulf of Mexico two years earlier — made even more tragic since his body was never recovered. And knowing the reason for the sudden silence on the other end of the phone, Charlotte rushed in to fill the gap. "Under the circumstances, I don't think a little spoiling will hurt her," she offered.

"Oh, Charlotte, that's what I truly miss about you. You always seemed to understand and know just the right thing to say. If it wasn't for Daisy being such a jewel, I'd try to steal you back from Marian in a heartbeat."

"I take it that Daisy is still with you then."

"Yes — yes, she is, and I can never thank you enough for recommending her. In fact, in a roundabout way, she's the reason I'm calling Marian. Daisy told me she'd heard that Marian is handling the Devilier apartments. Daisy knew that I've been looking for something to use as a guest residence for out-of-town friends during Mardi Gras and the Jazz Fest. Since those apartments are just down the block from me, they would be a perfect location. Is Marian in?"

Charlotte glanced up and was surprised to see Marian standing in the doorway.

How long had she been standing there? Charlotte wondered. How long had she been listening and watching? And why the strange look, a seething look of bitterness that was totally out of character?

Charlotte shifted uneasily, and though she averted her gaze, she couldn't shake the image of Marian's expression or the uncomfortable feeling it gave her.

Chapter Four

"Hold on a moment, Katherine, and I'll see if she can take your call."

"Thanks, Charlotte," Katherine replied, "and it's been really nice talking to you again."

"Same here," Charlotte answered. Muffling the receiver against her chest, she glanced over at Marian again. "It's Katherine Bergeron," she told her softly. "She wants to talk about leasing one of the Devilier apartments."

Several moments passed in which Charlotte feared that Marian was going to refuse the call. Finally, as if gathering her strength, Marian took a deep breath, and letting it out in a heavy sigh, she stepped over to the desk and took the receiver from Charlotte.

As Marian greeted Katherine, she was all business, her tone brisk as she paced back and forth in front of the desk.

Still puzzled by Marian's initial reaction to the call since, according to Katherine, she and Marian were such good friends,

Charlotte took her time gathering her supplies. Normally, she didn't make a habit of eavesdropping on her clients, but Marian's strange, erratic behavior worried her.

"No, I'm afraid I'm going to have to cancel our appointment," Charlotte heard Marian say. "Aaron is sick," she explained. "Just a stomach virus, I think, but I'm taking him to the doctor later this afternoon, and I expect to be tied up most of the weekend. If you want to, however, *you* could still look at the apartments on your own. B.J. should be home soon, and I'll leave an extra set of keys with him. One thing though," she added. "Right now the apartments aren't very presentable. They're a mess — construction and all of that. But if you wait until Sunday afternoon, they should be cleaned up by then."

Still puzzled but satisfied that Marian was handling things okay and not wanting to seem too obvious about eavesdropping, Charlotte chose that moment to slip out of the room. After loading her vacuum cleaner and supplies into her van, she returned to the office to let Marian know she was leaving.

She found Marian seated at the desk, her head slumped forward.

"Ah, excuse me, but I wanted to let you

know that I'm leaving now."

Marian slowly raised her head, and when she faced Charlotte and nodded, there was a glazed look of despair about her.

Charlotte stepped closer. "Are you okay?"

The younger woman gave a one-shouldered shrug that reminded Charlotte of Aaron's earlier gesture.

"Oh, Marian, what's wrong?" she asked, growing more concerned.

"It's just — I —" Marian shook her head. "Ever since Bill died, it's been a strain to even talk to Katherine. It takes everything I have to be civil. Katherine still insists on holding on to the fantasy that Bill was the one who quit working for Drew, that he resigned in order to start his own company. And she refuses to even acknowledge that the real reason Bill left the agency was that Drew out-and-out fired him. After it happened, things were never the same again between us, any of us."

When Bitsy had first told Charlotte about Drew's and Bill's relationship, Charlotte had ignored the information as simply gossip. But now it seemed as if the old lady had been right all along. It also explained Marian's initial reaction to

61

Katherine's call.

"It didn't use to be that way," Marian continued in a sad, longing voice. "There was a time when the three of us — Bill, Drew, and I — were inseparable. Then, when Drew married Katherine, we grew even closer . . . for a while. But that was a long time ago . . . an eternity."

Charlotte squeezed Marian's shoulder. "I wonder, have you ever considered that maybe Katherine truly doesn't realize what really happened, that Drew fired Bill? Maybe she only knows what her husband told her," she offered by way of explanation.

Marian simply stared at Charlotte. "Oh, I've considered it all right. At first. I even tried to set her straight about it. But ever since Drew's plane went down, she's been different. She only hears what she wants to hear, and she absolutely refuses to listen to anything negative about him. In her eyes, he was a saint." Marian laughed, a bitter sound without humor. "But I knew him long before he married Katherine. And I know what he's — what he *was* capable of. Drew Bergeron was no saint by any stretch of the imagination. But, hey —" Marian suddenly brightened, albeit assuming a facade that Charlotte recognized for what it was, a cover-up for her embarrassment. "I'm sure you have better things to do than to listen to my boring past."

Charlotte smiled gently. "Any time you need someone to talk to, my middle name is discretion." Then, to save Marian further embarrassment, Charlotte changed the subject. "I do have to get going though, but good luck with Aaron — I hope he feels better soon — and I'll see you on Monday."

After retrieving her purse from the kitchen, Charlotte stopped by Aaron's room on her way out to say good-bye. But the little boy was curled up on his bed, fast asleep.

The sleep of the angels, she thought. All little children looked like angels while they slept. How many times had she stood just inside her own little boy's bedroom and simply watched him sleep? Not enough, she decided as a heavy feeling settled in her chest. And her son was no longer a little boy but a grown man.

Unbidden, a quote from Agatha Christie popped into her mind. *One doesn't recognize in one's life the really important moments — not until it's too late.* No truer words had ever been spoken, Charlotte decided as the heaviness in her chest grew. If only she'd known then what she knew now, if she'd realized how fast the years would go by, just how soon she'd be facing her sixtieth birthday, wouldn't she have savored those moments a lot more?

Easing out of the room, Charlotte felt a tear slide down her cheek. Maybe she would have, she thought as she slowly made her way down the hall. At least she hoped she would have.

Outside, the afternoon sky was clouding over, giving the day a dreary cast that only seemed to deepen Charlotte's melancholy mood. As she trudged slowly down the narrow sidewalk to the van, it was all she could do to put one foot in front of the other. The temptation to simply go home and crawl into bed was strong. But she still had her hair appointment, and as she'd told Marian, she still had one more chore to do, one last walk-through at the old Devilier house, all before she could call it a day.

Charlotte glanced at her watch. If she hurried, she just might have enough time to do the walk-through before it got dark.

With a heavy sigh, she pulled the van keys out of her apron pocket, but just as she unlocked the door, a battered old truck pulled up behind the van.

Recognizing the white truck, she almost groaned out loud. "Great," she muttered. "Just what I need right now."

The driver's side of the truck opened. "Hey there, Charlotte. I was wondering if I'd have the pleasure of seeing you today."

Charlotte forced a friendly smile. *Careful though. Mustn't act too friendly,* she reminded herself. She'd learned early on that being discreet was the name of the game when dealing with the man approaching her.

Sam Roberts was a handyman of sorts who had been employed by Marian's husband first, then by Marian after her husband's death. If it hadn't been for the scraggly beard that Sam wore, he could have easily passed for a Willie Nelson look-alike.

But that was where any comparison between the two men came to a screeching halt. In Charlotte's opinion, Sam talked too much, for one thing. And he was loud. But it was the flirting that really got her goat. Not that she minded flirting. She'd been flirted with before and had done some flirting back, but Sam was different. She'd tried telling herself that his teasing was just his way of being friendly, but

65

every time she talked to him, he always managed to say *something* that was just off-color enough to be offensive and make her really uncomfortable.

Now be nice, Charlotte, her conscience cautioned.

Charlotte had always been the type of person to look for something positive about everyone she met, and she had to admit, albeit grudgingly, that Sam had his good points too. According to Marian, he'd proven to be indispensable since Bill's death. And in all fairness, he worked hard and was good at his job. He also appeared to really care about Marian and her boys. From what she'd observed, he was always patient and kind to the boys despite Aaron's endless questions and B.J.'s sullen ways. And come to think of it, she'd noticed a marked difference in B.J.'s rebellious attitude any time that Sam was around. The teenager actually seemed to admire Sam, even look up to him. The good Lord only knew, the boy needed *someone* he could respect.

"So how's everything going with you, pretty lady?" Sam's dark eyes slowly raked her from head to foot, then back again. "Got everything under control . . ." His words trailed away suggestively. "Everything's all neat and tidied up as usual? Up at the house?" he finally added.

His inference was offensive and Charlotte responded with chilly politeness. "Everything's just fine *up at the house*."

Sam grinned knowingly. "Now, Charlotte, if you'd be nicer to me, I might be persuaded to take you out on the town and show you a good time." He waggled his eyebrows, *à la* Groucho Marx. "Hey, a little jazz, a little razzmatazz . . ." He held out his arms and shuffled his feet, executing an intricate dance step. Then, without warning, he suddenly grabbed her. Before she could utter a protest, he whirled her around, and it was either follow him or stumble over her own feet. When she finally did open her mouth in protest, he abruptly stopped and released her, and Charlotte swallowed her protest.

In an instant, he grew sober, and a stilted expression came over his face as he took a step backward. "Or maybe *madame* would prefer something a bit more cultured around our fair city," he said in a pseudo cultured voice. Bending forward at the waist in a mock formal bow, he continued. "A museum? Or the symphony? Or perhaps the opera?" He suddenly smirked. "If we had an opera, that is," he added.

The whole thing had happened in a matter of moments, and Charlotte was still trying to recover from the shock of it all. He'd asked her out before, and she suspected that he already knew that her answer would always be no. He simply wasn't her type. Still, he asked every time he saw her.

Gathering her wits about her, she forced a saccharine smile. "Thanks for asking, but no thanks. Now, if you'll excuse me —"

He slapped his hand over his chest in an overly dramatic gesture. "Oh," he groaned. "You wound me deeply, fair lady."

"Yeah, right!" she retorted, unable to suppress the sarcastic rejoinder. "Sam Roberts, you're about as full of baloney as they come." The man was incorrigible and outrageous to boot. "Now — if you'll excuse me — I have places to go and things to do."

Sam threw back his head and roared with laughter. "That's what I like about you, Charlotte. You say what you mean and mean what you say — but here, let me get that door for you."

With one hand he opened the door of the van, and with his other hand, he made a wide sweeping arc. "Your carriage awaits, milady."

Charlotte stiffened, not sure of what to expect next, but she wasted no time climbing inside the van. To her relief, Sam simply shut the door.

"You take care now, Miss Charlotte," he told her, with a mock salute. "See ya next time."

Not if I see you first, Charlotte thought as she drove away.

Though Charlotte had good intentions, it was almost six before she finally pulled into the small parking lot behind the Devilier house. When she'd arrived for her hair appointment, Valerie was still busy with another customer and she'd had to wait a precious twenty minutes for her turn. Then she'd gotten stuck in a traffic jam, thanks to a malfunctioning traffic light and the usual Friday five o'clock rush of commuters trying to get a jump start on the weekend.

The parking area behind the Devilier house took up about half of the back property, and Charlotte estimated that it was just large enough to accommodate eight to ten vehicles.

The other half of the backyard had been turned into a small garden area, an oasis landscaped with azaleas, sweet olive, small

69

palms, and night-blooming jasmine.

At the edge of the parking lot was a magnificent live oak that had to be at least a hundred years old judging from its size alone. The oak offered shade both to the parking lot and to the garden.

As Charlotte admired the old oak, she wondered if the tree was a member of the exclusive Live Oak Society. It always made her smile when she thought about the unusual club where membership requirements were based on the age and size of the oak, and dues consisted of forty-five acorns a year.

"Nowhere but New Orleans," she murmured.

Charlotte's smile faded. Time was a-wasting. It was already twilight, and soon the twilight would fade into darkness. For safety's sake, Charlotte didn't like the idea of being caught all alone in the big old empty house after dark.

Vince Roussel, the owner of the construction company in charge of the renovation, had given her a master key. With the house key firmly in one hand and her car keys in the other, she locked the van and hurried to the back entrance of the house.

Thank goodness enough light poured in through the fanlight above the door for her to see, Charlotte thought as she stepped into the back hallway. Roussel had assured her that the electricity and the water would be turned on by the time her crew came in for the cleanup, but the moment she was inside, she tested the light switches just to make sure. Charlotte breathed a sigh of relief when lights in the dim entrance hall came on.

"Awesome," she whispered, as her eyes swept over the wide hallway. The Devilier house on the outside was a wonderful specimen of the Greek Revival era. Charlotte had been in many magnificent homes over the years she'd worked in the Garden District, but even with the thick layer of sawdust and dirt that seemed to cover every available surface, the inside of the Devilier renovation was a thing of beauty with its high ceilings, the crystal chandeliers, and the intricately molded ceiling medallions and cornices.

In keeping with the luxurious ambience of the house, along one wall was an Empire chaise longue upholstered in a bluish-green brocade with dark gold trim. Two matching, gilded lyre-back chairs flanked a small marble-top table on the opposite side. On top of the table was a gorgeous Tiffany-styled lamp.

Charlotte frowned. Why on earth had they already delivered the furniture, especially the lamp? All of that should have been delivered after her crew cleaned up. She swiped her finger along the back of the chaise longue. At least it was protected with a clear plastic wrap. Good thing it was, since the dust was as thick as mud. Her gaze strayed to the lamp again. She'd have to caution her crew to be careful around that lamp. It looked expensive, and she didn't want to have to replace it if someone got careless and broke it.

Eager to explore the rest of the house, and ever conscious of time passing, Charlotte dropped the keys in one side of her apron pocket and removed her notebook and pen from the other side.

The downstairs was divided into two small apartments, each almost identical and each consisting of a bedroom, a bathroom, and a combination living area and small galley-type kitchen. What truly impressed her and surprised her was the luxuriousness of each apartment. As in the grand entrance hall, great care had been taken to preserve and restore the original structure, and the workmanship was superb.

As she toured the first downstairs apartment, she was relieved to note that though it was certainly dirty, the cleanup work would be mostly routine stuff. And if the rest of the apartments were like the first one, there was a good chance that most of the work could be completed on Saturday. She might not need the crew for Sunday too, which would mean more money in *her* pocket.

Judging by the looks of the living room, the degree of cleaning needed in the second downstairs apartment was much the same as the first. Except this one had mosquitos, she thought as she swatted at one buzzing her head then slapped at one that bit her ankle.

With a frown of annoyance, she glanced around. Where were they coming from? she wondered as she walked over to the windows in the living room.

Both windows in the living room were closed and locked, though, and it was in the bedroom that Charlotte finally located the entry source of the pesky insects. There was one lone window in the room, and not only was it raised a couple of inches, but the outside screen was missing as well.

On her pad, Charlotte jotted down a note to call Vince Roussel about the missing screen and the open window.

Once Charlotte had finished her inspection downstairs, she climbed the wide spiral staircase to the second floor. At the top landing she made a quick note to report a deep gouge in the wood on the sixth step that needed repairing.

Like the downstairs, the second floor was also divided into two apartments. The first one she walked through had the same layout as the two on the bottom floor, and again, she figured that the cleanup would be routine.

Because of the open window on the first floor, Charlotte made sure she checked all of the windows before doing her tour of the fourth and final apartment.

As she checked the last window in the bedroom, she suddenly realized that the very thing she'd feared had already happened. Twilight was gone, and darkness had set in for the night.

Even as an uneasy feeling crawled through her, Charlotte hurried across the hall to the final apartment. The moment she entered the apartment, though, she forgot about the dark, forgot about everything.

"What on earth?" she exclaimed as she stared at the living area.

Chapter Five

Unlike the other three apartments, the fourth had more in it than just grime and dust.

Several empty beer bottles littered one of the windowsills, and below the window on the floor there were a couple of empty food sacks, one from McDonald's and one from Popeye's. Besides the food sacks, a collection of wadded-up napkins and dirty plastic eating utensils also littered the floor.

Charlotte felt a sudden chill as she recalled the missing screen and open window downstairs. Had someone broken into the house or was the trash simply an oversight of the construction crew?

Even if there was an intruder, theft couldn't have been the motive, since there was nothing to steal . . . except the Tiffany lamp. Besides, a thief wouldn't take the time to eat and have a beer. She also dismissed the idea of vandalism. As far as she could tell, nothing had been damaged and there was no graffiti on the walls.

Though still a bit uneasy, Charlotte admonished herself for her overactive imagination. "You've been reading too many mystery novels again," she mumbled. The trash was more than likely left by the construction workers. Nothing more and nothing less.

Even so, the uneasy feeling grew as she walked into the bedroom. One look at the small room was all it took to dismiss the possibility that workers had left the trash behind.

In the middle of the dirty floor was the distinct outline of a large rectangular area that was relatively free of dust, just the right size for a sleeping bag, and there were even more beer bottles and food sacks strewn about. To Charlotte, it looked suspiciously like someone had been staying there, camping out.

Like most large cities, New Orleans had its share of homeless people, and though Charlotte hadn't witnessed any hanging around the Garden District, she didn't dismiss the possibility that one could have migrated from the Quarter to the Garden District. And what better place to take up residence than in an empty house?

After checking the windows to make sure they were all locked, Charlotte went into the bathroom. "Now that's odd," she muttered as she stared at a smear of something in the vanity sink that looked suspiciously like dried toothpaste.

Did homeless people brush their teeth? Somehow the picture of a tattered, dirty man brushing his teeth didn't quite fit the image she'd always had of a homeless person. But even more disturbing, she wondered if whoever was camping out in the house would return. She truly hoped not, at least not while she was there all alone.

Still, the thought that the intruder could return any minute chased her all the way down the stairs and out into the dark night. Only when she was once again safely locked inside her van and driving down St. Charles Avenue did she feel even a modicum of safety.

Whom should she call? she wondered as she slowed to a stop for a traffic light. Vince Roussel, Marian, or the police?

If Louis was home, she could ask him.

And since when did you start needing Louis' advice anyway, or any man's advice, for that matter?

Charlotte sighed deeply. Though she'd had her qualms about renting out the other half of her double to the detective, she had to admit it had been nice to know there was a man living next door. But not just any man. Louis could be exasperating at times and they'd butted heads on more than one occasion due to his chauvinistic attitude, but he was a man of principle, a man she could trust, a man she could learn to care about. . . .

The traffic light turned green. Suddenly uncomfortable with the direction of her thoughts, Charlotte felt like squirming in the seat. On more than one occasion, her niece had taken delight in teasing her about her relationship with Louis Thibodeaux simply because she'd expressed her distaste for the man.

Or could it be that you like him a little too much? Judith's teasing accusation played through her mind. Was her niece right about her feelings for the detective? Charlotte felt her face grow warm at just the thought.

"Ridiculous," she muttered. "I'm too old for such nonsense anyway." Besides, even if she'd had *those* kinds of feelings or thoughts about Louis Thibodeaux, he didn't feel that way about her.

And why would he after you told him off?

Charlotte still cringed each time she thought about that awful scary night. Even so, he'd deserved every scathing word she'd thrown at him. She'd caught his killer for him, then he'd treated her like a child who didn't have sense enough to come in out of the rain. To top it off, he'd purposely led her to believe that he was arresting her for interfering, just to teach her a lesson.

But she'd called his bluff and won, and since that night, they'd settled into an uneasy truce.

No, she thought. Louis Thibodeaux was the last person she'd ask advice from. But she could call Judith. She'd meant to call her anyway to grill her about her new partner, so this would be a good excuse.

Charlotte braked upon approaching her house. When she turned into her driveway, for a brief moment, her headlights flashed on the front porch. "Speak of the devil and he appears," she murmured. There, sitting in the dark on her front porch swing, was the very man who had been the center of her thoughts.

A bit disconcerted, Charlotte swallowed hard as she pulled under the carport. She switched off the engine, then gathered her purse.

"Getting home kind of late, aren't you?" Louis called out when she rounded the corner of the porch.

Detecting just the slightest hint of censure in his tone, Charlotte felt her temper rise in response. Whatever time she chose to come home was really none of his business.

You're overreacting, a little voice whispered in her head. *And you're just tired.*

She *was* tired, she suddenly realized. Weary to the bone. Too weary to spar with Louis Thibodeaux. Ignoring the detective's question, she asked one of her own as she trudged up the steps. "How's the house coming along? I figured you'd still be working on it late tonight."

"I ran into a snag and left early," he told her. "The Sheetrock and paneling were supposed to be delivered early this morning — or so I thought. After a few calls, I found out different. Now they aren't being delivered until tomorrow afternoon." He shook his head. "It's times like this that I wish I had a truck. If I'd had a truck, I could have gone after the stuff myself."

"That's too bad."

"Tell me about it. But hey, the day wasn't a total loss. Since there wasn't much point in hanging around the camp, I was able to stop off at Home Depot and pick up some tile and carpet samples, and some brochures on cabinets and fixtures. And — I might add — I had time left over to cook up a fresh pot of seafood gumbo. Have you eaten supper yet?"

"Supper? Ah . . . Why, no — no I haven't."

"Well, I make a mean gumbo, but I never figured out how to make just a little. I've got enough in there to feed the whole neighborhood. So how about it?"

The backhanded invitation caught her completely off guard, and Charlotte hesitated. *So what's the problem, Charlotte? He's only asking you to share a meal with him.*

The problem was Louis Thibodeaux. And the problem was her mixed emotions concerning the aggravating man.

But food was food, and there was nothing she liked better than a good seafood gumbo, so Charlotte forced her lips into a smile. "Let me get this straight. Are you inviting me to eat supper with you, or are you offering me leftovers?"

Louis chuckled. "Since I haven't eaten either, there are no leftovers yet, so I guess that means I'm inviting you to eat supper with me."

"In that case, give me about ten minutes and I'll be over. I should check my answering machine," she explained, "and I promised Sweety I'd let him out of his cage for a while tonight."

"Sure, no problem. I still need to warm the French bread and heat up the gumbo anyway." Louis shoved out of the swing and stood. "And speaking of that bird, how is the savage little beast?"

A smile pulled at her lips. "Aw, come on now. You're not still holding a grudge, are you?"

"Nope, but it will be a cold day in — Let's just say I won't be sticking my finger back inside his cage again any time soon."

Louis' remark made her grin. The first time he had been introduced to Sweety Boy, the little bird had taken an instant dislike to him. To Charlotte's acute embarrassment, Sweety had attacked the detective and tried to bite a plug out of his finger. The only excuse Charlotte could come up with for the bird's behavior was that something about Louis must have reminded Sweety of his previous owner, a deadbeat tenant Charlotte had rented to. The tenant had not only mistreated the little parakeet but had trashed the place before skipping out on Charlotte without paying the two months' back rent he'd owed her.

Louis snickered. "I'm tempted to buy a

cat and let him loose inside, just to aggravate the little sucker," he continued.

Charlotte gave him her sternest look. "That would be grounds for immediate eviction."

"Hey —" He threw up his hands. "Just kidding."

Charlotte nodded. "Good. Now, is there anything I can bring over when I come?"

He shook his head. "Nope. Just bring yourself."

"Be there in ten then," she said. With a parting nod, she walked briskly to her front door, and Louis headed toward his side of the double.

As she unlocked the door, she wondered if she had time to take a quick shower. After working all day, then tramping through the dusty Devilier house, she felt as if she were carrying around half the dirt in the world.

All of her life, Charlotte had been blessed with the ability to accomplish a lot in a short space of time. Some called it having good organizational skills, and most of the time she considered it a plus, especially in her line of work. But at other times, like now, when she was dog tired, she considered it a curse, simply because her mind never stopped categorizing and organizing.

She'd told Louis ten minutes. Would that be time enough? "Why not?" she muttered. Since she didn't have to wash her hair, she could be in and out of the shower in five minutes . . . if she hurried. Checking her messages could wait until after supper, she decided. That way, once she'd checked them, she could go straight to bed.

The moment she entered the house, Sweety Boy burst into a series of chirps and whistles as he pranced back and forth on the perch in his cage. It was his usual routine, one meant to attract her attention.

"As for you" — she shook her finger at the little bird — "just be patient a few minutes longer, and I'll let you out when I leave again."

"When you say ten minutes, you mean ten minutes," Louis told her at the door. "And you changed clothes —" His eyes narrowed. "Don't tell me you took a shower too — not in just ten minutes."

Charlotte shrugged. "Okay, I won't tell you."

With a chuckle, he motioned for her to come inside. "That has to be a record of some kind, especially for a woman."

Charlotte was able to bite back the sharp retort that came to mind, and she did her best to ignore his chauvinistic remark, but only because she was curious and much more interested in what he'd done in the way of decorating his half of the double than in chastising him.

It was the first time she'd been in the half he was renting since he'd moved. Though she'd rented it to him furnished, she noted that he'd added several pieces of his own furniture — a well-worn recliner, a bookshelf, and a gun cabinet — along with some paintings and sculptures. And it was hard to miss the large-screen television and state-of-the-art stereo system that took up almost a complete wall.

But the paintings were what really interested her. All but one, which was a portrait of a young girl, were magnificent wildlife scenes. Though the identity of the angelic child certainly stirred her curiosity, she was equally fascinated by the wildlifes.

She walked over to one in particular that depicted a Louisiana swamp scene. The artist had used various shades of grays, greens, and browns to capture just the right mood and essence of the murky, still waters of the swamp and the cypress trees dripping with lacy gray moss.

"These are breathtaking," she told him. "And so realistic," she added. Then she noticed the signature in the lower left-hand corner, and she frowned. "S. Thibodeaux. Any relation?" she asked.

Louis nodded. "My son."

"Your son painted these? I didn't realize you had children." Or even a wife, for that matter, she silently added.

"I don't," he retorted. "Not anymore."

Charlotte frowned. "You don't?" What on earth did that mean? she wondered as a sinking feeling of dread filled her. Was his son dead?

"What happened? An accident?" The second she asked, she immediately wished she hadn't. For a fleeting moment, so fleeting that she almost missed it, his dark eyes radiated pain and something else she could only describe as torment. Then, as if she'd dreamed it, the look was gone, replaced by a mask that was devoid of emotion.

"Sorry," she quickly added. "It's really none of my business." Though she'd often wondered if he'd ever been married or had a family, she'd never felt comfortable enough around him to just come right out and ask . . . until now. Of course it didn't necessarily follow that just because he had a child, he had to have a wife. After all, she'd never been married, but she had a son.

"No, it's not any of your business," he told her bluntly. "And I *don't* like to talk about it," he added, glaring at her as if daring her to contradict him.

"Sometimes talking helps," she suggested softly.

"Not this time — and not to you. If I want to talk, I'll go to a shrink — a professional. Last time I checked, you don't qualify." He stared hard at her for several heartbeats. Then, abruptly, he sliced the air with his hand, motioning toward the kitchen. "The bread should be ready by now, so we can eat. What would you like to drink?"

Well, I guess he told you, Miss Busybody. Charlotte's cheeks burned with embarrassment and his rude comments stung. If he'd thrown cold water in her face, he couldn't have stunned her more, and suddenly, just the thought of having to sit through a meal with him was intolerable.

Chapter Six

The next few moments were the most awkward that Charlotte had experienced in a long time. She desperately wanted to leave, and she would have, in a heartbeat, but pain and loss were things she understood all too well. She too had lost people she'd loved. She too had lashed out at those around her because of her losses. And even now, so many years later, at times, the pain was still unbearable.

She drew in a deep breath and lifted her chin. "I'll just have water, please." Without waiting for a response, she turned and walked purposefully toward the kitchen.

The moment she stepped inside the kitchen, the wonderful aroma of French bread warming in the oven assailed her. Bread of any kind was her Achilles' heel, but she especially loved fresh French bread.

The kitchen itself was neat and orderly, and she noted that Louis had already set the table, complete with place mats, matching napkins, silverware, and beautiful china.

Would wonders never cease? she thought. And what a contradiction. Never in a million years would she have guessed that the gruff detective could be so . . . so civilized.

While Louis busied himself taking the bread out of the oven, Charlotte seated herself at the table and tried to think of some safe, neutral topic that would end the strained silence between them.

"These dishes are beautiful," she ventured. "I've always loved this particular rose pattern."

His only reaction was a dismissive shrug and what sounded like a grunt.

What now? she wondered, glaring at his back. With a sigh of impatience, she glanced around the room. Then she saw it. Stacked haphazardly on the countertop, near the back door, she spied what she hoped would be just the thing to end the awkward tension between them.

"Are those the carpet and tile samples you mentioned earlier?"

When he finally glanced over his shoulder, she tilted her head toward the countertop.

"Yeah, they are," he answered.

"Mind if I look through them? I've been thinking about doing some renovations," she quickly added, since she certainly didn't want him to think that she was being nosy . . . again.

"Actually —" He slipped the hot bread into a small wicker basket. "I had an ulterior motive for inviting you to supper. I was hoping I could persuade you to give me some pointers. I figured that since you've been in so many different houses, you'd know which types of tiles or carpet were the best to use, and which types require the least amount of upkeep."

Feeling as if she were walking on eggshells, Charlotte ventured a small smile. "Ah-ha! The truth finally comes out. So that's why I get a free meal."

Her ploy to ease the tension worked like a charm. The strained look on his face faded.

"*After* we eat, though," he said as he brought the basket to the table and set it down near the edge. "Sorry I don't have a salad, and I thought we'd just serve ourselves from the pot if that's okay with you."

"Hey, I'm for whatever is easiest," she told him.

At the stove, Charlotte spooned a generous helping of rice into her bowl. The gumbo was a dark, rich color, and as she ladled it over the rice, she noted that it was chock-full of shrimp and crabmeat. "This looks delicious," she commented.

Seated back at the table, Charlotte helped herself to the bread. Still warm from the oven, the bread was exactly how she liked it, crunchy on the outside and soft on the inside.

When Louis finally joined her, he brought her a glass of ice water, along with his own bowl of rice and gumbo.

"So — why were you so late getting home?"

It was a good thing that Louis' question caught her with a mouthful of bread. Otherwise she might have been tempted to tell him that it was none of *his* business and let him see how it felt.

But getting back at someone was not her way, and she had always tried her best to live by the golden rule. Besides, since he'd asked, why not take advantage of the situation? Why not tell him what she'd discovered at the Devilier house. That way she could get his reaction without really asking for his advice after all.

Charlotte finally swallowed the bread. "You know that old Devilier house that's been renovated into apartments?"

He looked up and his expression grew hard. "Yeah. What about it?"

Though she thought his reaction was a bit odd, she explained. "I submitted a bid for the cleanup and won the contract. We're scheduled to start early tomorrow morning, so after work today, I went over there to look things over."

"So Roussel and his bunch are finally done there."

Charlotte nodded, puzzled by his contemptuous tone.

"Well, that's a relief! I say good riddance to bad rubbish."

"I — I'm afraid I don't understand."

"What's to understand? That whole crew is nothing but a bunch of thugs and troublemakers. Most of them have rap sheets as long as your arm. And Roussel and that delinquent son of his are the worst of the lot. They're nothing but trash, Charlotte. Does Judith know about this contract of yours?"

Charlotte slowly shook her head. "Why, no. But I don't make a habit of checking out my clients with my niece," she replied curtly.

"Well, maybe you should, especially considering your recent track record."

Every defensive bone in Charlotte's body

stiffened. "If you're referring to the Dubuissons, you can —"

Louis raised his hands. "Sorry! Guess that was a pretty cheap shot."

Charlotte narrowed her eyes. "Yes, it was," she snapped.

"Hey — I said I was sorry. But seriously, Charlotte —" He lowered his hands to the table and leaned closer. "You really shouldn't be dealing with the likes of Roussel."

"But he seemed like such a nice man," she stressed.

His lips tightened into a grim line. "Well, he's not. But you don't have to take my word for it. Ask Judith. She'll tell you the same thing."

"Oh, no," she whispered, as a sinking feeling settled in the pit of her stomach. "Poor Cheré."

Noting Louis' bewildered look, she explained. "Cheré Warner is one of my employees — a bright young woman working her way through school. Anyway — she's been seeing young Todd. It was through her connections that I knew about the bids going out for the cleanup to begin with."

"Well, she couldn't be too bright if she's hooked up with Todd Roussel."

"I'll have you know that she's a lovely girl. She's dependable, smart, and has —"

"Okay, okay. I get the picture. But if you care so much about this Cheré person, you'd better warn her to steer clear of the Roussels. We're talking Mafia ties here — the kind of men that nice girls run from if they know what's good for them. And believe me, Vince Roussel is in up to his eyeballs. We've never been able to prove anything — not and make it stick — but we've been after Vince for years."

"But just because you believe the father is shady," she argued, "that doesn't necessarily mean that the son is part of it."

"Not just shady, Charlotte. Corrupt! Through and through. As for his son, he's nothing but a rich-boy hoodlum. He already has a juvy record. And if you ask me, I say a rotten apple never falls too far from the tree."

"Guilt by association," she challenged.

"Well," he drawled, "you know the old saying about birds of a feather."

"That's ridiculous. Todd can't help what his father is."

"No — no, he can't, but there's another saying too, something about children learning what they live."

Charlotte didn't want to believe it, didn't

want to think that Cheré would have such poor judgment in men. But she was a realist too, and she knew that even the brightest, most intelligent women were sometimes fooled into falling for the wrong men.

"Charlotte, all I'm saying is that your friend needs to be warned. If you really care about her, just urge her to be cautious."

Charlotte nodded, but during the rest of the meal, as she tried concentrating on eating the gumbo, she kept thinking about what Louis had said. The gumbo tasted just fine, and in fact, was surprisingly good, almost as good as her own. But Louis' revelation about the Roussels had succeeded in chasing away any appetite she'd had. Though she managed to eat what was in her bowl, her concern for Cheré took all of the enjoyment out of the meal.

To Charlotte, her employees were like an extension of her family. And Cheré in particular was dear to her heart. She'd long admired the young woman's spunky approach to life. Like herself, Cheré hadn't had an easy time of it, but had made the most of what life had dealt her.

Once they had finished, to her relief,

Louis quickly cleared the table. Then he dragged out every sample of tile and carpet that he'd collected, along with several brochures on cabinets, kitchen appliances, and bathroom fixtures.

"Why don't you show me what appeals to you?" she suggested. "Then I'll try and give you the pros and cons about it."

"I think I'd rather see what appeals to you first," he countered.

Charlotte stared at him thoughtfully for a moment. Then she narrowed her gaze and a shrewd smile pulled at her lips. "You haven't picked out anything yet, have you?"

A sheepish look came over his face. "Caught red-handed," he admitted. "But I like how your place looks," he hastened to add. "It's comfortable but nice without being fussy."

"Fussy?"

Louis waved a dismissive hand. "You know, frilly, woman-type stuff."

She was certain that in his mind, he thought he was paying her a compliment, and though she wanted to point out how chauvinistic he sounded, she held her tongue and tried not to take offense.

Going through the samples and brochures did serve a good purpose, though.

Not only did she get some ideas for updating her own home, but it took her mind off the disturbing revelation about the Roussels and provided a brief diversion from her concerns for Cheré.

When Charlotte returned to her own half of the double, the cuckoo clock was signaling the hour. "Great," she muttered, when she realized that it was already ten o'clock. "That's just great," she added tiredly.

All too soon, it would be time to go to work again . . . to the Devilier house. As she locked her front door, it suddenly hit her that she never had told Louis about the open window or the intruder.

"Tomorrow," she told Sweety Boy, who was perched on his favorite spot on top of the cuckoo clock. "I'll call Marian and report it tomorrow."

But Sweety ignored her and continued squawking with each sound the cuckoo made. "Not that you care, huh, you little rascal?" Charlotte shook her head and laughed. She'd long suspected that the silly little parakeet thought the cuckoo was a real bird, but what she couldn't figure out was if Sweety was jealous or simply starved for companionship.

While she listened to her phone messages, she coaxed the little bird back into his cage. Once she'd covered him for the night, she prepared the coffeepot and set the automatic timer. The last thing she always did before climbing into bed was brush her teeth and wash her face, and tonight was no exception, despite her exhaustion.

She'd told her crew to meet her at the Devilier house at seven Saturday morning, so she set her alarm clock for five-thirty, figuring that an hour and a half would give her plenty of time to go through her regular morning routine. Then she automatically picked up the book sitting beside the clock.

There were few things she enjoyed more than burying herself in a good mystery novel, and she tried to make time to read at least a little each night at bedtime.

But not tonight, she decided as the words blurred and swam before her eyes after she'd read only a few lines. With regret, she placed the book back on the table. Just as well, she thought. Five-thirty would come around all too soon.

Once she'd switched off the bedside lamp, she snuggled down in her bed. Though faintly, she could hear music coming from Louis' half of the double, and she smiled when she recognized an old Righteous Brothers song. She and Louis might disagree on a lot of things, but evidently, one thing they had in common was their choice in music.

She was just drifting off when Louis' words about Todd Roussel intruded. *He's nothing but a rich-boy hoodlum.* Again she thought of Cheré and wondered what, if anything, she could do.

Then the song ended, and within seconds, yet another one she recognized all too well began. Charlotte felt her throat grow tight as she listened to the familiar lyrics, a sad song full of longing . . . of lovers separated yet hungering for each other.

For her, it had been a lifetime of hungering for someone she could never have. There was no wondering if *he* was still hers. And it did no good to wait for him. A terrible war in Asia and death had ended her wait . . . forever.

Chapter Seven

On Saturday morning, Charlotte was still a bit uneasy when she unlocked the back door to the Devilier house. Before she left home, she'd called Marian and told her about the missing screen and the raised window, as well as the evidence she'd found that indicated someone had been camping out in the old house.

Marian hadn't seemed concerned in the least. She'd quickly assured Charlotte that *if* someone had been staying in the house, they weren't there anymore. Marian had said that she knew for a fact that Katherine Bergeron had gone by around eight the night before to check out the apartments, and Katherine hadn't mentioned finding anyone there then.

Taking a deep breath for courage, Charlotte stepped just inside the Devilier entrance hall. For several seconds she stood perfectly still and listened for any sounds of life in the old house. But there was nothing. No squeaking floorboards, no footsteps. Nothing at all.

Charlotte hesitated a moment longer. Then, as an added precaution, she cupped her hands on either side of her mouth and shouted out, "If anyone's here, you'd better leave now!"

Her voice echoed throughout the cavernous hallway, and then there was silence. Still a bit uneasy, but somewhat satisfied that she'd given fair warning just in case someone was still lurking around inside, she backed out of the entrance hall and firmly pulled the door shut. All she could do now was hope that if anyone was hiding out, they would leave the same way they got in. With one last backward glance at the door, she walked purposefully to the patio table in the small garden to wait for the rest of her crew. While she waited, she stared at the back of the old house and debated whether or not to tell her crew about the possibility of an intruder. She didn't want to frighten them, but she didn't want them going into a possibly dangerous situation without being forewarned either.

Charlotte wasn't surprised in the least that the first of her crew to arrive a few minutes later was Cheré Warner. Dependable and energetic were Cheré's middle names, and for the two years she'd been employed by Charlotte, not once had a client ever complained about her work.

Charlotte smiled, and as she motioned for the attractive younger woman to join her, she decided that Cheré would be the perfect one of the crew to ask about warning the others.

Like Charlotte, Cheré was dressed in the Maid-for-a-Day standard uniform that Charlotte insisted all of her employees wear. With Cheré's dark, bouncy hair and her shining black eyes, the cotton navy top and pants covered by a white bib-type apron were a perfect foil for her slim figure.

Cheré flashed her a smile as she seated herself across the small table. "Please tell me you brought extra coffee," she said. "I intended to stop at P.J.'s on the way, but when I passed by, there was a crowd and I didn't want to be late."

With a grin, Charlotte reached down beside her and pulled a thermos from a tote bag. "It's not that fancy stuff you prefer, but it's strong and hot." She set the thermos on the table. "I figured the least I could do was furnish everyone a cup of coffee."

While Cheré was busy unscrewing the lid off the thermos, Charlotte pulled out a stack of Styrofoam cups and a Ziploc bag containing plastic spoons, sugar packets, and creamer packets.

Cheré sniffed the coffee. "Hmm, if your coffee's as good as your iced tea, who cares if it's fancy?"

Charlotte laughed. "I brought some of that too, for later on." But as she watched the younger woman pour herself coffee and stir in sugar and creamer, her laughter died.

"Cheré, I need your advice about something."

"Sounds serious."

Charlotte shrugged. "It could be." Then she went on to tell the younger woman about what she had found the night before.

When she got to the part about shouting out a warning, a look of horror came over Cheré's face. "I can't believe you went in there by yourself. You should never have gone back inside without someone else being here."

Charlotte shrugged. "I didn't exactly go all the way in — just inside the back door — but that's not the point. The point is, should I warn the others?"

"That is the point, but no, I don't see any reason to warn anybody. If anyone was in there, he'd be pretty stupid to stay there after all of that. Besides, with all of us trooping in, he'll be outnumbered. But if you're really worried, I can call Todd to come over. I think he's working over on Seventh Street today."

At the mention of Todd Roussel, Charlotte suddenly grew decidedly uncomfortable. *He's nothing but a rich-boy hoodlum.* She quickly shook her head. "No — I mean, I don't think that's necessary."

Was Louis right about Vince and Todd Roussel? *It's really none of your business.*

Yes it is, Charlotte argued with her conscience. *Cheré is my employee and that makes it my business.* But what to do about it? she wondered. Only one way to handle it, she thought. Just say it, straight out.

Charlotte squared her shoulders. "I need to talk to you about something else too."

Cheré nodded. "Sure, what's up?" Then she narrowed her eyes. "Uh-oh. I don't like that look. You're not firing me, are you?"

Charlotte quickly shook her head. "No, of course not, silly. It's nothing like that." She hesitated, choosing her words carefully. "I learned something disturbing that I think you should know," she finally said. "It's about —"

Behind her, the sound of an approaching car intruded, and Charlotte glanced over her shoulder to see the other half of her cleaning team pulling into the parking lot. "Later," she murmured as Janet Davis and Emily Coleman climbed out of the vehicle. "We'll have to talk about it later."

"Charlotte?"

"Not now, dear." She nodded meaningfully toward the two women approaching them. "It's a private matter, just between you and me."

Besides Cheré, Emily Coleman was another of Charlotte's full-time employees. Emily, a stout woman in her late forties with salt-and-pepper hair, had been with Charlotte for five years. The other woman, Janet Davis, was in her early thirties. Tall and thin, with dishwater-blond hair, Janet had worked for Charlotte on and off as a temporary, part-time employee for the past three years.

"Good morning," Charlotte called out. "There's coffee." She motioned at the thermos. "Join us."

After greeting Charlotte and Cheré, Janet and Emily poured themselves coffee, then seated themselves around the table.

"Is Nadia coming too?" Emily asked as she added sugar to her coffee.

Nadia Wilson was another of Charlotte's full-time employees, a young single mother who had worked for Charlotte for a couple of years.

Charlotte shook her head. "She couldn't find a baby-sitter for Davy."

Emily frowned. "That poor girl has really had a time of it, hasn't she?"

Janet let out a sound of disgust. "That Ricco character should be hung up by his toenails," she snapped. "First he gets the poor girl pregnant, then lives off her like a leech for the past three years and treats her like dirt, and now he's just upped and disappeared."

Though Charlotte agreed with Janet about Ricco Martinez, it was a strict policy of hers never to discuss her employees or clients, but before she had a chance to steer the conversation in a different direction, Cheré added her two cents worth.

"What a louse," she said. "If you ask me, good riddance to bad rubbish." Cheré made a face. "I always figured he was the criminal type, but stealing artifacts from a graveyard —" She shuddered. "I say they should have let him rot in jail — him and all those antique collectors who sold the stuff, as well."

"I heard poor Nadia had to borrow money to bail him out," Emily added. She turned to Charlotte. "Is that true? Come on, Charlotte. If anybody knows, you do."

"Yeah, Charlotte, do tell," Janet urged.

Charlotte sighed. "Ladies, ladies, ladies." She shook her head. "I think that's enough gossip for one morning. It's time to get down to business."

Though they groaned in protest, the women finally settled for quietly sipping their coffee while Charlotte spent several minutes briefly outlining what needed to be done in each apartment.

"There's a lot of sawdust and dirt that's been tracked in," she finally concluded, "so I brought along extra vacuum cleaner bags. And I think working as teams would be best." She nodded at Cheré. "You and Janet will be a team, and Emily and I will work together."

Charlotte caught the sly look that passed between Janet and Cheré, but she ignored it. Though Emily was dependable and thorough doing her job, the middle-aged woman was also slow and tended to get distracted easily. Both Cheré and Janet knew that Charlotte had teamed herself up with Emily on purpose, to keep her on track.

"There are four apartments — two up and two down," Charlotte explained. "Emily and I will work downstairs, and you two will be upstairs. And if we get a move on, I'm hoping we can finish up today. I really don't like working on Sundays."

Cheré laughed. "I think that's a hint, ladies. Just Charlotte's way of saying we need to work our butts off."

Janet gave a dramatic sigh. "Well, Harry will be relieved. I promised the kids a trip to the zoo tomorrow, and he was really dreading having to take them by himself." She suddenly grinned. "Last time he took them, he made the mistake of making faces at one of the monkeys." She snickered. "The monkey retaliated though. He spit at him, and there my darling husband was, with this big glob of who knows what all over the front of his shirt."

"Oh, gross," Cheré squealed.

Emily groaned, then added, "I could have gone all day without hearing that."

Charlotte rolled her eyes. "Well I wouldn't want poor Harry to get stuck going to the zoo again, so let's get to work, ladies."

While the three other women unloaded the cleaning supplies from Charlotte's van, she packed up the thermos and stuffed the used cups inside a trash bag.

One of the things that Charlotte liked

about her employees was that they all shared her appreciation for the beauty of the elegant old homes they cleaned. As they entered the back hallway, each woman in turn ooh'd and aah'd over the superb workmanship that had gone into the renovation as they divided up the cleaning supplies.

Once Janet and Cheré were armed with their supply carriers, they headed up the stairs.

When they were about midway up, Cheré shouted down, "Hey, Charlotte, did you know there's a deep gouge on the sixth step?"

Charlotte smiled. Of the three women, she wasn't surprised that Cheré had been the one to notice the flaw. But she also figured Cheré was using it as an excuse to issue her own warning to the would-be intruder, just in case he'd been stupid enough to hang around.

"I saw it last night," Charlotte told her, just as loudly. "It's on my list of things to bring to Mr. Roussel's attention."

Out of the corner of her eye, Charlotte could see that Emily was looking at her oddly.

"What's with all the shouting?" Emily asked. "Geez, you'd think you both suddenly went deaf or something."

Charlotte just smiled. "Echoes," she explained. "Big old empty houses always echo and sound louder."

Charlotte could tell that Emily wasn't buying her excuse, but when Charlotte didn't offer any other explanation, Emily simply shrugged and picked up her supply carrier. "Where do you want me to start?" she asked.

Charlotte motioned, indicating they would begin cleaning in the apartment on their left. "Your choice," she told her as they entered the living room of the apartment. "But I know how the dust gets to you, so why don't you do the bathroom, and I'll work on wiping down the walls and cleaning the windows? Then we'll both tackle the kitchen."

Emily nodded. "Thanks, Charlotte. My allergies *have* been acting up, ever since that front came through night before last."

"I know exactly what you mean," Charlotte told her, thinking of her own minor allergy irritations.

For the next half hour, as the women worked, the only sounds that broke through the silence were the rumblings of traffic along the avenue in front of the house and an occasional honking horn.

Charlotte had almost finished cleaning the last window in the living room when there was a sudden, ear-splitting shriek from upstairs.

"Charrrrlotte!"

For a moment, she was too stunned to move as the sound echoed throughout the empty house.

Not a cry of pain, her mind registered, but terror. It was a cry of sheer terror.

Chapter Eight

"Charrrrlotte!"

Janet, Charlotte thought, her heart pounding. Janet was the one screaming out her name.

It was the thump-thump of running footsteps above her that finally jerked her into action. Was someone chasing Janet and Cheré? Were they in danger?

A weapon. She needed a weapon of some sort. Charlotte glanced frantically around the room. Nothing. There was nothing she could use except . . . her fingers tightened on the spray bottle of ammonia in her hand. *Better than nothing.*

Vaguely aware that Emily had bolted from the bathroom, Charlotte dashed out into the hallway and sprinted for the stairs. "You stay down here," she shouted at Emily.

Halfway up the staircase, she met the other two women scrambling down.

"What on earth?" Charlotte cried. "What's going on?"

Janet was shivering so hard she could

barely talk. Crowded close behind her, Cheré's face was drained of color, and her dark eyes were wide with horror.

"D-dead," Janet stuttered, her voice cracking. "I — I turned on th-the light, and th-there's a dead man in — in the closet."

A dead man . . . dead . . . Charlotte's stomach turned queasy, and she heard Emily utter a startled cry from the foot of the stairs.

"Okay, okay, hon." Charlotte squeezed Janet's arm. "Now just calm down. Are you sure — sure he's dead?"

"Well, he's not moving," Janet cried. "And — and I don't th-think he's breathing."

Charlotte squeezed her arm again. "But you don't know for sure." Janet shook her head with short, jerky motions.

Cheré shuddered. "He — he looked dead to me," she whispered.

"But neither of you felt for a pulse?" One look at the horrified expressions on their faces told her they hadn't. "No, of course you didn't." She took a deep breath, and though she was already pretty sure what the answer would be, she asked anyway. "Which apartment — which one were you cleaning?"

"The one to the left of the landing," Cheré told her.

Charlotte swallowed hard. It was the same one, the one she'd found the food sacks in during her walk-through, the one that had the toothpaste smeared in the bathroom sink. "Which room?"

"The m— master bedroom," Janet whispered. "He — he's in the walk-in closet."

Charlotte knew what she had to do. Whether she wanted to or not — and she most definitely did not want to — she was going to have to check it out for herself. What if the man wasn't really dead? What if he was just unconscious and needed help?

"Okay, here's what we're going to do," she told them. "You two join Emily downstairs while I go check. And here —" She handed Janet the bottle of ammonia. "Take this with you." Then she pulled her cell phone from her pocket and thrust it at Cheré. "You take this and call the police. Be sure and ask for my niece."

Cheré took the phone. "But Charlotte!"

Charlotte shook her head. "It'll be okay. Just go." Willing her legs to move, she squeezed past the two women and hurried up the remaining stairs.

Once she was inside the apartment,

though, she hesitated at the door to the master bedroom to catch her breath.

A sleeping bag was spread out in the middle of the room on the floor. Near the foot of the sleeping bag was an open duffel with clothes spilling out of it, and in the midst of the clothes was a small camera, one of the disposable kind, she noted. And beside the camera were several pictures scattered about.

"Weird," she murmured. For one thing, the sleeping bag and the duffel bag both looked almost brand-new. And expensive. *And don't forget the toothpaste in the sink.*

It was just as she'd suspected, she thought, eying the dark green sleeping bag. Someone, probably the man in the closet, *had* been camping out in the empty house after all.

With a heavy feeling of dread, Charlotte moved farther into the room. Maybe she'd been wrong about the homeless angle after all. But if the man in the closet wasn't a homeless person, then who was he? And why had he been camping out in the old house?

The walk-in closet door was open. A wave of apprehension swept through her as she edged nearer the opening. Any minute she expected to see a hand or foot or some evidence of a body. But there was nothing yet, nothing but an odd-looking, half-smoked cigar that had been ground out into the floor.

Charlotte took the last two steps that would bring her to the closet door. Swallowing hard, she leaned forward and peeked around the door.

"Oh, dear Lord," she whispered, as she reached out and grabbed the door frame to steady herself. The man was in the back corner of the closet, half sitting, half slumped sideways against the wall.

Though she wasn't exactly sure what she'd expected, the one thing she hadn't expected to see was a half-naked man wearing nothing but a purple feathered Mardi Gras mask and boxer shorts.

A Mardi Gras mask?

For what seemed like forever, all she could do was stare at the mask. It was a cheap one, the kind sold mostly to tourists, but it wasn't so much the mask itself that kept her gaze riveted as it was the dried blood along the side of the man's head.

The blood and his eyes. She was only about four feet away from him, but under the harsh glare of the closet light she could see that his eyes were wide open, staring out at her from behind the rounded eye slits of the mask. Like huge black holes, the pupils were already fixed and dilated.

Other than at funerals, she'd never actually seen a dead body, but she'd read enough mystery books and true-crime novels over the years to know the signs of death. She was almost ninety-nine point nine percent sure that the poor man was truly dead.

With a sinking heart and drawing in a deep breath for courage, Charlotte approached the man. Her eyes still glued to the mask, she leaned over him and touched him near the underside of his jaw, checking for any small sign of life.

Just as she'd expected, his skin was death cold to her touch, and there was no pulse.

She frowned. Strange; now that she was closer to him, something about the man seemed almost familiar, as if she'd seen him before. There was something about his build, or maybe it was because of the reddish-brown color of his thick hair.

For a moment more her hand hovered near the mask. If she could just see his face without the mask. . . .

The muted sound of a distant siren suddenly broke through the silence. The police were coming . . . Judith.

It was then that the reality of the whole

situation really hit her. With a cry of horror, Charlotte jerked her hand away and backed quickly toward the closet door. This was not fiction. This was not some murder mystery out of a book. This was the real thing.

Charlotte kept backing up until she was once again out of the closet and inside the bedroom. Only then did she realize how badly she was trembling. Wrapping her arms around her middle, she hugged them tightly as she stared downward.

Outside the house, the police siren grew louder. But inside, it was several moments before Charlotte could stop shaking, before she felt more in control.

She needed to vacate the room, she thought. It was a crime scene, and without thinking, she, along with Cheré and Janet, had already contaminated it. Charlotte winced. Judith would have a conniption fit.

Then suddenly, Charlotte narrowed her eyes as her vision once again focused. She'd been staring downward without really seeing what she was looking at. And what she'd been staring at was the stack of pictures beside the camera.

The top photo was a picture of a little girl who looked to be about four years old. It had been taken in an outside setting.

Behind the little girl, a white gazebo sat beneath a huge oak. Again, a feeling of familiarity swept through her and niggled at Charlotte's memory. She'd seen that setting before . . . but where?

Think, Charlotte! Think! But it was no use. No matter how hard she tried, she simply couldn't remember. First the dead man, and now this. What was wrong with her? Lord, maybe she *was* getting old after all. Or worse. Maybe she was in the beginning stages of Alzheimer's?

Abruptly outside, the police siren died with a squawk. Then, in the distance, another siren sounded.

The police had arrived and more were on the way, which meant that even now, Judith could be coming through the front door. With one last searching glance at the photo, Charlotte hurried from the room.

Downstairs in the front foyer, two uniformed police officers were already questioning Cheré, Janet, and Emily by the time that Charlotte reached the first floor.

Though Charlotte didn't recognize the older officer, she was pretty sure she recognized the younger of the two. If she remembered right, his first name was Billy, and though she couldn't recall his last name, she did recall that he'd been pushy and rude the last time they'd met.

The last time they'd met . . . the day she'd learned that Jackson Dubuisson had been murdered. . . .

A sinking feeling settled in the pit of her stomach as she approached the small group. She nodded a greeting at both of the men; then, ignoring them, she turned to Cheré. "Did you speak to Judith?"

"Yes, ma'am. She said she was on her way."

"Ah, excuse me," the older officer interrupted in a no-nonsense voice that dripped with sarcasm. "But who are you?"

Before Charlotte could answer, the younger officer spoke up. "It's okay, Hal," he told his partner. "She's Detective Monroe's aunt." He turned to Charlotte. "Isn't that right, ma'am? Aren't you Judith's aunt?"

"Yes — yes, I am," Charlotte answered. "And your name is Billy —" Still unable to recall his last name, she shrugged.

"Wilson, ma'am. Billy Wilson."

Charlotte felt something tickle the back of her neck, and when she reached up to rub it, she realized she was sweating. "Well, I'd say it was good to see you again, Billy," she murmured, suddenly distracted by the realization that she was sweating profusely, "but under the circumstances . . ." How could she be sweating when she felt so cold?

"I understand, ma'am. And speaking of circumstances, what can you tell us about the situation here?"

Charlotte began by explaining that her crew had been hired to do the cleanup of the Devilier house, but just as she got to the part where Janet had discovered the dead man, Judith burst in through the doorway. Following close behind her was a man Charlotte didn't recognize. Must be Judith's new partner, she thought.

"Hey, Aunt Charley, are you okay?"

Was she okay? Even as Charlotte nodded, she felt her knees go weak. And why, all of a sudden, was it so hot . . . and stuffy?

"What's this about a dead body?"

Dead body . . . dead body . . . Again Charlotte opened her mouth to explain, and again she was interrupted when Louis Thibodeaux barged through the door. Charlotte frowned and felt a sudden chill again. Why was Louis there? He was supposed to be off duty and on his way to the camp.

Judith glanced his way and voiced the exact same thing Charlotte had been thinking. "Hey, Lou. What are you doing here?"

But Louis' dark eyes were boring a hole through Charlotte, and he ignored Judith and her question. "Charlotte? What's going on?" he demanded. "Who's dead?"

Dead . . . someone's dead . . . He was there because he'd been worried about *her,* Charlotte realized. He must have heard something over his radio about a dead body and thought that she was —

The room blurred, and it was all that she could do to motion toward the ceiling. "Upstairs," she whispered, swaying on her feet. "A — a dead man upstairs."

Before she knew what was happening, Judith grabbed her on one side and Louis grabbed her on the other. "Whoa now, don't you pass out on us," he said.

Charlotte was horrified. She shook her head. "Never — never passed out in my entire life," she said. But her voice sounded strangely weak and distant, even to her own ears. In an effort to prove her point, she made a feeble effort to pull away from him, and that's when the lights went out.

Chapter Nine

Charlotte came to with a start. She was flat on the floor and Judith was hovering over her, waving a foul-smelling vial under her nose. She could hear voices murmuring somewhere just behind her . . . Cheré and Janet. She shoved Judith's hand away.

"No — don't try to get up — not yet," her niece ordered softly, gently pushing on her shoulder. "You're still pale, Auntie, so just lie still a moment more. Please," she added.

As if someone turned up the volume, the voices grew more clear and distinct.

"She's coming to." Janet's voice.

"I knew I shouldn't have let her go up there in the first place." Cheré.

Charlotte was confused. What were they talking about? And what on earth was she doing on the floor? "Wh— what happened?" she whispered. But as soon as the words left her mouth, it all came back.

"You passed out, Auntie," Judith told her, confirming Charlotte's own conclusions.

"Here, Monroe." Louis' face swam into her vision just behind Judith. He handed Judith what looked like a wet cloth of some kind. "All I had was a handkerchief, but it's clean."

"Thanks, Lou." When Judith began blotting Charlotte's forehead and cheeks, Charlotte pushed away her niece's hand yet again.

"I'm okay, hon. Please stop making such a fuss."

"Yeah, right, Aunt Charley. You're just peachy. That's why you passed out."

"Judith." Emily Coleman appeared. "Here's some water." She handed Judith a cup.

"Thanks, Emily." Judith took the cup. "Drink this, Auntie."

"I'm not thirsty."

"Drink it anyway."

Only because arguing was too big an effort did Charlotte finally give in and allow Judith to lift her head enough to drink the water.

Behind them, out of Charlotte's line of vision, a gruff male voice called out, "Hey, Judith!"

Judith gently lowered Charlotte's head back onto the floor again, then turned toward the direction of the voice. "Yeah, Will."

"I'm going on up and check out the D.B.," he said.

Judith stiffened, and Charlotte saw her hand tighten around the wet handkerchief. "Wait up a minute, Will, and I'll go with you."

Only because Charlotte knew her niece so well was she able to detect the slight edge in her tone. That and the panicky look on Judith's face confirmed what she'd suspected when she'd first talked to Louis about her niece's new partner. Something was going on between the two, something that Louis was aware of and didn't like, judging from his attitude.

"I'm okay, hon," Charlotte reassured Judith. "Go do your job."

"I've got a better idea," Louis drawled. "Monroe, you stay here with Charlotte, and I'll go baby-sit Willy boy."

"Now, Lou. Take it easy."

Louis shot Judith a smug look. "I've been around a long time, little girl, and believe you me, I can handle that snotty hotshot with one arm tied behind my back."

"Lou, don't —"

But either Louis didn't hear her or he purposely ignored her. "Hey, Richeaux," he yelled. "Wait up."

125

Charlotte caught the look of alarm on Judith's face, and while her niece was distracted, she pushed herself up off the floor. "What on earth is going on?" she asked, easing herself into a sitting position. "Is there a problem with this Will character?"

"Nothing," Judith murmured distractedly, her gaze following the two men heading for the stairs. "Nothing's going on."

"Nothing, my foot," Charlotte scoffed. "Something's going on and I want to know what."

Judith didn't answer until the men had disappeared up the staircase. "Give it a rest, Auntie," she said, turning her attention back to Charlotte. "Believe me, now is not the time or the place." She cast another worried glance toward the stairs. Then, with a sigh, she turned back to Charlotte. "I hate to, but if you're feeling up to it, I need to ask you some questions, Auntie. But when we're finished here, I want you to have one of your crew drive you home. And when you get there, I want you to promise me that you'll call Hank and tell him about this fainting spell you just had."

The best defense is an offense. Charlotte knew her niece was worried about her, but

126

she was also well aware that Judith was purposely changing the subject. Before she could protest, though, Judith shook her finger at her. "If you don't tell him, I will," she threatened. "When's the last time you had a good checkup?"

Charlotte pursed her lips stubbornly and glared back at her niece.

Judith's eyes narrowed. "Uh-huh! Just as I thought. You can't even remember, can you? Well, it's past time. Now promise me you'll call him."

Charlotte released a heavy sigh. Judith was right. She *couldn't* remember the last time she'd had a checkup. But there hadn't been a reason to go running to a doctor, she consoled herself. It was probably just the stress of the moment. After all, it wasn't every day that she found a half-naked dead man. And up until then, she'd felt just fine.

Liar, liar, pants on fire. Well, almost fine, she amended. She had been a bit more tired than usual lately. But the thought of turning sixty was enough to make anyone tired. Wasn't it? Of course it was.

But you fainted . . . you passed out cold. . . . Charlotte grimaced. Bottom line was that in spite of all of her excuses, and as much as she would have liked to pretend that she hadn't fainted, she had.

"Aunt Char-ley. I'm waiting."

Charlotte never had been one who could give in graciously, and she most certainly didn't like to be bullied, not even by her niece whom she knew loved her and meant well. "Okay, okay, I promise," she muttered irritably.

While Judith questioned Charlotte and each of her crew, Charlotte rested on the chaise longue. Cheré had wiped most of the dust off of the plastic cover, and she, along with Judith and the others, had insisted that Charlotte sit there until they were allowed to leave.

Though Charlotte was extremely uncomfortable with all the fuss everyone was making over her, she still felt a bit weak in the knees and was glad to have somewhere to sit.

When Louis and Will returned from upstairs, Judith broke away to confer with her new partner.

From where Charlotte sat, she had a perfect view of all the goings-on. Cheré, Emily, and Janet huddled around the marble-top table across from where she sat, Will and Judith were talking near the entrance door, and over by the foot of the staircase, Louis was grilling Billy Wilson and his partner, Hal.

Watching Louis cross-examine the patrolmen, Charlotte thanked her lucky stars that Judith, and not Louis, had been the one who had interrogated her crew.

Louis could be intimidating when he chose to, and though they had called a truce of sorts since he'd begun renting her double, the gruff detective seemed to have a gift for getting on her last nerve. Part of her bias toward him, she knew, had a lot to do with his outdated macho, chauvinistic attitude, but she also still felt the sting of humiliation every time she remembered his harsh accusations and the shabby way he'd treated her during the Dubuisson investigation.

As if he could feel her watching him, he glanced her way. For a long moment, he stared at her, and the searching look of concern he gave her did funny things to her insides. After what seemed like forever, as if satisfied that she was okay, he turned back to the patrolmen.

Such an enigma, she thought. The man was a puzzle she'd yet to figure out. In his own way, he truly cared about people, and he was completely trustworthy and honest to a fault, albeit sometimes brutally so.

And if she were equally honest, she'd have to admit that, all in all, despite his many shortcomings, he'd be one of the first people she'd call if she were ever in a real bind.

Louis pointed up the stairs; then, with a nod to the two patrolmen, he walked over to where Judith and Will were standing.

At that moment, more police arrived. From the looks of the equipment they were carrying, Charlotte figured they were from the crime scene division. With all of the commotion, she couldn't quite hear what Louis said to Judith, but she had no trouble whatsoever hearing Judith's response.

"No way!" she argued.

"I swear it," he retorted.

"This I've got to see." Judith did an about-face, and with Louis and Will trailing after her, she threaded her way through the crowd of policemen who had gathered near the foot of the stairs.

"Ah, Charlotte?"

Charlotte turned her head to where Cheré was standing.

"How are you feeling now?"

Charlotte made a face. "Contrary to everyone's opinion, I'm doing just fine. My goodness, such a fuss over nothing."

"It wasn't just nothing and you know it. Judith's right. You need to get a checkup." Then she waved a dismissing hand. "But meantime, about right now I think we could all use some of that iced tea you brought. No — no, don't get up. Just tell me where it is and I'll get it."

Charlotte sighed. "Oh, for pity's sake. Look behind the driver's seat in my van. It's in the blue ice chest. Cups are in the plastic grocery sack beside the ice chest. And while you're at it, you might as well bring me some too, since it looks like we're going to be here a while."

Cheré only got as far as the door, where a policeman stopped her. "Sorry, ma'am, I can't let you leave until the detectives say so."

"I'm not leaving," Cheré told him. "I'm just going to the van to get something to drink for Ms. LaRue — Detective Monroe's aunt."

He shook his head. "No can do, but if you'll tell me where it's at, I'll send someone after it for you."

"Oh, good grief," Cheré retorted. "In the ice chest in the back of that white van — a jug of tea. And tell whoever you send to bring those plastic cups in that grocery sack too."

A few minutes later, Cheré returned with the tea. She had just poured Charlotte a cup when Judith came down the stairs.

"Gather around, ladies," she told the crew. "I've got some more questions to ask — and if there's any to spare, I'd love to have some of that tea."

She waited until Cheré poured her a cup of the tea, took several swallows, then set the cup on the marble-topped table. After a searching look at each of the women, she motioned toward the stairs. "I know I asked this before, but I have to ask it again. Did any of you recognize the man in the closet?"

"I didn't go up there," Emily said.

"Yes — yes, I know," Judith replied. "You said you stayed downstairs. Right?"

Emily nodded.

"How about you, Cheré? Janet?"

Both women shook their heads.

"Aunt Charley?"

Charlotte hesitated a moment before she answered. "Not right off the bat," she finally said. "I kinda thought he looked familiar, but I really couldn't see him that well, what with that mask he has on."

Judith nodded. "He looked familiar for a good reason, Auntie. Lou — Detective Thibodeaux — says the man is Drew

Bergeron, and I believe I remember that you once worked for him and his wife."

Drew Bergeron. Charlotte's insides quivered with disbelief. "That's impossible," she blurted out. "Mr. Bergeron died over two years ago. Why, I went to his funeral."

Chapter Ten

"Surely Louis is mistaken," Charlotte insisted. But even as she denied the possibility, she knew that the half-naked dead man in the closet upstairs was truly Drew Bergeron. That was why he had seemed familiar, why she'd thought she had seen him before. She *had* seen him before.

Because he was supposed to have already been dead, her conscious mind had rejected recognition, but her subconscious had identified him as someone she knew.

"The victim still has to be officially I.D.'d," Judith told her, "but since Lou once had some dealings with Bergeron, unless the body upstairs is a twin, he's almost one hundred percent certain the I.D. will check out. No trace of Bergeron's body was ever found in the wreckage after his so-called accident, so it's very likely that he bailed out before his plane exploded."

"But why — How is that possible?" Charlotte asked.

"Easy," Judith said. "His plane exploded

twenty miles out into the Gulf of Mexico. Since there were a lot of sharks around, everyone just assumed . . ." She shrugged.

"No." Charlotte shook her head and waved a dismissive hand. "That's not what I meant. If the man is Drew Bergeron, then, like you said, he probably bailed out. Either he was rescued and had amnesia — which isn't very likely — or he had to have staged his first death. What I meant was, why would he have done such a thing?"

"That's what we're going to have to find out," Judith replied. "Once we know why, then we might have a better idea as to who killed him."

Judith turned to Janet and Cheré. "I know we've already been over everything, but this time I need you to tell me exactly what happened again, starting from the time you entered the house. We need to know just how much of the evidence has been disturbed. Let's start with you, Mrs. Davis."

As Charlotte watched Janet and Judith walk off toward the end of the hallway, memories of the first time she'd met Drew Bergeron and his wife, Katherine, swirled through her mind . . .

Katherine. "Oh no," she groaned.

Abruptly, Judith and Janet glanced her

way, and Cheré turned toward her. As if by design, almost in unison they asked, "What's wrong?"

"I just thought about Katherine — Drew's wife," Charlotte explained. She shook her head slowly. "That poor, poor woman."

Judith and Janet walked back to join Charlotte and Cheré. "What about Katherine?" Judith asked her.

"Can you imagine? For the past two years she's thought that her husband was dead. And now this." She shuddered. "Horrible — it's just horrible. She's already been through one funeral for him, and now —" She shook her head again. "Now she'll have to go through it all again."

"I wouldn't feel too sorry for her yet," Judith cautioned in a stern tone. "She might have been in on it."

Charlotte frowned. "In on it?" she repeated. "But why would she —"

"All kinds of reasons, Auntie. *All* kinds," she emphasized. "And money's at the top of the list. Now —" She motioned at Cheré. "Your turn, Ms. Warner."

In spite of what Judith had implied about Katherine Bergeron, Charlotte couldn't seem to stop thinking about her as she watched Judith question Cheré at the end of the hallway.

When Cheré and Judith joined Charlotte and Janet again, Judith addressed them all. "I'm going to need written statements from each of you. I'll get one of the patrolmen to take you to the precinct, and once you've given your statements there, you're free to go home." She reached out and took Charlotte's hand. "How about it, Auntie? Are you up to giving a statement?"

Charlotte rolled her eyes toward the ceiling. "I'm fine," she snapped. "Please stop being such a worrywart."

Judith squeezed her hand before releasing it. "You just remember what I said about calling Hank."

"I'll make sure she calls him," Cheré offered.

"Gee, thanks, Cheré," Charlotte drawled sarcastically. "Just what I need. Two conspirators."

Cheré flashed her a sassy smile. "You're welcome," she quipped. "And it's only because we love you."

Judith cleared her throat to get their attention. "One last thing. I'm going to need the shoes you're wearing, fingerprints, and a DNA sample — head hair will do — everyone but you, Ms. Coleman, since you didn't go upstairs at all."

Judith ignored their protests. "And Aunt Charley —" Her lips thinned with disapproval. "I understand why you did it, but if you ever run across a dead body again — God forbid — *do not* go near it."

"But I didn't know if —"

Judith held up a hand. "I realize that, Auntie, but you can get into big trouble. You might even be taken into custody as a suspect, and I might not be around to smooth things over."

It was midafternoon before Charlotte was finally able to go home. Despite her vigorous protest, none of her crew would hear of her driving herself home. Instead, Cheré drove Charlotte's van. Since Janet had caught a ride with Emily that morning, she followed in Cheré's car. Emily brought up the rear of their little caravan in her vehicle, so she could pick up Janet.

True to her word, Cheré refused to leave until Charlotte phoned Hank. While Charlotte dialed the number, Cheré entertained herself by playing with Sweety Boy. From the moment they had entered the room, the little parakeet had begun his normal routine of squawking and pacing back and forth on his perch, all designed to get attention.

As it turned out, Hank had to be paged.

"Are you as hungry as I am?" Charlotte asked Cheré as she hung up the phone.

Cheré had her finger in the birdcage, rubbing the back of the little bird's head. "Starving," she quipped, pulling her finger from the cage. "Hey, we could order a pizza?"

"Sounds good to me. Why don't you order while I see about a salad? I think I have some of that prepackaged stuff in the refrig. I usually add a few carrots and tomatoes to it, if that's okay with you?"

"Sounds great. Pepperoni, mushrooms, and onions on the pizza okay with you?"

Charlotte nodded. "And order extra sauce too," she suggested. "They never put enough sauce on it," she muttered.

While Cheré ordered the pizza, Charlotte headed for the kitchen. Within minutes, Cheré joined her. "The pizza should be here in about twenty minutes," she told Charlotte. "Now, what can I do to help?"

Charlotte held out a tomato and a bag of raw baby carrots. "You can wash these."

Within minutes, the salads were ready. Cheré suggested that they should go ahead and eat while waiting for the delivery of the pizza, and Charlotte agreed. They had just sat down at the table when the phone rang.

"That's probably Hank," Charlotte murmured as she stood. Motioning toward Cheré's plate, she added, "Don't wait on me. Go ahead and eat."

Charlotte hurried into the living room and snatched up the phone receiver. "Maid-for-a-Day. Charlotte speaking."

"Momma, what's wrong?" Hank asked with an edge of worry in his voice.

"Why does anything have to be wrong for me to talk to my own son?"

"Mother, the only times you've ever paged me was because *something* was wrong."

"Yes, well, I guess you have a point." Charlotte hesitated, dreading having to explain everything. She hated giving him any more excuses than he'd already come up with to nag her about retiring.

"Mother?"

"Well, *I* don't think there's anything wrong," she hedged, "but Judith insisted that I call you."

"Call me about what?"

"It's nothing — really it isn't. Judith's just being a worrywart as usual."

"Mother! Out with it."

"Oh, okay, I fainted." She said it quickly, as if by doing so, it wouldn't be such a big deal.

"You fainted! And you don't think anything's wrong? What am I going to do with you? Mother, people don't faint for no reason."

"Well, I was a bit stressed out at the moment."

"O-kaay." When he stretched the word out, then sighed heavily, she almost grinned. In her mind's eye, she could picture the exasperated frown he always got when he was at the end of his patience. "Start from the beginning, please," he finally said, "and tell me *exactly* what happened."

Once she'd told him everything, she had to listen for endless minutes while he lectured her on the dangers of ignoring certain warning signs at her age, and it seemed to take forever to end the conversation.

"Enough, already," she finally told him, interrupting his spiel about regular check-ups. "I get the message, loud and clear."

"Now, Mother, don't go getting stubborn on me. You know I love you, and it's for your own good."

"And I love you too," she told him, "but

141

I'm not senile yet, son. Besides, I'm sure you have better things to do than stand around lecturing your mother."

When Charlotte returned to the kitchen, Cheré took one look at her and asked, "Gave you a hard time, didn't he?"

With a sigh, Charlotte seated herself at the table again. "He wants me to have some tests run, and he's setting up an appointment with a colleague of his for me to see next week."

"Good. Better safe than sorry."

Charlotte scooped up a forkful of salad. "I suppose so," she agreed, somewhat grudgingly, "but if you ask me, it's just a lot of fuss over nothing." Or was it? she wondered uneasily. Were Hank and Judith right? Was she just being too stubborn for her own good? She had been feeling more tired lately, but she also had been working longer hours than usual. She'd just put the bite of salad in her mouth when the door-bell rang.

"Pizza time," Cheré quipped.

"Oh, great," Charlotte grumbled around the mouthful of food as she shoved away from the table.

Cheré pointed at her. "Stay put and eat your salad. I'll get it."

Charlotte was more than ready for a hot shower and bed by the time Cheré finally left. She'd just stepped into the shower when she heard the muted ring of the telephone.

"Too bad," she muttered as she turned her face into the warm spray. Whoever was calling would just have to leave a message on the machine.

By the time she'd finished her shower and pulled on her favorite cotton pajamas, Charlotte was sorely tempted to not even check the answering machine. She was tired, both mentally and physically, and images of Drew Bergeron's dead eyes staring out at her from beneath the purple Mardi Gras mask kept swimming through her mind. If she could just sink into the oblivion of sleep, maybe the images would stop haunting her.

But even as she neatly folded back the comforter and quilt on her bed, the thought of that infernal blinking light on the message machine kept nagging her.

"Oh, all right, already," she muttered, finally giving in. She'd always been too curious for her own good, and at times, it drove her crazy. And though she hated to admit it, she knew the real reason she couldn't ignore the call was because of her superstitious nature. It never failed that the one call she ignored would end up being something really important.

Charlotte stomped off toward the living room. Besides, she reasoned, she still had to cover Sweety Boy's cage for the night, and just because she listened to the message didn't necessarily mean she had to return the call.

Charlotte hit the play button on the machine then walked over to Sweety Boy's cage.

"Hi, Charlotte, it's me."

The message was from her sister, Madeline, and Charlotte felt the old familiar dread well up from within as she pulled the cover over the birdcage. She hated feeling that way about her own flesh and blood, but Madeline could be a real pain to deal with at times.

"What's this about you fainting? You've never fainted in your life, not that I remember anyway."

Charlotte rolled her eyes as she checked to make sure she'd locked and bolted the front door. Having a close family had its advantages, and her family was closer than most. Their parents had been killed when Madeline was fifteen. Charlotte, only twenty herself at the time and a single mother, had taken over raising her sister as well as her own two-year-old son. But having a close family also meant that everyone knew everyone else's business. Evidently Judith had wasted no time in calling her mother.

"And why aren't you answering this call?" Madeline continued. "Surely you haven't gone to bed already. It's only eight o'clock, for Pete's sake. Only old people go to bed this early, and just because you're turning sixty doesn't mean you're that old yet — unless — unless you've passed out —" Madeline suddenly groaned. "Please tell me you haven't passed out again! But what if you have?" she murmured. "Charlotte? Charlotte!"

Several moments passed and Charlotte could hear her sister's harsh breathing on the recording. "Listen," Madeline finally said. "If I don't hear back from you within the next fifteen minutes, I'm calling 911 and coming over there, so you'd better call me back."

Sudden panic knifed through Charlotte. She rushed over to the phone and snatched up the receiver. How much time had passed? she wondered as she punched out her sister's number. Surely not a whole fifteen minutes yet. The very last thing she wanted was to have to deal with Madeline tonight, and she certainly didn't want the police or an ambulance showing up on her doorstep.

The call was answered on the second ring. "Charlotte?"

"Yes, Maddie, it's me. Please tell me you haven't called 911."

"Why didn't you answer the phone the first time?"

"Not that it's any of your business, but I was in the shower."

"Well of course it's my business," she snapped back. Then she snickered. "At least now I know how to get you to return my calls."

"That's not funny, Maddie."

"Neither is you fainting," she shot back.

Charlotte sighed. *Give me patience, Lord.* "Look, I've already gotten one lecture tonight from Hank, so I don't need another one. Why Judith felt she had to call you anyway is beyond me."

"Well that's a fine how-do-you-do," Madeline snapped. "In case you've forgotten, I am your sister. And why wouldn't my own daughter call me?"

Why indeed? thought Charlotte as the words unstable, irresponsible, and selfish came to mind.

Madeline's divorce from her first husband had devastated her. She had truly loved Johnny Monroe, but Johnny had a roving eye that not even the love of his wife or two little children could compete with. For years after the divorce, Madeline had been barely able to function on a daily basis, and much of the care of her two children had fallen on Charlotte's shoulders. Even Madeline had admitted on more than one occasion, albeit out of jealousy, that Charlotte had always been more of a mother to her children than she had.

Truth was, Judith and her brother, Daniel, were more likely to call Charlotte about something than call their own mother. It was one of those family things that everyone knew but no one ever talked about.

Charlotte sighed. "Oh, now Maddie, don't get in a snit. You know I didn't mean anything," she said. "And I do appreciate your concern. It's just that — well, it's just been one of those days. I'm fine. Really I am. It was probably just the circumstances. It's not every day that I find a dead man. But of course Hank insisted on setting me up with an appointment for a checkup next week anyway."

"I suppose you're right. Finding that dead man and all would certainly be enough to make *me* pass out for sure. But you might as well get a checkup anyway, just to be on the safe side." Madeline paused, then, "Another reason I called was to find out if you're feeling up to coming over tomorrow now that you won't be working."

Originally, Charlotte had excused herself from the family's regular Sunday lunch after church due to the Devilier job. Because their family was small, years ago she and Madeline had started the tradition of taking turns hosting the Sunday lunches after church services on alternating Sundays. Even with the busy lives that their children led, without fail, everyone always tried to show up.

"Yes, I'll be there," Charlotte replied.

"Good. Daniel is going to barbecue and I needed to know how much chicken to buy in the morning."

"Just a breast will be plenty for me," Charlotte told her. "Now at the risk of sounding like an old lady, I *am* going to bed. See you tomorrow."

"Sorry about that," Madeline admitted. "You know I don't think of you as getting old. Besides, sixty really isn't that old, not in this day and time."

"Good night, Maddie, and just remember, you're only five years younger than me."

Maddie groaned. "Thanks for reminding me, dear sister of mine. And by the way, why don't you go to bed now?" With a giggle, Madeline hung up the phone, and Charlotte did the same.

She was just too tired to sleep, Charlotte finally decided two hours later as she switched the bedside lamp back on. That had to be the reason she couldn't sleep.

After she'd hung up from talking to Maddie, she'd gone straight to bed. She'd read a bit, just enough to relax her into thinking she could finally fall asleep. But the minute she'd turned off the lamp, visions of Drew Bergeron's dead eyes staring at her filled her mind. She'd tried deep-breathing exercises, and she'd even resorted to counting sheep. But nothing had worked. Those dead eyes just wouldn't go away.

Charlotte reached for the book she'd been reading earlier, but not even a chapter later, the detective in the novel stumbled upon a dead body.

With a groan, Charlotte slammed the

book shut and dropped it on the floor. Maybe a glass of milk would help, she decided, pushing herself out of the bed. And maybe if she watched a little television . . . something nice and boring like one of the old black-and-white movies that sometimes played late at night.

He was on the porch . . . From the front window she could see the shadowy figure skulking around. Then, suddenly he turned and saw her staring out at him. He looked straight at her with those dead eyes of his, then he disappeared.

Thwack, thwack . . . Oh, dear Lord, he was trying to break down her front door. . . .

Chapter Eleven

Charlotte awoke with a start, her heart racing beneath her breasts. A dream, it was just a dream, she kept telling herself. But no, it had been far worse than *just* a dream. It had been a full-blown nightmare . . . every single woman's nightmare.

Still feeling a bit disoriented even as her heart slowed to a steady thud, she frowned when she suddenly realized that she was on the living room sofa instead of her bed.

And the television was on.

Her frown deepened. "Oh great," she grumbled. "Just wonderful." On the TV screen, Clint Eastwood had his gun drawn and was trying to break down a door. It was a scene from an old *Dirty Harry* episode that she recognized all too well. That was what had probably awakened her to begin with.

So what time was it anyway? When she turned her head to look up at the cuckoo clock on the wall above the sofa, she suddenly groaned with pain and grabbed the back right side of her neck. Not only was it just barely six o'clock — not even daylight yet — but worse, now she had a crick in her neck.

"That's what you get for falling asleep on the sofa," she muttered.

From beneath the cover over his cage, Sweety Boy squawked.

"No, it's not time to get up yet," she said irritably. "Go back to sleep."

Careful to keep her head straight, she eased herself up. Once she was standing, she decided that maybe an aspirin would help, that and another hour or so of sleep . . . in her bed, this time.

It seemed that only minutes had passed when Charlotte again awoke with a start, this time to the sound of a ringing in her ears. Several seconds passed before she realized that the ringing was actually the doorbell, and several more seconds passed before it dawned on her that tiny jets of sunlight were peeping through the closed blinds that covered her solitary bedroom window.

A quick glance at her clock radio on the bedside table told her it was almost nine, but who on earth would be at her door this early on a Sunday morning?

As if he'd heard her unspoken question, Louis Thibodeaux's muffled voice called out, "Charlotte, answer the door. I know you're in there."

Charlotte groaned, "Oh, good grief!"

"Charlotte!"

"Hold your horses!" she yelled. "Just a minute!"

When she tried to sit up, the dull ache in her neck reminded her of the crick she'd gotten from sleeping on the sofa. Though the aspirin had numbed the pain somewhat, the crick was still there.

Wondering why on earth Louis was at her door so early, she slipped into her housecoat and the moccasins she favored for house shoes. Then she quickly brushed her hair.

At least her hair wasn't sticking out all over the place the way it had been on Friday morning, she thought, eying her reflection in the mirror one last time before heading for the living room. The new haircut had helped, and despite her restless night, her hair had fallen nicely in place. She'd have to remember to tell Valerie how pleased she was with it the next time she saw her.

Now if she could only have a cup of coffee before facing Louis, she thought irritably as she unlocked the front door to let him in.

Unlike Charlotte, Louis was dressed. His hair was still damp from the shower, and there was a tiny telltale cut on his chin where he'd nicked himself shaving.

The moment Louis said, "Good morning," and stepped through the doorway, Sweety Boy began squawking inside the covered cage as if he was being terrorized.

"That bird doesn't like me."

Ignoring Louis for the moment, Charlotte turned her attention toward the cage. "It's okay, Boy," she soothed, easing the cover off the cage. "Calm down now. It's okay."

After a moment, the little parakeet's squawks quieted to an occasional pitiful chirp as he hovered on his perch, and Charlotte faced Louis again.

With a quick scowl directed at the cage, he asked, "Were you still sleeping?"

The hint of disapproval in his tone grated on her caffeine-starved nerves, and Charlotte simply glared up at him. "Duh, it is Sunday morning," she told him.

"But you're always up by seven at the latest. And no, I haven't been spying on you or playing Peeping Tom," he added, "so just get that look off your face. You and I both know that the walls in this old

154

house are almost thin enough to see through."

It was true. The dividing wall between his half of the double and hers wasn't that thick or insulated, if at all, and too many nights and mornings, she'd heard his movements on the other side of that wall. It stood to reason that if she could hear him, he could hear her as well.

"Are you sick?"

"No," she snapped. "I am not sick, and I'm getting pretty tired of everyone insisting that there's something wrong with me. But — if you must know — I simply didn't sleep very well last night."

Louis' eyebrows slanted into a frown. "Okay, you're not sick, so what's wrong with your neck?"

Charlotte shot him a withering glance, and instead of answering him, she motioned toward the kitchen. "Do you mind if I put on a pot of coffee first, Mr. Detective? *Before* you interrogate me," she added.

"No need to get sarcastic," he answered. "And by all means, have some coffee. Maybe it will improve your disposition." Then he suddenly smirked. "Fell asleep on the sofa and got a crick, didn't you?"

To keep from hauling off and punching

him, Charlotte did an about-face and stomped off toward the kitchen.

"Hey, Charlotte," he called out from behind her. "Don't get mad. The only reason I knew about the crick was because I've done it myself a few times."

Charlotte paused in the doorway of the kitchen, but she didn't turn around. Between gritted teeth, she asked, "Is there a specific reason you're over here this morning, or is this a social visit? Because if this is a social visit —"

"Actually, I'm here on official business," he said, cutting her off. "Official police business," he added, moving closer toward her. "I have to ask you some more questions about yesterday."

"I should have guessed as much," she grumbled, heading for the pantry where she kept the coffee.

"Well, given your — ah — attitude, the questions can wait until after you've had coffee."

He was right, she thought as she filled the coffeepot with water and scooped coffee into the filter basket. She did have an attitude. But why? she wondered. Why did everything and everyone seem to irritate her lately, and for no real reason? Just because she felt as if she could chew nails was no excuse to take it out on Louis.

Hoping a few moments alone would help, and conscious of the time, Charlotte excused herself for a few minutes to put on her makeup while the coffee dripped. Church services began promptly at ten-thirty, and she figured if she allowed an hour for Louis' questions, she should still have time to finish dressing before she needed to leave.

By the time she'd applied a bit of makeup, she felt somewhat better and a little more in control. When she returned to the kitchen, Louis was seated at the table staring out the back window. He'd already poured them each a cup of the freshly brewed coffee, and the smell was heavenly.

"I hope you don't mind that I helped myself," he told her as she sat down opposite him.

Charlotte started to shake her head but winced when a sharp pain shot through the side of her neck. "No, not at all," she finally told him with a dismissive wave of her hand once the pain subsided.

"What you need for that crick is a good massage," he told her, and before she realized his intentions or could protest, he had shoved out of his chair and was standing behind her.

The touch of his warm hands on her neck was a shock at first, and she went still even as her senses leaped to life.

"No, now don't tense up," he told her. "Just relax and drink your coffee."

Relax? Yeah, right, she thought as the palms of his hands slid against her skin while his thumbs gently but firmly kneaded the sore muscles in the side of her neck.

She should probably protest. She really should. But at the moment she was still too stunned to utter a sound, and there was no way on God's green earth that she could casually sit there and drink coffee while he was doing such delicious things to her stiff neck.

How long had it been since she'd experienced a man's hands on her? she wondered, relaxing somewhat in spite of herself. Too long, she decided as an unexpected warmth surged through her when his forefingers brushed just below her earlobes.

"You're tensing up again," he warned as his fingers slipped down to just beneath the top edge of her pajamas and housecoat to knead the top of her shoulders as well.

A part of her wanted to relax, and she

tried. She really tried. But that other part of her, the sensible, practical part, kept whispering all the reasons she shouldn't.

Then suddenly, it was no longer even an issue. "There now," he said, with one last, warm squeeze before he withdrew his hands. "That should feel better."

Almost as quickly as it had begun, it had ended, and within moments, he was once again seated across the table from her.

All Charlotte could do was stare at him while her cheeks burned and her thick tongue refused to function. *Ridiculous,* she thought. *This is ridiculous.* In a few days she would be sixty years old, and here she was, acting like the worst cliché of a simpering virgin just because a man had touched her intimately.

"Ah — th-thanks," she finally blurted out as she slowly rotated her head from side to side. "That does feel a lot better."

"You're welcome," he told her. Then, as if he suspected how awkward the moment was for her, he pulled a small notebook and pen from his pocket and got right down to business.

"Why don't we start from the beginning," he suggested as he thumbed through the notebook. "Start from the time you first arrived — no, on second thought, start further back than that. On Friday night, when you did your walkthrough, did you notice anything unusual or out of place then?"

Charlotte's throat suddenly went dry. Knowing Louis, he wasn't going to be too pleased with her answer . . . if she told the truth. To give herself a moment to think about how she should answer, she took a slow sip of the still-warm coffee. By the time she finally set the cup down, she'd decided that there was no way around it, no choice but to tell the truth, straight out.

"I meant to mention this Friday night during dinner," she said. "And I started to — if you recall — but I got sidetracked when you began talking about Vince Roussel and his son, Todd. Once we got caught up in picking out all of that stuff for your house —" She shrugged. "I forgot about the Devilier house."

Louis never once interrupted her as she began explaining about all the signs she'd found that made her think that someone had been camping out in the old house. And throughout her explanation, he maintained a poker face that didn't give her a clue as to his reaction to what she was telling him, one way or another.

"I really meant to tell you," she said

when she had finished. "But —" She shrugged.

"And I suppose you conveniently forgot to mention it again yesterday when Judith was questioning you."

The tone of his voice should have warned her, but Charlotte ignored it. "If you remember right," she continued, "I was a bit upset yesterday, what with finding poor Drew's body and all. Then, after I fainted, I —"

Suddenly, without warning, Louis slammed his fist against the table so hard that coffee sloshed over the edge of the cups. "Poor Drew, my hind foot!" he roared. "I can't believe this crap! Of all the asinine stunts you've pulled, this one takes the cake." He leaned menacingly across the table. "Did it ever occur to you even once that after finding that stuff on Friday night, going back in there by yourself on Saturday might have been dangerous? And what about *poor Drew?*" He spat the words out as if they were bitterly foul. "Maybe, just maybe, if you had mentioned this stuff on Friday night, then *poor Drew* might still be alive instead of dead meat on a slab at the morgue?"

All Charlotte could do was stare at him in stunned disbelief. She'd expected him to be upset that she hadn't told him what she'd found. And she was both gratified and annoyed that he was concerned with her safety, but the very idea that *she* was somehow responsible for . . .

Shock quickly yielded to fury, and she jumped to her feet, her hands clenched into fists at her sides. "How — how dare you!" she sputtered. "How dare you sit there and say such things to me! And how dare you insinuate that Drew Bergeron's death is my fault."

"Sit down, Charlotte!" he warned in a no-nonsense tone.

"I will not sit down. You owe me an apology, and either you apologize or you can get out of my house right this minute."

"And if I don't?"

"I — I'll —"

"You'll do what?" Louis shot back. "Call the police?"

Long seconds ticked by as Charlotte tried, and failed, to come up with a response. Then, from the doorway, an unexpected voice suddenly intruded.

"Hey, you guys!"

Charlotte and Louis both turned to stare as Judith marched into the kitchen.

"Did I hear someone say something about calling the police? And what's all the shouting about? I could hear you two all the way out in the driveway."

"Detective Thibodeaux was just leaving," Charlotte snapped as she marched over to the cabinet and yanked a paper towel off the towel rack beside the sink.

"No, Detective Thibodeaux was not just leaving," Louis drawled. "Detective Thibodeaux was just fix'n to apologize to your aunt for being so rude and disrespectful and losing his temper. But your aunt did a very foolish thing."

"Yeah, so I gathered from the parts I heard," Judith replied. "In fact, the whole neighborhood probably heard it." She turned to Charlotte. "Well?" she asked. "Is he leaving or staying? Whichever, I would love to have a cup of that coffee."

"What are you doing here?" Charlotte asked, ignoring her niece's question as she blotted up the coffee off the table.

"I came to offer you a ride to church." Judith looked pointedly at Charlotte's housecoat. "But since you're obviously not dressed yet, I don't think we're going to make it on time."

"Don't blame me." Charlotte turned to glare at Louis. "It's all his fault."

"She's right," Louis said. "I came over to ask her some questions and — well — I guess things sort of got out of hand." He slid his gaze to Charlotte. "Again, I apologize."

Charlotte stiffened. "As well you should," she retorted.

"Don't push it, Charlotte," he warned.

She wanted to say more, was tempted to really give him a piece of her mind. But what good would it do? After all, he had apologized. Now all that was left was to either back down gracefully or come off looking like a shrew.

"Oh, for Pete's sake, this is ridiculous." She motioned at Judith. "Sit down, and I'll get you some coffee."

"I guess this means that you're not going to tell me what started the squabble to begin with?"

"Have you had breakfast yet?"

Judith stared at her a moment too long, then a tiny smile pulled at her lips as she shook her head. "Have it your way, Auntie," she said as she seated herself at the table. "I'm sure Lou will fill me in. And no, I haven't had breakfast yet. No time," she added. "Actually, I'm still working on the Bergeron murder. I intended on dropping you off at church, then I was going to come back here and see if I could pick Lou's brain. I figured that after the service, you could catch a ride with either Mother or Hank to her house."

Charlotte deposited the paper towel in the trash. "It won't take but a minute to fix some eggs and toast, and since it's too late to go to church —" She shot Louis a quick accusatory glare. "You can kill two birds with one stone, so to speak. You can eat and talk to Detective Thibodeaux at the same time."

Charlotte started toward the pantry, but after a couple of steps, she paused. "Oh, and by the way." She turned and gave Judith a knowing look. "Offering me a ride was a sweet and thoughtful gesture, but let's get one thing straight. In spite of what you and my son think, one little fainting spell does not mean I need chauffeuring around. I'm perfectly capable of driving myself anywhere I need to go. And one more thing, while I'm at it." She turned to glare at Louis again. "Though I appreciate your concern for my safety, Detective Thibodeaux, I've been looking out for myself a long time now, and I'm perfectly capable of knowing what's safe and what's not safe."

Louis' response was a grunt that indicated otherwise. Then, he leaned toward Judith. "Well, I guess she told us."

Judith nodded gravely. "She always has been a bit on the stubborn side."

Charlotte simply shook her head in annoyance and busied herself gathering the ingredients she needed from the pantry and the refrigerator for the impromptu breakfast.

Eavesdropping was not something Charlotte ordinarily approved of, but as she prepared the food, there was no way she could ignore the conversation between Judith and Louis.

"So, little girl," Louis asked, "where's that hotshot partner of yours this morning?"

"Don't start that with me, Lou," Judith warned. "But if you must know, he's back at the precinct, going over the reports from the crime scene."

There it was again, Charlotte thought as she cracked the last of a half a dozen eggs, dumped the yolk and egg white into the bowl, then poured in a dollop of milk. Why the contempt every time Louis mentioned Judith's new partner? she wondered as she added a dash of salt and pepper, then began beating the mixture with a fork. What was wrong with Will Richeaux? What had he done that would cause Louis to be so hostile?

Making a mental note to question Judith about it later, she dropped a glob of butter into the skillet she had heating on the stove burner.

By the time she had the eggs and toast ready and had set the table, Charlotte had learned that Drew Bergeron was killed by a single gunshot to the forehead, execution style. The gun used was a twenty-two caliber. Since, according to Louis, it was the type of gun that could be bought just about anywhere, it would be almost impossible to trace.

But what Judith seemed most interested in was Louis' impressions as to why Drew Bergeron would have been in town to begin with, especially after going to all the trouble of faking his own death.

"He had to have known he would be recognized by *someone*," Judith said. "Surely he wasn't that stupid."

"That I can't say," Louis told her. "All depends on if and why he faked his first death to begin with. Have you talked to his wife yet?"

Judith shook her head. "I wanted to talk to you first, then I'm heading over there. And I have to say, that's one chore I'm not looking forward to."

At the mention of Katherine Bergeron,

Charlotte felt her chest grow heavy with pity. She couldn't begin to imagine how it would feel to have to cope with something like that.

"Well, there could be all kinds of reasons he showed up here again," Louis told Judith, "but it would be a safe bet to put money at the top of the list as the number-one reason. Seems like it always boils down to money."

When Charlotte placed the food on the table, Judith got up to refill everyone's coffee cup.

Once Judith was seated again, she continued her questions. "So, yesterday you said you recognized Bergeron because you'd had dealings with him, Lou. What kind of dealings?"

"Way back when," he told her as he spooned a generous helping of eggs on his plate, "before his first so-called death, it was rumored that Bergeron was connected with Vince Roussel's crowd. I was investigating a murder that involved one of Roussel's crew at the time — a muscle-bound lowlife that we suspected of being Roussel's enforcer. We'd found this low-life's body floating in the river. At first we figured that he'd crossed Roussel, and Roussel killed him.

"Anyway — the lowlife had been seen with Bergeron the day before he was killed, so" — Louis shrugged — "I questioned Bergeron. According to what he told me, his only connection to Roussel had to do with a so-called business deal, a real estate venture on the North Shore. He claimed he and Roussel's enforcer just met by coincidence. What he didn't tell me and what I learned later was that his deal fell through and he owed Roussel a ton of money."

Judith chewed thoughtfully on a piece of toast while Charlotte took a bite of her eggs.

"Think that could have anything to do with why Bergeron might have faked his own death?" Judith finally asked. "From what I gathered, Vince Roussel isn't someone you'd want to be in debt to."

Louis shrugged. "It's a good place to start. Roussel could have sent the enforcer after Bergeron, and Bergeron offed him, then staged his own accident to get Roussel off his back. But of course there's no way to prove it."

Chapter Twelve

From what I gathered, Vince Roussel is not someone you would want to be in debt to.

Judith's words still haunted Charlotte long after her niece and Louis had left. As she pulled her van into an empty parking spot at her sister's apartment complex, she wondered what, if anything, she could say or do to persuade Cheré that these people were not the kind that she should be associating with.

Charlotte frowned as she climbed out of the van and locked it. She should have talked to Cheré yesterday about Todd Roussel, when she had the chance.

So why didn't you?

An uneasy feeling settled in the pit of her stomach as she walked toward her sister's apartment, and her footsteps slowed. She'd forgotten. Plain and simple, it had completely slipped her mind. Oh, it was easy enough to excuse her lapse of memory, what with everything that had happened at the Devilier house. But this wasn't the first time that she'd forgotten something important lately. There had been other instances over the past few weeks, other tiny details that she'd overlooked.

First the forgetfulness, then the fainting spell. Were Judith and Hank right? Could something be wrong with her?

Charlotte took a deep breath, then released it with a heavy sigh. . . . *just because you're turning sixty doesn't mean you're that old yet . . .*

Though Charlotte didn't usually put much stock in anything her sister said, for once, Madeline was right, she decided. Sixty wasn't really that old, and it certainly didn't automatically mean she was going senile. Not yet. And there was no use worrying about any of it anyway. Worrying was counterproductive and wouldn't change anything. *If* and *when* she found out there was something wrong with her, *then* she'd do whatever had to be done to cope with it. She always had.

Charlotte raised her hand to knock, but the door swung open before she got the chance.

"I was watching for you through the window," her son explained as he reached out and pulled her into his arms for a quick hug. Charlotte breathed in the scent of him and smiled. He was wearing the cologne she'd bought him for his birthday, a brand that smelled similar to the one she'd once given his father so many years ago.

When Hank pulled away, he said, "I missed you at church. How are you feeling today? Any more fainting spells?"

Patience, she reminded herself as she looked up at him. *Patience is a virtue.* Besides, Hank's concern was because he loved her. She smiled. "I'm fine, hon," she told him, patting his freshly shaved cheek.

A tall and lean man, her son had piercing blue eyes and sandy-colored hair with just a hint of gray at the temples. Just the sight of him filled her to overflowing with a mother's pride, and there were times, like now, when he so resembled his father that it took her breath away.

Charlotte felt her eyes grow misty and her throat tighten. Oh, how she wished her son and his father could have known each other, had wished it a thousand times. She'd often wondered if it would have made a difference if Hank Senior had known he'd fathered a son. Many a lonely night she'd thought that he might have tried harder to stay alive if he'd known.

But he hadn't known. There hadn't been time to tell him. Instead, he'd died, just one of the many first casualties of a war in Southeast Asia that should never have been fought to begin with.

Charlotte swallowed hard and shoved the painful memories back into that tiny compartment of her mind reserved for those she'd loved and lost.

Clearing her throat, she asked, "Who all's here?" She peeped around his shoulder. "Did Carol come with you?"

A slim, attractive woman with warm brown eyes suddenly appeared in the doorway leading from the kitchen to the small living room. "Yes, I'm here, Charlotte," she called out.

Carol Jones was a nurse whom Hank had been seeing for several months, and Charlotte had high hopes that any day now, Hank would announce their engagement and impending marriage. Unlike her son's ex-wife, Mindy, Carol was a generous, caring woman who was sensible as well as practical, all traits that strongly appealed to Charlotte. And, in Charlotte's opinion, Carol was the best shot she had of ever becoming a grandmother. Carol loved children.

Again, sadness pulled at her heart, sadness for her unborn grandchild that Hank's ex-wife had so heartlessly aborted.

"Everyone's on the patio," Carol told her, drawing Charlotte's attention back to the present.

After a quick hug, Carol looped her arm through Charlotte's and urged her toward the kitchen. "Madeline gave us strict instructions to bring you out there as soon as you arrived. But what's this I hear about you fainting yesterday?"

Charlotte chose to ignore the question. "I like your hair that way," she said instead. Normally, Carol wore her dark, shoulder-length hair in a classic pageboy style, but today, she'd pulled it back and secured it with a large barrette, a style that strongly emphasized her high cheekbones.

Carol shrugged. "Thanks. This is what happens when I don't have time to wash it. I worked the evening shift last night and didn't get relieved until half the night shift was over. I ended up oversleeping because someone we both know and love" — she shot Hank a pointed look — "forgot to call me when he was supposed to."

Hank just shrugged. "I figured you needed sleep more than your hair needed washing."

Suddenly, a child's ear-piercing squeal rent the air, and all three of them froze.

"Is that who I think it is?" Charlotte asked Hank.

Hank groaned but nodded. "Little Davy, in the flesh. According to his mother, that horrible noise he just made is his latest trick to get her attention."

Charlotte grinned. "So Daniel finally did it. I had wondered when he was going to get up enough nerve to invite Nadia and Davy to one of our little gatherings."

When Nadia's live-in boyfriend had been arrested for theft five months earlier, she hadn't been able to afford an attorney. She'd shown up on Charlotte's doorstep in tears. She said her son kept crying for his father, and she didn't know where to turn or what to do.

Though Charlotte had never cared for Ricco Martinez, she felt sorry for Nadia and Davy, and she had persuaded Daniel to take Ricco's case pro bono. Daniel had been willing, but once he'd gotten Ricco out on bail, Ricco had abruptly disappeared without a word to anyone.

At first Daniel had continued seeing Nadia, using the excuse that he was simply lending legal support. But he hadn't fooled Charlotte. She knew better. She had sensed right away that her nephew had fallen for Nadia and Davy. Nadia had been reluctant in the beginning, but with Ricco out of the picture, Daniel's persistence and kindness was finally paying off, and nothing could have pleased Charlotte more.

"How's your aunt taking it?" Charlotte asked Hank.

"Better than I would have thought," he answered. "She was a little distant at first — you know how Aunt Maddie can get — but I think she knows that she doesn't have much say in the matter. Once my cousin sets his mind on something, he can be every bit as stubborn as you ever thought about being."

"Well, he could do a lot worse," Charlotte avowed, ignoring her son's gibe. "Nadia is a lovely person, and Davy is as cute as a button. And speaking of children, when are —"

Hank immediately cut her off. "Don't even go there, Mother."

Charlotte sighed and Carol grinned. It wasn't the first time she had tried to hint that she wanted a grandchild, and it wouldn't be the last, she vowed. After all, she certainly wasn't getting any younger and neither was her son.

Then Hank, like the gentleman his mother had raised him to be, opened the back door and ushered the two women through to the backyard.

Though Madeline's patio and backyard were small, the area was adequate for the small gathering. Daniel was hovering over the smoking barbecue pit near the fence, and Madeline and Nadia were setting out food on the picnic table, while Davy was busy stalking something through the tall grass near the corner of the fence.

"Hey, Aunt Charley," Daniel called out. "You're just in time."

Madeline and Nadia glanced up from their tasks. "Not just in time, but about time," Madeline scolded. "Where have you been? Judith said she left your place over two hours ago. And another thing." Her stern expression suddenly softened, and a secretive smile played at her lips. "What's this I hear about Louis being there with you still in your robe?" she teased. "Come on, Charlotte, do tell."

At that moment, Charlotte could have happily choked her sister. When she ventured a quick glance at her son and found him staring at her with an amused but curious expression on his face, she felt a slow flush creep up her neck.

Telling herself that she was too old to be embarrassed so easily over a bit of teasing, and that the warmth that had now reached her cheeks was not a blush, she smiled sweetly. "Police business, sister *dear*. Detective Thibodeaux had some more questions about yesterday."

"Yeah, right," Madeline quipped with a giggle. Then she quickly sobered. "Speaking of yesterday." She made a face. "As usual, my daughter was tight-lipped and wouldn't tell me any of the real juicy stuff when she called." She nudged Nadia with her elbow. "Maybe now we can get the real scoop."

Nadia simply smiled indulgently. "Not if I know Charlotte. She's the last person you'll get to gossip about anything."

Little Davy chose that particular moment to let out another of his earsplitting squeals, diverting everyone's attention.

"Oh, Davy, honey, no-no." Nadia rushed toward her son. In his pudgy fingers was what appeared to be a small green lizard, wriggling frantically in an attempt to regain its freedom. "Let that poor thing go," Nadia told him as she pried his fingers apart.

Evidently none the worse for wear, the tiny reptile promptly scurried away. When it disappeared in the grass, Davy screwed up his face and began to wail as if his little heart had been broken.

Seizing upon the opportunity to avoid discussing the events of the previous day, Charlotte hurried over to help comfort the little boy.

"Hey, little man," she cooed. "What's all this crying about?" She knelt down beside him, and seeking something to distract him, she pointed at his T-shirt. "I sure do like your shirt, but who's that silly-looking bear on it? I'll bet his name is Tigger."

Davy shook his head. "Not Tigger," he whimpered.

Charlotte pretended to be confused. "Maybe Piglet?"

"Pooh Bear," the little boy declared, the lizard forgotten momentarily. He patted the figure on his shirt. "Name Pooh Bear."

"Hey, Davy —" Without warning, Daniel suddenly appeared beside them and scooped the little boy up in his arms. "How about an airplane ride?" Amid Davy's giggles of delight, Daniel lifted the little boy above his head. Making a guttural roaring noise, Daniel began loping back and forth around the small backyard.

With Davy distracted, Madeline continued as if she'd never been interrupted. "You know that after Drew Bergeron's father-in-law died, the firm I work for began handling City Realty's bookkeeping," she said.

In spite of her earlier reluctance to discuss the matter, Charlotte found herself curious. "His father-in-law was Maurice Sinclair, wasn't he?"

Madeline nodded. "After the old man's death, Drew stepped in and took over City Realty, and the first thing he did was move their account to our firm."

"I wonder why," Charlotte murmured.

"Probably had something to do with the deal he was working on with Roussel Construction," Madeline said. "My boss and Vince Roussel go back a long way, and since we handled their books, I guess he figured it would be easier all the way around."

"Do y'all still handle City Realty?"

Madeline shook her head. "A couple of months after Drew's funeral, his wife switched everything back to the firm her father had always used before."

"Hey, Mom," Daniel called out, interrupting them. "Davy and I think the chicken looks like it's about done, so could you bring that platter over?"

"I'll take it," Nadia volunteered.

"Thanks," Madeline told her. "And I guess that means I need to get the rest of the food out so we can eat."

"I'll help you," Charlotte offered.

"And Hank and I will put ice in the glasses," Carol volunteered.

By the time they had all settled around the table and said the blessings, much to Charlotte's relief the Devilier house and Drew Bergeron's murder were forgotten for the moment . . . or so she'd thought.

While everyone stuffed themselves with Daniel's barbecued chicken and Madeline's sour-cream potato salad and baked beans, conversation turned to All Saints' Day and Halloween.

"I wonder which cemetery they'll bury Drew Bergeron in this time," Madeline commented, tongue in cheek. "Whichever, he couldn't have picked a better time to have another funeral."

"Madeline!"

"Mother!"

Ignoring Charlotte's and Daniel's gasps of disbelief, Madeline shot them a defiant look. "Well, it's true," she said. "Why, just last Friday, I noticed a group already working in Lafayette Number One."

Lafayette Number One, located on Washington Avenue, was just one of over thirty aboveground cemeteries located throughout the city. As in most of Louisiana, the two weeks leading up to All Saints' Day was a time when everyone gathered to pay homage to their dead by cleaning and beautifying the cemeteries. Armed with buckets of whitewash, scrubbing brushes, and gardening tools, families would gather in the cemeteries and spend hours laboring away so that the tombs and grounds were tidy and neat for All Saints' Day.

Madeline cast a wary eye toward Charlotte. "Are you going this year?"

Though Charlotte was Protestant, Hank's father had been Catholic. For years Charlotte had honored his memory by attending the special All Saints' Day services held at the cemetery where his remains had been buried.

"If Mother wants to go this year, I'll take her."

Charlotte gave her son a grateful look, and he, in turn, gave her a knowing smile.

"Better you than me," Madeline quipped. "Those places give me the creeps. It's still hard to believe that people used to go there at night and do those weird rituals and stuff."

"They weren't weird," Charlotte argued. "Lighted candles were blessed by the priests, then placed on the tombs, and a mass was held. The priests performed what they call the ancient rites for the souls of the departed."

Madeline shuddered. "I don't care what they called it." She shuddered again. "No way would you ever catch me there after dark."

Sensing that a change of subject was needed, Daniel turned to Davy. "Davy and I are going trick-or-treating this year for Halloween, aren't we, big guy?"

Since Charlotte had a couple of errands to run after she left Madeline's house, it was late that afternoon before she finally returned home. Waiting for her was a fractious Sweety Boy and several messages on her answering machine.

"I know, I know, Boy," she told the little parakeet as she opened the cage door. "You're tired of being penned up in there, aren't you, fellow?"

His answer was a squawk as he scurried through the open cage door and spent several minutes flying back and forth from one corner of the room to the other. When he finally settled on top of the cuckoo clock, Charlotte walked over to the desk and hit the play button of the answering machine.

The first message was from Bitsy, and Charlotte sighed.

"My goodness, Charlotte, where are you?" the old lady said reprovingly. "I didn't hear about Drew Bergeron until this morning at church, what with Jenny's being here and all. And by the way, Jenny and I had a lovely visit. But I'll tell you all about it when you come on Tuesday." Bitsy paused a moment, then said, "You *are* coming on Tuesday, aren't you? Someone said that you were the one who found poor Drew dead and that when you found him, you fainted. What a dreadful experience. I do hope you're okay."

"Oh, great!" Charlotte exclaimed as Bitsy paused again. Already the rumors were circulating. Inaccurate rumors to boot.

"Well — anyway," Bitsy continued. "Give me a call as soon as you get home."

"Not likely," Charlotte muttered as the message ended and the beep sounded.

The machine beeped again, and the next message began.

"Ms. LaRue. Vince Roussel here. Just calling to tell you that I'll be in touch as to when your crew can finish up at the Devilier house. The police are dragging their feet, though, and I doubt you can get back in there before next weekend."

The brief, but curt message reminded Charlotte of what Louis and Judith had told her about Vince Roussel and his son, and it left her with an uneasy feeling as well as a sense of urgency. The sooner she talked to Cheré, the better, she thought.

"Speak of the devil," Charlotte murmured when the machine beeped and she recognized Cheré's voice as her last caller.

"Just checking up on you, Charlotte, to see how you're feeling today. Give me a call if you have time."

Long after the message ended, Charlotte continued staring at the machine. Even though she had already decided to talk to Cheré about Todd Roussel, the thought of interfering in her employee's personal life left a bad taste in her mouth.

From the beginning, she'd always made it a rule to mind her own business when it came to employees or clients. Unless an employee sought out her help or asked for advice, as Nadia had done, Charlotte never interfered in their personal lives. More times than not, and knowing human nature, uninvited meddling just caused hard feelings and resentment.

But if Louis and Judith were right . . . if

the Roussels were mixed up with the mob . . .

Suddenly another thought hit her. What was it that Louis had said about some kind of business dealings between Vince Roussel and Drew Bergeron? Something about a real estate deal that had gone sour, if she remembered right.

Charlotte frowned, deep in thought. But there was something else that Louis had said about Vince Roussel too. Something — Then she remembered.

We'd found this lowlife's body floating in the river . . . we figured he'd crossed Roussel, and Roussel killed him.

As Louis' words played through her mind, Charlotte's knees grew weak, and she stumbled to the sofa. It was obvious that Louis thought that Vince Roussel was capable of murder, and if that was true, then . . .

Charlotte shivered. Was it possible? Could Vince Roussel have murdered Drew Bergeron?

Chapter Thirteen

The sky was overcast and dreary, and the air was once again heavy with humidity by Monday morning, none of which helped the depressed mood that threatened to overwhelm Charlotte as she locked her house and climbed into her van. Already, she felt as if she'd put in a full day's work, and for the first time in a long time, she wished she could simply stay home and climb back into bed.

Within reason, Charlotte knew that her lethargy and depressed mood were simply the results of lack of sleep after a restless night of tossing and turning due to worry.

After much soul searching, she had finally placed a call to Cheré before she'd gone to bed the night before. But Cheré wasn't home, and Charlotte had been forced to leave a message on the young woman's answering machine. Charlotte's message had been short and to the point. She'd simply told Cheré that she needed to see her right away. Then, Charlotte had suggested that Monday around five would be a good time if Cheré could drop by her house.

To make matters worse, along with worrying about Cheré, no matter how hard she'd tried, she kept thinking about Drew Bergeron. Recurring visions of how he'd looked, all slumped over and wearing nothing much more than that silly feathered mask, kept haunting her.

But underlying all of her other worries were the nagging thoughts about her health . . . the tiredness she'd felt lately, the forgetfulness, and the fainting spell. Each symptom could be excused or explained away individually, but all of them together . . .

"Stop it," she muttered as she turned the van down the street where Marian lived. "Just stop it right now."

Hank had set her up with an appointment to see a colleague of his on Tuesday afternoon, she reminded herself again. Until then, there was no use in even speculating about it, just as there was no reason to speculate about Drew Bergeron's death. How or why he had been murdered was none of her concern. As for Cheré, she would have her talk with her that afternoon, but ultimately, the young woman would have to decide for herself what was best.

Firmly shoving the thoughts aside, Charlotte pulled in front of Marian's house and parked. From the back of the van, she gathered her cleaning supplies along with two of the candles that she'd bought after leaving her sister's house the day before.

All the talk about All Saints' Day and candles had started her thinking. There were all types of scented candles now that were designed to alter moods. Maybe there was one she could get for Marian, one that might help calm her. Since she'd been on Magazine Street anyway, she'd decided to stop in at one of the specialty shops and check it out.

While in the shop, she had noticed a display that was devoted solely to aromatherapy. There were also brochures explaining the theory behind mood-altering scents. When she'd read how the scent of lavender had the power to soothe, she'd immediately purchased several lavender-scented candles.

"Should have used the candles myself," she muttered as she locked the van.

Within mere seconds of ringing Marian's doorbell, the front door swung open. One look at Marian, and Charlotte figured the poor woman needed more than a few candles to calm her down.

Once again she was still in her night-gown and robe, but unlike on Friday, today there were dark circles beneath her eyes, and her hair was tangled and in dire need of a good shampooing. But it was the wild look in Marian's eyes that disturbed Charlotte the most.

"Oh, Charlotte, come in, come in. I've been waiting for you."

Despite the distance between them, Charlotte wrinkled her nose when she caught a distinct whiff of alcohol. "Where are the boys?"

"Is it true?" Marian asked breathlessly, her eyes glittering with some emotion that Charlotte couldn't readily identify. "Did you really find Drew Bergeron's body at the Devilier house?"

Charlotte felt like groaning out loud as she stepped past Marian into the entrance hall.

"The story was splattered all over the front page of the *Picayune* yesterday," Marian continued without waiting for a response. "But even before the story came out in the paper, I heard about it from Sam. He said he heard about it Saturday afternoon at the Rink when he stopped in for a cup of coffee.

"If you ask me," Marian rushed on, "the S.O.B. got exactly what he deserved. But then, that's exactly what I thought two years ago after his so-called plane crash.

"Well?" Marian grabbed Charlotte's arm. "Is it true? Were you the one who found him? Please tell me you were and that he truly is dead this time."

Charlotte was taken aback by Marian's vehemence. But she was equally disturbed that her name was being connected with all of the gossip flying around — not to mention the clawlike grip Marian had on her arm.

Charlotte gently patted Marian's hand. Then, under the pretense of setting down the supply carrier, she eased back a step to free herself from Marian's grasp. Once she'd set her supplies down on the floor, she finally replied to Marian's question. "I was in the house when Drew's body was discovered. But *I* didn't find him," she avowed. "Rest assured, though, the body was definitely identified as Drew Bergeron."

Since that was all she intended to say about the matter, Charlotte tried to change the subject.

"How's Aaron feeling? What did the doctor have to say about him?"

"Aaron's fine — nothing but a virus." Marian dismissed the subject of her son's illness with an impatient wave of her hand. "So if you didn't find Drew, then who —"

"And B.J.'s okay too?" Charlotte interrupted, determined to change the subject. "He didn't come down with the virus?"

"No!" Marian glared at her. "Aaron's just fine," she snapped. "B.J.'s just fine. *I'm* just fine. Now, who —"

At that moment the phone rang, interrupting further discussion, to Charlotte's vast relief.

With a look of frustration, Marian spun away, marched to the extension, and jerked up the receiver.

Charlotte fully intended taking advantage of the phone call to make herself scarce. After all, she'd come there to work, not to gossip about Drew Bergeron. But a sudden gasp from Marian stopped her in her tracks.

"He's been what?" Marian sputtered. As Marian listened to the reply, she paled and leaned heavily against the wall. "For fighting?" she whispered. "Fighting with who?" Several moments passed before Marian finally said, "Yes, of course I understand. I can come pick him up within the hour."

When Marian finally hung up the receiver, she pushed away from the wall and turned to face Charlotte. "That was B.J.'s school," she said, her eyes welling with tears. "He's been suspended for — for fighting, an— and I have to go get him."

"Oh, hon, I'm so sorry." Charlotte rushed over to her and wrapped her arm around the younger woman's shoulders. "I just can't believe that B.J. was fighting. Surely there's been a mistake of some kind."

Marian gave a one-shouldered shrug and swiped at the tears that had spilled over onto her cheeks. "I don't find anything hard to believe anymore. But th-thanks, Charlotte." She pulled away from Charlotte's embrace. "Thanks anyway. Guess I'd better go get dressed."

As Charlotte watched Marian walk away, her head down, her steps dragging as if she were wading through ankle-deep mud, her heart went out to the younger woman and to B.J. as well.

From all indications, the boy was well on his way to trouble with a capital T, and Marian, poor thing, was well on her way to the breaking point.

With a sigh, Charlotte picked up her supply carrier. "Such a shame," she murmured. "A crying shame."

Almost half an hour passed before Marian came looking for Charlotte to let her know she was leaving. Though makeup had been artfully applied to cover the dark circles beneath Marian's eyes, and she had twisted her hair up and secured it into a presentable French roll, nothing could disguise the worried, defeated look in her eyes.

"If the phone rings, just let the machine pick up the calls," she told Charlotte. "I don't have any appointments this morning, but if anyone does drop by, I should be back within the hour."

Once Marian left, Charlotte strategically placed the two candles she'd brought with her and lit them — one in Marian's office, and one in the kitchen-living area — in hopes that the soothing scent would have time to permeate those portions of the house by the time Marian returned. Then she focused on the task of cleaning the stove.

If possible, the kitchen was in worse shape than she had found it in on Friday. Not only was the cooktop of the stove splattered and caked with what appeared to be dried spaghetti sauce, but something had boiled over and congealed in one of the drip plates.

The stove was all-electric, so it was simple enough to disassemble it. Since all four of the drip plates needed a good cleaning anyway, Charlotte filled the sink with hot, sudsy water and let them soak while she scrubbed the cooktop.

After she'd thoroughly scrubbed the stovetop, she liberally applied an appliance wax, a thick, creamy liquid that when rubbed off and polished would leave the whole stove glowing and would help make subsequent cleanups easier.

Charlotte had just begun wiping away the wax when a loud crash broke the silence. "What on earth," she cried as she jerked her head around to stare toward the dining room.

Dropping the towel she'd been using onto the cabinet, she hurried toward the dining room.

The dining room was at the front of the house, and a large double window overlooked the porch and the street. The first thing she spotted was a small pile of lumber on the porch, lumber that hadn't been there when she'd arrived earlier. Beyond the porch was a battered white truck parked behind her van.

"Of course," she murmured, immediately recognizing the truck. It was only Sam making all the racket. From the looks of the planks, he'd brought in the load of lumber to do some repairs, probably to the porch, she decided, eying two cans of paint sitting beside the lumber. The last few times she'd swept it, she'd noticed that there were some rotting boards that needed replacing.

But where was he? Craning her head, she scanned the front yard. When she finally spotted him, he was coming around the corner of the house, headed back toward his truck.

She watched for a moment more until she saw him heave a large toolbox from the bed of the truck. Her curiosity satisfied, she returned to the kitchen.

As she finished cleaning the stove and the rest of the kitchen, she was able to trace Sam's progress through the sounds she heard coming from the porch . . . the creaking of boards being pried loose, the whine of an electric saw, followed finally by the banging of a hammer.

Charlotte had finally finished in the kitchen and living area and was dusting and waxing the tables in the hallway when she heard the rattle of the back door screen, then the groan of the back door being opened.

"Charlotte!" Marian called out. "It's just us."

When Charlotte walked into the kitchen, Marian was unloading small boxes of food from a sack onto the kitchen counter. Her mouth watered at the smell of fried chicken wafting from the boxes. But when she glanced to her left and saw B.J. perched on one of the bar stools at the island that separated the kitchen from the living area, all thoughts of food were forgotten.

He gave her a sullen look. The white knit shirt he wore was filthy and spotted with what she could only guess was dried blood. But it was his bruised and puffy face, along with the large bandage he was sporting just above his swollen right eye, that made her wince with sympathetic pain.

Marian glanced over her shoulder. "Oh, hey, Charlotte. I see that Sam started on the porch. Did anyone call or drop by?"

Charlotte dragged her gaze away from B.J. and shook her head. "No calls, no visitors," she answered.

"That's good," Marian continued, "because things took a bit longer than I expected." She motioned toward her son.

"As you can see, B.J. had a nasty cut, so we had to make a side trip by the doctor's office. Had to wait an eternity, but thank goodness he only needed a couple of stitches." She pointed to the boxes on the cabinet. "Since it's so close to lunchtime, I went ahead and picked up some Popeye's chicken. You're welcome to join us if you'd like."

"Thanks," Charlotte told her. "I'm really tempted, but I've put on a couple of pounds, so I guess I'd better stick to the salad I brought."

Then, placing her hands on her hips, Charlotte abruptly turned her attention back to B.J. "Well, young man," she said. "I certainly hope the other guy looks at least as bad as you do."

"Don't encourage him, Charlotte," Marian warned. "He's in enough trouble as it is."

"Believe me, encouraging him to fight is the last thing I'd do. Well?" she addressed B.J. again. "Does he? Does he look as bad as you do? Did *he* have to get stitches?"

When B.J. finally shook his head, Charlotte leveled a stern, narrow-eyed look at him. "Then what was the point?"

"He started it," the teenager blurted out defensively.

"And you finished it by getting yourself beat up. Like I said before, what was the point?" She let him mull it over a moment. Then, with a sympathetic smile on her face, she moved closer. "You know sometimes it takes more courage just to walk away than to fight," she said gently. "Fighting doesn't always solve the problem, and knowing when to fight and when to walk away is one of the real differences between being a boy and being a man."

Charlotte didn't kid herself that B.J. would necessarily take her advice or even listen to her homegrown philosophy. She could only hope that emphasizing the differences between being a man and a boy would make an impression, especially since she suspected that trying to be the man of the family was one of B.J.'s problems. She'd raised a son and the signs were all there. She also knew that sometimes just planting a small seed of wisdom did a lot more good than an all-out lecture.

"Just think about it, okay?" Moving even closer, she asked, "So — are we still friends?" After a brief hesitation, when he finally nodded, Charlotte grinned and held out her hand, palm side up. "Well, then, give me five, my friend."

Though he rolled his eyes toward the ceiling and let out an indignant groan, he finally relented and slapped his hand against hers.

"All right, out of sight!" she drawled, which produced yet another indignant groan.

"Go wash up, B.J.," Marian interrupted. "And change your shirt. It's almost time to eat."

Though B.J. cast a resentful look at his mother, he did as he was told.

As soon as he was out of earshot, Marian turned to Charlotte. "Any suggestions?" she asked.

Because of Charlotte's experience with the Dubuisson family, the last thing she wanted or needed was to get sucked into yet another client's personal life or problems. But this situation was different, she told herself. There was just no way she could ignore it, not when the welfare of two children was at stake. Marian was sick, possibly mentally ill from all accounts. Grown-ups and their problems were one thing, but when it came to children . . .

Charlotte didn't even try to pretend that she didn't know what Marian was talking about. "Have you thought about some professional counseling?"

"Oh, I've thought about it, but B.J. would never cooperate in a million years."

Whether Marian had genuinely misunderstood or had deliberately misunderstood was hard to tell; Charlotte couldn't be sure. Since she couldn't be sure, she suddenly found herself reluctant to correct her employer's assumption. Still . . . there was more than one way to get a point across.

"You're probably right," Charlotte agreed. "B.J. might not cooperate, not if he thought *he* was being singled out. But what if you used another approach? What if you made it a family affair and all of you went in for some counseling sessions?"

The expression on Marian's face was contemplative, as if she were seriously considering Charlotte's suggestion. She was about to answer when, much to Charlotte's frustration and disappointment, the chimes of the front doorbell interrupted.

Marian, looking as frustrated as Charlotte felt, said, "I'd better see who that is."

Since Charlotte needed to finish waxing one of the tables in the entrance hall anyway, she followed Marian.

When Marian opened the front door, Charlotte's mouth dropped open at the sight of the couple standing on the other side of the threshold. What on earth were *they* doing here? she wondered as shock turned into an uneasy feeling of dread deep in the pit of her stomach.

Chapter Fourteen

Charlotte's imagination went wild as one terrible scenario after another ran rampant through her mind. Surely the only reason for Louis and Judith showing up where she worked was because something horrible had happened to one of the family . . . Hank . . . Madeline . . . Daniel . . .

But after only the briefest nod of recognition, Judith turned to address Marian instead. Only then did Charlotte remember to breathe again.

"Mrs. Hebert, I'm Detective Monroe with the New Orleans Police Department."

With a confused frown, Marian stared hard at Judith, then turned to stare at Charlotte. Even without Marian saying a word, Charlotte could tell from her confused frown what she was thinking. The resemblance between Charlotte and her niece was amazing. More times than not, to Madeline's constant aggravation, anyone meeting Judith for the first time wrongly assumed that Charlotte and Judith were mother and daughter instead of aunt and niece.

"And this is Detective Thibodeaux," Judith continued. We're here —"

"Who's at the door, Mom?" B.J. stepped out of his room near the end of the hall and shuffled past Charlotte to where his mother was standing. He'd changed from his soiled shirt and chinos into a pair of baggy jeans shorts and a T-shirt, Charlotte noted with satisfaction.

But Marian's mouth tightened with irritation as she glared at her son. "Detectives from the police department, son." She gave Judith an apologetic look. "Sorry. Now, what were you saying?"

"I was saying that —"

"What do the cops want with us?" B.J. blurted out as he glared first at Judith, then at Louis.

"B.J.! Mind your manners," his mother admonished. "Now apologize to Detective Monroe for being so rude."

"I wasn't rude, and I didn't do anything," he all but snarled. "So why do I have to apologize, especially to a couple of stupid cops?"

"B.J.! Stop it!"

"But I didn't do anything!"

"We'll discuss it later," Marian told him

firmly between gritted teeth. "Now go to your room, young man."

When B.J. didn't budge, Marian took a step toward him. "Go *now!*" she ordered, a warning tone of *or else* in her voice.

For a moment, Charlotte wasn't sure who was going to win the battle of wills, but finally B.J. relented. With daggers of resentment shooting from his eyes, he whirled around, and muttering what Charlotte could only guess were expletives beneath his breath, he stomped off down the hallway.

He didn't go to his room, though, Charlotte noticed. At the last second, he abruptly changed directions and headed into the kitchen instead. But Marian had already turned back to Judith and Louis, so she didn't see that he had disobeyed her.

"Again, I'm so sorry," she told Judith. "Come in, come in," she said, motioning for the two detectives to come inside. With a sigh of defeat, she added, "And please excuse my son." She pulled the door closed behind them. "My husband was killed back in January, and my son was here when the police came to inform us of his death. Unfortunately, he heard all of the grisly details, and ever since, he gets

this way whenever he sees a policeman."
She shrugged. "I guess seeing or being
around the police brings back all the
painful memories for him."

"I'm sure it does," Judith murmured, her
eyes narrowed in an expression that Charlotte recognized all too well, an expression
that said Judith wasn't buying the excuse.

Marian sighed again. "Now, how can I
help you?"

"We're investigating the murder of Drew
Bergeron," Louis said, stepping up beside
Judith, "and it's our understanding that
your real estate company is handling the
rentals of the Devilier apartments."

While Marian talked, Louis kept shooting reproachful glances Charlotte's way,
glances that irritated her, but made her feel
self-conscious and conspicuous as well.
Since she had finished waxing the table
anyway, and since her initial curiosity had
been satisfied as to why Judith and Louis
had shown up at Marian's, she decided
that now was as good a time as any to
make herself scarce.

But Charlotte didn't go far, just to the
dining room. There, she was out of sight
but still within hearing distance of the conversation taking place in the entrance hall.

As Louis began questioning Marian

about potential clients who had shown an interest in the apartments, a movement just outside the front dining-room window caught Charlotte's attention. Curious, she stepped closer, just in time to see B.J. drop down into one of the wicker chairs on the porch. The chair was located near enough to the front door that he could probably hear the conversation between the detectives and his mother even though it was closed.

At first she thought his actions were a bit strange, but then she figured that like her, he was simply curious as to what the detectives were doing there. Charlotte turned away and began the tasks of dusting and waxing the mahogany extension-leaf table.

It was while she was clearing off the centerpiece that another, more plausible excuse came to mind. Maybe, just maybe, B.J. was afraid that the police showing up had something to do with the fight he'd been in at school.

Out in the hall, Charlotte heard Judith say, "We'd like a list of anyone who might have access to keys to the house."

"No need for a list," she heard Marian respond. "Besides myself, only two others had keys. Jefferson — Jefferson Harper, the owner — has a master set, and Drew's wife, Katherine, picked up a set on Friday afternoon. Katherine was thinking about buying one of the apartments to use for out-of-town guests, mostly during Mardi Gras," she explained. "Since I couldn't show her the apartments myself on Friday because of a doctor's appointment, I told Katherine she could pick up the keys and look around on her own."

"Mrs. Hebert, we understand that you and your husband were friends with the Bergerons. Were you close friends?"

The question came from Louis, and as Marian explained about the former relationship between the two couples, for the first time since Louis and Judith had arrived, it suddenly dawned on Charlotte that Judith's new partner, Will Richeaux, should have been with Judith instead of Louis. So where was Will? she wondered. And why was Louis there instead?

Once again, Charlotte wondered about the obvious antagonism between Louis and Will that she'd witnessed on Saturday.

She'd have to remember to ask Judith later. Yeah, right, she thought uneasily. The way her memory was lately, she'd probably forget . . . again.

Since Charlotte had finished in the dining room but didn't want to disturb the group in the hall, she resigned herself to the fact that there was nothing more she could do for the moment but wait until Judith and Louis had finished questioning Marian.

Maybe this would be a good time to take a lunch break. Usually she enjoyed eating her lunch out on the front porch in the fresh air. Then she remembered that Sam had been working out there, and the last time she'd looked, B.J. was still on the porch too.

Hoping that Sam had finished by now and that B.J. had grown tired of just sitting and eavesdropping, Charlotte wandered over to the window to check out the situation.

To her disappointment, B.J. was still slouched in the wicker chair. So where was Sam?

In the hall, Marian was talking, nonstop, about the business relationship between her husband and Drew Bergeron. That Marian was bitter was more than evident, and though she didn't exactly come right out and say it, it was plain that she blamed Drew Bergeron for her husband's state of mind before his accident.

Charlotte was so caught up in what Marian was saying that the sudden appearance of Sam within her view gave her a start. Even if she hadn't noticed the can of paint he was carrying, it was obvious from the smears on his overalls that he'd been painting, and even more obvious that he'd finished the task as he began gathering the tools lying near the toolbox.

If he was finished, though, then she might be able to eat her salad on the porch after all . . . except that B.J. was still there.

Sam closed up the toolbox, but instead of loading it back into his truck, he approached B.J. After a few words to the teenager, he turned and walked to the steps. Within moments, B.J. pushed himself out of the chair and followed Sam. Then the two of them disappeared around the corner of the house together.

It was almost four when Charlotte turned onto her street that afternoon. So much for the soothing scent of the lavender candles, she thought. Her restless night combined with work and the tensions between Marian and B.J. had left her feeling drained, and definitely not soothed.

Maybe once she was home, she'd forgo her usual shower and take a long, relaxing hot bath instead. Maybe she'd even start on that new Joanne Fluke mystery she'd picked up the last time she was in the Garden District Bookshop.

Yep, Charlotte decided, a hot soak in the tub and a good book were always a surefire way to relax and forget . . .

And what about Cheré? You told her to meet you at five.

"Oh, no," she groaned. Today of all days, the last thing she felt like doing was getting embroiled in yet another human being's personal problems.

Charlotte glanced at the dashboard clock. She could always cancel the meeting. She was almost home, and it was just a little past four. Maybe there was still time if she hurried.

Charlotte pressed her foot a little harder against the accelerator and was halfway down her block when she spotted the tan Toyota parked in front of her house. Her heart sank. It was too late. Cheré was already there waiting for her.

But why was Cheré there so early? she wondered. She was almost certain that she'd left word that they were to meet at five, not four . . . well, almost certain.

Warning spasms of alarm erupted within Charlotte, quickly followed by the same uneasy feeling that had plagued her for weeks. Had she told Cheré four o'clock and just thought she'd said five? Was this yet another example of her forgetfulness lately?

"Oh, for Pete's sake," she muttered. "This is ridiculous!" One way or another, she'd find out for sure on Tuesday when she kept her doctor's appointment, so why borrow trouble? Besides, she had other, more pressing things to worry about at the moment, mainly Cheré. Somehow, some way, she had to find the right words to tell Cheré about the Roussels.

As Charlotte turned into her driveway, Cheré waved to her from the porch swing, and Charlotte, forcing a smile she didn't feel, waved back.

Once she'd parked the van, she locked it. Then, taking a deep, fortifying breath, she headed toward the porch.

"Hey, Charlotte."

"Hey, yourself," Charlotte answered as she climbed the steps. "Have you been waiting long?"

Cheré shook her head. "Just got here a few minutes ago," she answered, pushing out of the swing. "I know you said five in your message, but I took a chance that you wouldn't mind if I came by a little early."

"Of course!" Charlotte suddenly gushed, so relieved that she felt like shouting. "You *are* early, aren't you? And no, I don't mind. No siree, I don't mind at all."

Cheré gave her a strange look. "Charlotte? Are you okay?"

Charlotte figured that the poor girl probably thought she was either drunk or high on something, but she really didn't want to have to explain. She waved away Cheré's concern.

"I'm fine," she told her. "Just a bit — ah, overtired," she quickly improvised. "Haven't you ever been so tired that you either started acting silly or got the giggles?"

"I guess," Cheré answered, not looking very convinced.

The moment Charlotte unlocked and opened the front door, Sweety Boy started his usual routine of squawking and preening to get her attention. But unlike most days, Charlotte ignored the little bird as she switched on the light, then set down her purse.

Cheré followed her inside and pulled the door closed behind her. "You haven't had any more fainting spells, have you?"

Charlotte shook her head as she slipped off her shoes and stepped into the soft moccasins beside the front door. "No fainting spells. Just —" She shrugged. "Just tired." She motioned toward the sofa. "Why don't you have a seat, and I'll get us something to drink. Iced tea okay with you?"

"Sounds great," Cheré responded as she sank down on the sofa.

Minutes later, Charlotte returned with two tall glasses of tea.

"So what's up?" Cheré asked as she accepted the glass Charlotte handed her. "Why did you want to see me?"

Charlotte settled in the chair opposite the sofa. With a sigh, she plunged in. "I don't know any way to say this but straight out. But please, just remember that I'm not being nosy. I just care about you and I don't want to see you get hurt."

Cheré frowned. "I don't understand."

"I know you don't, hon. Not yet. But you will . . . I hope. You see, over the past few days I've been hearing some really disturbing things about your friend, Todd, and his father. Things that I think you need to know about."

Cheré's frown deepened. "What kind of things? And from who?"

Charlotte explained about the conversations she'd had with Louis and Judith, and she repeated the things she'd been told about the Roussels. To Cheré's credit, she didn't flinch or interrupt, or even offer a word of protest.

"Ordinarily, I wouldn't interfere," Charlotte assured her when she had finished. "But whether the allegations are true or not, my main concern is for you. I'm not blaming you, mind you, but if I had known all of this stuff before, I'm not so sure I would have accepted the Devilier job. And now, with everything that's happened, I'm wishing I'd never heard of the Devilier house or Drew Bergeron."

For long seconds, Cheré simply stared at Charlotte. Then, to Charlotte's utter distress, the girl's eyes filled with tears that overflowed down her cheeks.

"Oh, hon —" Charlotte moved immediately to the sofa. She set her glass down on the coffee table and put her arm around the younger woman's shoulders. "Please don't think I'm blaming you, because I'm not. I know this is upsetting, but I just couldn't stand by and not say anything. I care too much about you."

Cheré closed her eyes and shook her head. "Not upset — not with you." She bowed her head. "Mostly upset with myself. I've known for some time that something was wrong, that Todd and his father weren't . . ." Her voice trailed away. "It's just that finally, I had someone of my own, someone —" She shook her head. "It's hard to explain."

She opened her eyes and turned to Charlotte. "I know you mean well, Charlotte, and it's not that I don't believe you, but it's just been a long time since I had anyone who cared enough to —" She hesitated, then continued. "My mom died when I was twelve, and after she died, my dad — Well, he did the best he could, but with three other children besides me and his job, he's just never had a lot of time. I've been kind of on my own, and —" Suddenly, she leaned over and hugged Charlotte. "Thanks," she whispered against Charlotte's shoulder. "Thanks for caring."

Charlotte was beyond words as tears filled her own eyes and painful memories filled her head. Like Cheré, she knew how it felt to lose someone you loved. All within the space of a couple of years she'd lost the man she'd loved with all of her heart, then she'd lost her beloved parents. She knew all too well how it felt to be all alone without anyone to care about you. And she understood.

Charlotte swallowed hard and sniffed back the tears. "No thanks required," she finally told Cheré when she could speak again. "Like I said before, I don't want to see you get hurt."

"What a Difference a Day Makes." Charlotte hummed the tune of the old song as she turned down First Street on Tuesday morning. It had been one of her mother's favorites, and for whatever reason, she'd awakened with the song playing in her head.

The lyrics of the song were right on, she thought. Just one day, along with a good night's sleep, could make a huge difference in a person's whole outlook.

Once Cheré had left, Charlotte had treated herself to a long, luxurious bath and a light supper of cheese, fruit, and crackers. Then she'd curled up in bed with the mystery novel she'd been wanting to read. She'd only gotten through the first two chapters when she realized that she either had to quit reading or she'd end up pulling an all-nighter, just to discover who the killer was. But the whole process had relaxed her just enough so that when she did turn out the lights, she fell asleep almost immediately. And she'd stayed asleep until her alarm sounded that morning.

Now if only she didn't have to face Bitsy

Duhe, she thought, easing off the accelerator as she approached Bitsy's house. Like Bitsy, the raised-cottage-style Greek Revival was old; according to the old lady, the house had been built in the mid-eighteen-hundreds.

Charlotte sighed heavily. She hadn't returned the old lady's phone call, and knowing Bitsy as she did, she would have a million questions about the discovery of Drew Bergeron's body. Any and every tidbit of information would be grist for Bitsy's gossip mill.

"But I don't want to talk about Drew Bergeron," Charlotte muttered as she pulled alongside the curb and parked. *And you sound like a petulant child,* an inner voice taunted.

Maybe so, she argued back, but for once, she didn't care. All she wanted was to forget that she'd ever seen Drew Bergeron, to wipe the memory of his half-naked body and his dead eyes from her mind forever.

Charlotte barely had time to park the van in front of Bitsy's house when the elderly lady appeared at the doorway, then stepped out onto the gallery. Bitsy was a spry, birdlike woman, and as usual, she was wearing one of her many loose, mid-calf floral dresses.

The minute Charlotte emerged from the van, Bitsy waved at her. "Do hurry up, Charlotte," she called out in her squeaky voice. "I've fixed a fresh batch of muffins, but we need to eat them while they're hot. And we can talk," she added.

Oh, great. Just what I need — muffins full of calories and fat grams to go along with a conversation about a dead man. The minute the sarcastic thought entered Charlotte's mind, guilt reared its ugly head. *Be nice, now. She's an old lady, and she really doesn't mean any harm.*

"Be there in just a sec," Charlotte spoke up as she unloaded her supply carrier from the back of the van.

A few moments later, as Charlotte climbed the steps leading to the front gallery, she couldn't help noticing that something about Bitsy was different. She looked younger and . . . *happier* was the only word she could think of.

Then suddenly it hit her. Of course! Bitsy had changed her hairstyle. For as long as Charlotte had worked for Bitsy, the old lady had worn her hair pulled straight back into a tight little bun that she secured at the nape of her neck. She'd once confided in Charlotte that pulling her hair back so tightly helped smooth out the wrinkles around her eyes and was like getting an instant face-lift.

"Why, Miss Bitsy, you've had your hair cut," she drawled, then smiled. "I love it. I absolutely love it. That shorter look is just beautiful."

Preening at the compliment, Bitsy reached up and patted her hair. "That's thanks to your girl, Valerie, down at the Lagniappe Beauty Salon," she quipped.

"Oh, right — Valerie. Of course," Charlotte murmured, her smile fading as she followed Bitsy inside. "Now that you mention it, I believe I do recall her telling me that you had switched over to —"

"Didn't you get my message, Charlotte?"

Charlotte raised her eyebrows. "Message?"

"Now that's strange. I called you on Sunday and left a message."

Charlotte neither denied nor confirmed that she'd gotten the message. "What was it you needed?" she asked innocently as she followed Bitsy into the house. *Liar, liar, pants on fire,* a voice whispered in her head, and shame washed through her. She'd always despised the act of lying. And she'd always figured that lying by omission and outright lying were the same thing.

"Why, I wanted to know all about Drew

Bergeron. What else?"

Charlotte purposely ignored the statement. "When did you get your hair cut?" she asked, hoping to steer Bitsy onto something else, anything else but rehashing the events that had taken place on Saturday. "I just can't get over how lovely it looks."

"Friday morning, and Jenny — you remember, that's the granddaughter who lives in New York, the one who visited this weekend — well, she really liked it a lot too. Said it made me look twenty years younger." The old lady suddenly giggled. "She also said I was a real hip granny now."

Charlotte smiled again as she set down her supply carrier in the kitchen. "Well, it does look nice on you," she acknowledged. "Valerie is a very talented stylist."

"And so smart," Bitsy added, as she bustled over to the cabinet. "How many muffins can you eat?"

"Ah, Miss Bitsy, I —"

"Now I won't take no for an answer. They're blueberry. It's a new recipe I got out of a book I'm reading —"

Charlotte cleared her throat, interrupting. "The title of that book doesn't happen to be *Blueberry Muffin Murder* by Joanne Fluke, does it?"

"My goodness, Charlotte, how did you know?"

Charlotte smiled. "I'm reading it too."

Bitsy beamed. "Well, then, you simply must try one or two. I baked them in my new toaster oven and I'm dying to get your opinion — on the oven, that is. According to the advertisement it's supposed to bake just as good as a regular oven but use half the electricity — not that I always believe everything I read."

Typically Bitsy, and to Charlotte's relief, the old lady momentarily forgot about Drew Bergeron and took off on a tangent about how cautious elderly people needed to be about advertisements these days. To be polite, Charlotte tried to pretend interest, but her eyes strayed to the newest addition in a long line of kitchen gadgets that Bitsy had accumulated over the years.

Bitsy's entire kitchen was a maid's nightmare, not because it was especially dirty or messy, since the elderly lady adhered to the old philosophy of a place for everything and everything in its place, but because it contained every modern kitchen gadget imaginable, all of which collected dust and grease.

As best Charlotte could recall, at last count, Bitsy already owned two toaster ovens, both of which sat on a special shelf that she'd had built to display all of the appliances that wouldn't fit on the over-crowded countertops.

When Bitsy finally finished her tirade about misleading advertisements, she paused long enough to thrust a plate con-taining two muffins at Charlotte. "Here. Now try these and tell me what you think. Then, I want to hear all about Drew Bergeron."

Charlotte's heart sank as she accepted the plate and seated herself at the kitchen table. In hopes of delaying what was begin-ning to look like the inevitable, she took a huge bite out of one of the pastries. Maybe if she kept her mouth full, then she wouldn't have to talk, at least not for a little while longer.

"I was going to bake them for Jenny, and get her opinion," Bitsy continued, "but never got the chance." She seated herself across from Charlotte. "Jenny was out so late Saturday night, and it was almost noon before she woke up. By then it was lunchtime."

Charlotte swallowed. "Speaking of Jenny, did you enjoy her visit?" Maybe if she kept Bitsy talking about her grand-daughter, she'd forget about Drew Bergeron. *Yeah, right. Fat chance.*

"Oh, my, yes — yes, I did," Bitsy gushed. "I just wish she could have stayed longer though. But she's promised to come back for Thanksgiving this year and spend more time. Now —" She waved at Charlotte's plate. "Eat up."

Left with little choice and under Bitsy's watchful eye, Charlotte dutifully ate every crumb of the two muffins.

"Well? What do you think," the old lady asked her when she'd finished.

"Delicious," Charlotte replied in all honesty. "I think your new oven works just fine."

Bitsy beamed. "Me too, but I wanted another opinion. Now, what's all this I've been hearing? Someone said that *you* were the one who found Drew's body."

"Well, I —"

At that moment the phone rang. Though a shadow of annoyance crossed Bitsy's face at the intrusion, Charlotte felt like grinning from ear to ear. There was no way Bitsy would ignore a phone call. When the phone rang a second time, Bitsy glared at the extension hanging on the wall above the countertop, then gave a disgusted grunt. "Guess I'd better get that," she said as she pushed away from the table. "I'll take the call on the portable in the hall-way," she told Charlotte as she walked past the extension. "If it's who I suspect it is, it might take a while. Help yourself to some more muffins," she called out over her shoulder, "and we'll talk later." Then she disappeared through the doorway.

Charlotte was able to get the kitchen clean and had started dusting in the parlour when Bitsy wandered in with the portable phone still pressed to her ear.

"Any time, Norma," Charlotte heard her say. "Talk to you later, then. Bye now." The old lady clicked the phone off. "My good-ness, how that woman can talk," she said to Charlotte. "And what a gossip!"

Given Bitsy's penchant for gossip, Char-lotte almost choked to keep from laughing, and she quickly turned away to hide her reaction.

"Now! About Drew — Oh, no!" Bitsy suddenly gasped. "Look at this."

When Charlotte turned to see why Bitsy sounded so distressed, the old lady had set the phone down and had picked up a large book off the coffee table.

She held the book out to show Char-lotte. "Jenny went off and forgot her year-book," she explained. "She'd brought it with her so she could brush up on everyone's names for the reunion."

"You can always mail it to her," Charlotte suggested.

"Hmm, I suppose so." With a shrug, Bitsy placed the book back onto the table. "It sure came in handy, though. I knew a lot of Jenny's friends back then, and she and I went through it before she left Sunday evening, so she could bring me up to date on what's happened to the ones who showed up.

"Drew Bergeron was in that class, you know," Bitsy continued. "Here, I'll show you." She leaned over and thumbed through the pages. "Jenny said that everyone at the reunion was in shock when they heard what happened, especially since he was already supposed to be dead. She said there were all kinds of stories going around about him." She thumped one of the pages. "Look at this, Charlotte."

Curiosity was a vice and possibly a sin, Charlotte decided. Unable to resist the temptation to get a glimpse of a younger Drew Bergeron, she moved closer to the table. From the looks of the photo, it had been taken at a party, probably a fraternity party, she figured, since the two men and the woman in the picture were holding out beer cans, as if toasting some occasion.

"That's him," Bitsy said, pointing to the man on the left side of the picture. "And that's Bill and Marian Hebert with him. Of course, they weren't married then," she added.

Charlotte leaned closer to get a better look. Though she'd never met Bill Hebert, she'd seen pictures of him. But if Bitsy hadn't told her who the couple was, she would never have recognized either of them. "I knew they had all been friends," she murmured, "but I guess I didn't realize just how long they had been friends."

"Oh, my, yes — all three of them grew up together. In fact, Jenny said that it had always been a toss-up as to which of the two men Marian would end up with."

Unbidden, Marian Hebert's bitter words about Drew suddenly popped into Charlotte's head. *The S.O.B. got exactly what he deserved.* How sad, she thought. A lifetime friendship ruined, and all because of business dealings. She'd always heard that you should never do business with friends or relatives, and if nothing else, the Bergerons and the Heberts were perfect examples as to why the old adage was true.

"Jenny called them the wild bunch," Bitsy continued, "but then, what can you expect? All of them were spoiled rotten.

But that's what happens when parents give a child anything and everything that money can buy." Bitsy shook her head. "Lord knows, they were bad enough in high school, but by the time they got to Tulane, they were holy terrors." She abruptly paused. Then her expression grew thoughtful. "Hmm . . . Of course, that was the year there was all that hoopla about that chemistry professor too, so nobody paid much attention to their antics or pranks — and believe me, they pulled some. But here, let me show you."

Bitsy flipped over several pages and pointed out a large picture of a man dressed in what appeared to be a lab coat. "That's him. That's the infamous Professor Arthur Samuel."

The name sounded vaguely familiar to Charlotte, but the details as to why it seemed familiar escaped her.

"And what a delicious scandal that was," Bitsy said with relish. "Why I remember it like it happened yesterday. Jenny was in his chemistry class that semester. Of course it was all in the papers too — remember, that was when we still had the *States Item* as well as the *Picayune*." She waved a dismissing hand. "Anyway, the professor was arrested for a hit-and-run accident."

"Of course," Charlotte murmured. "Now I remember. Didn't the hit-and-run happen over on St. Charles Avenue, not far from Tulane?"

Bitsy nodded. "Yep, it sure did. He ran a red light and hit some poor man who was crossing the avenue. Everyone said he was drunk as a skunk when he did it, but of course the professor denied it all. Claimed he was home that night. But the jury didn't buy it, especially when it came out that the professor was an alcoholic. Convicted him of vehicular homicide and sentenced him to ten years." Bitsy snickered. "Evidently his wife didn't buy it either, since she divorced him, took the kids, and moved back to Kansas where she was from."

Bitsy closed the yearbook. "Funny thing, though," she said, patting the top of the book. "No one at the reunion seemed to know what happened to him after he got out of prison. You'd think *someone* would know." Bitsy suddenly made a face. "But that's old news. And Drew Bergeron isn't. Now, Charlotte, you simply must tell me what happened. Someone said that when you found him, he was naked as a jaybird. Well? Was he?"

There was no way around it, Charlotte decided. Like a dog gnawing on a bone,

Bitsy wasn't going to give up until she told her what she wanted to hear. Maybe if she gave the old lady just a brief rundown of the facts, she would stop obsessing about it. And just maybe she could stop some of the false rumors flying around. Working for the Dubuissons had taught her that having her name and maid service associated in any way, shape, or form with a murder simply wasn't good for business . . . or her own peace of mind.

"He was not naked," Charlotte finally replied a bit more sharply than she'd intended. "And I wasn't the one who found him," she added, toning down her agitation.

Since Charlotte's doctor's appointment was scheduled for two-thirty, she had just enough time to run a few errands after she left Bitsy's house at noon.

Later, as she sat in the crowded waiting room of the doctor's office, she idly thumbed through a magazine in an attempt to distract herself. Anything, any distraction at all so she could stop thinking about the reason she was there to begin with.

But none of the articles held her attention for long. Feeling definitely fidgety, she glanced at her watch. It seemed as if she'd been sitting and waiting for an eternity. Her lips thinned with irritation when she saw the time. Almost an hour had passed since she'd arrived.

Ten more minutes, she decided. She'd wait ten more minutes, then, appointment or not, she was out of there.

"Charlotte LaRue? Ms. Charlotte La-Rue?"

When Charlotte glanced up and saw the nurse waiting by the door that led back to the examination rooms, a cold knot formed in her stomach. She could still leave, she thought. She could just pretend that she didn't hear her name being called, get up, and walk out the door. Couldn't she?

Over two hours later, Charlotte was wishing she had left. Since she had no fever, her blood pressure was normal, and from the basic physical, she appeared to be just fine, the doctor had insisted that she go ahead and get her flu shot while she was there.

"You can get dressed now, Ms. LaRue."

Charlotte simply smiled at the nurse as she climbed off the examination table. Already her arm was feeling achy from the shot.

The nurse capped the needle, then dropped it into a small plastic container. "We should have all of your test results in by next Thursday, so be sure and make an appointment on your way out."

Once the nurse left the room, Charlotte's smile faded. "Thank goodness that's over," she muttered as she made her way back to the tiny cubicle where she'd left her clothes. She'd been prodded, poked with needles, and submitted to other indignities that she'd just as soon forget about before they had finished with her. But the worst part of the whole ordeal was yet to come.

"Another whole week," she grumbled as she pulled off the hospital gown and dressed. Now, she had to wait a whole week before she could find out the results of all the tests. But she should have known better than to expect an answer right away. Hurry up and wait seemed to be the norm for everything nowadays.

Chapter Fifteen

For a change, Marian was already dressed when Charlotte arrived on Wednesday morning. Only minutes after she stepped inside the Hebert house, she found out the reason why.

"As soon as I eat a bite, I'll be leaving for a while," Marian told her when they entered the kitchen. "I'm meeting with Jefferson Harper to decide what kind of damage control is needed for the Devilier house because of Drew's murder." Her expression turned grim as she walked to the pantry and retrieved a box of cereal. "Not too many people want to rent a place where a murder's been committed."

Charlotte began unloading the dishwasher. "I suppose not," she murmured.

Marian shrugged, then poured the cereal in a bowl and added milk. "Anyway, I need to ask a favor." She carried the bowl of cereal over to the table and seated herself. "Ordinarily, I would just let the machine catch any phone calls," she explained. "Or I would forward them to my cell phone.

But silly me, I forgot that the battery needed recharging. And with B.J. being back in school and all, just in case there's a problem, I was wondering if you'd mind too much answering any calls that come in. I'll leave a number where I can be reached," she added.

"No problem," Charlotte told her. "And speaking of B.J. —" She removed the basket of silverware from the dishwasher and placed it on the countertop. "Did you ever find out what the fight was about?"

Marian finished chewing the bite of cereal she had taken, swallowed hard, and blinked several times. "Unfortunately, yes — yes, I did. You know how worried I've been about him. He just hasn't been the same since his father died. And now, with all this stuff going around about Drew's murder, all the gossip has started up all over again about Bill's death as well."

Charlotte frowned. "But what does all of that have to do with B.J. fighting?"

"B.J. claims he was defending his father's honor. One of the boys he fought with taunted him about Bill. Said that he'd committed suicide and made it look like an accident because of the insurance money." She dropped her head, and covered her face with her hands. "Kids can be so — so mean," she whispered, tears in her voice.

For several moments, Charlotte was speechless. When she found her voice, she was furious on B.J.'s behalf. "I wouldn't call that just mean. I'd say that was down-right cruel. But why would the boy have said such a thing to begin with? Drew's murder had nothing to do with your husband's accident."

Marian dropped her hands and stared out the window. "Gossip," she replied. "The boy was probably repeating something he'd heard his parents say." She turned her head and faced Charlotte. "Everybody knew there were hard feelings between Bill and Drew after Drew fired him. And Bill made no secret of the fact that he blamed Drew when we began losing clients. He made sure everyone knew about Drew's threats." She grimaced. "For all the good that did."

"What kind of threats?" The second Charlotte uttered the words, she wished she hadn't. "Oh, Marian, I'm so sorry. It's really none of my business."

"Don't apologize, Charlotte. I'm the one who should apologize for burdening you with my problems to begin with. And like I said, it was no deep, dark secret anyway. But to answer your question, it all started when Maurice Sinclair died. Maurice left the business to Katherine, so Drew took over running things. Problem was, Drew was too busy playing big shot and didn't take care of the business or their clients. Bill saw what was happening and began to get worried since our livelihood was in jeopardy too.

"At first he tried talking to Drew, friend to friend — ha! Some friend he turned out to be," she added with a sneer. "Drew ignored him, of course, and things went from bad to worse. As a last-ditch effort, Bill more or less told Drew to either get his priorities straight or he was going straight to Katherine. Giving Drew warning was a mistake, though. A week after they'd had their little confrontation, Drew up and fired Bill. But just firing him wasn't enough for the bastard. To add salt to the wound, he threatened him too. Threatened to ruin him in the real estate business if Bill ever went to Katherine."

Marian paused. Then she sighed. "Of course Bill went anyway, and of course Drew made good his threats. From that point on, our business went from bad to worse.

"At first I didn't want to believe what everyone was saying. But those last few weeks before — before Bill died, he was so worried and upset that —" Marian shook her head. "I keep thinking that maybe if I'd been stronger, more supportive, he — he might still be alive —" Her voice broke and her shoulders quivered with silent sobs.

"Oh, hon." Charlotte rushed over to Marian, and placing her hand on the younger woman's shoulder, she knelt beside her chair. Some of what Marian was saying made sense, but some of it didn't, and no wonder. The woman was clearly distraught, so it was understandable that she might be confused. "You can't blame yourself," Charlotte told her.

"Oh, can't I?" she cried.

"It was an accident," Charlotte insisted. "The police said it was, so how can you blame yourself for an accident?"

Marian slowly shook her head. "I wish I could believe that — wish it with all of my heart. Then maybe I could sleep at night. Lord knows, I want to believe it. But I don't," she added in a whisper. "In spite of what the police said, I don't think Bill's death was just an accident, and I still have nightmares. It haunts me, and now it's haunting my son too."

The memory of Marian's last words lingered long after she had left for her appointment. Even after Charlotte had finished up and was on her way home that afternoon, the desperation and anguish in Marian's voice kept echoing in her mind. By the time she turned down her street, she was sick at heart from thinking about all of it.

Once inside her house, though, there were other things to occupy her thoughts. Sweety Boy provided some relief as he burst into chirps and whistles the minute she walked through the door.

"Hey, Boy, did you miss me?" She set down her purse and slipped off her shoes. "Come on, Sweety. Say, 'Missed you, Charlotte. Missed you.'" After pulling on her moccasins, she walked over to the little bird's cage.

"If you talk for me, I'll let you out for a while." A loud squawk was the only answer she got, but she unlatched the cage door anyway. The second she opened the door, the little parakeet was out like a flash.

Charlotte watched him flutter from one perch to another in the living room for a few minutes; then she walked over to the desk to check her answering machine. The blinking light indicated that she had three messages, and Charlotte tapped the play button.

After a long beep, the first message began. "Hi, Mother. Just checking in with you to see how you're feeling after your tests yesterday. Give me a call. Love you."

"I love you too," she murmured, as the machine beeped again.

"Charlotte, it's Madeline. I meant to call yesterday but got busy. Anyway, how was your doctor's appointment? Find out anything yet? Call me."

Charlotte sighed and shook her head as the machine beeped again.

"Hey, Aunt Charley. It's Judith. Just checking up on you. How'd the doctor's appointment go? Any news yet? Call me."

Charlotte glared at the machine. "Oh, for pity's sake," she muttered. "You'd think I was dying or something."

Normally, Charlotte tried to keep Thursdays free from commitments so she could catch up on paperwork or do whatever was needed to keep her maid service running smoothly as well as take care of personal errands.

After her early-morning walk, she put on a load of clothes to wash while she hurried through her own housekeeping chores. Then she settled at the desk.

It took her until almost noon to enter expense receipts into the ledger she kept for tax purposes. When she'd finally entered the last of the receipts, she shoved away from the desk with a sigh and walked to the front window.

Feeling a bit stiff from sitting too long, she rolled her head from side to side, then flexed the fingers on her writing hand. As she stared out of the window, she thought again about the offer her son had made. Maybe it was time to give in. For months he'd been nagging her to get a computer, but she'd resisted. He'd argued that if she was going to continue being stubborn about retiring, the least she could do was to let him get her a computer so that she could run her service more efficiently.

Not only had he offered to buy a computer, but he'd assured her that he would have someone set it up for her and even pay for lessons. Of course, as usual, he'd followed up the offer with yet another pitch aimed at getting her to retire.

Charlotte suddenly frowned when she realized what she'd been staring at out the window. For the second day straight, Louis' blue Ford was still parked in the driveway. Funny. She hadn't seen or talked to him since their confrontation Sunday morning. Come to think of it, even though his car was parked in the driveway, she hadn't heard the first peep coming from his half of the double.

Just about the time she'd decided that maybe she'd better check up on him, Judith's tan Toyota pulled up alongside the curb. When Judith emerged from her car, Charlotte saw that her niece was carrying a plastic sack.

Wondering what could be in the sack, she walked to the front door in anticipation of Judith's knock. When several minutes passed and nothing happened, Charlotte opened the door and stuck her head out just in time to see Judith disappear through the front door of Louis' half of the double.

"Oh, well," she murmured, unable to stem her disappointment as she closed the door. "Time for lunch."

One of the luxuries Charlotte allowed herself on Thursdays, if time allowed, was an afternoon nap after lunch. She'd just stretched out on the sofa with a book when her doorbell rang.

Probably Judith, she thought as she hurried to the door. Sure enough, when she opened it, her niece was standing on the other side of the threshold.

"Hey there, Auntie. Got a cup of coffee?"

"Hey there, yourself." Charlotte gave Judith a quick hug. But when she pulled away, she frowned. "You look tired, hon."

"I am," Judith told her as she followed Charlotte back to the kitchen. "Not only is the Bergeron case going nowhere fast, but half the department is out with the flu, and we've had three other homicides since Saturday. No rest for the weary, that's for sure."

Charlotte motioned toward the kitchen table. "How about a bite to eat?"

"Just coffee, Aunt Charley. Lou's down with the flu too, so I took him lunch and ate with him."

"Well, that explains it," Charlotte murmured as she prepared the coffeepot. "I knew I'd seen his car parked in the driveway, but I hadn't actually seen or talked to him since Sunday morning."

"Yeah, he started with the chills and fever Sunday night — which reminds me. Did you get your flu shot yet?"

Charlotte switched on the coffeepot and nodded. "Yesterday, while I was at the torture chamber, otherwise known as the doctor's office."

A slight smile pulled at Judith's cheeks. "That bad, huh?" she drawled. "And that's another thing. You never did return my call last night. So — other than being tortured — how was your appointment?"

While the coffee dripped, Charlotte gave Judith a rundown of the various tests that had been done. "The very worst thing of all, though," she said when she'd finished, "is that I have to wait a whole week to find out the results."

"Yeah, waiting is always the hard part with everything. I'm still waiting on some lab results that I should have had two days ago."

Charlotte frowned. "About the Bergeron murder?"

Judith nodded. "That and others."

"Any suspects yet?"

Judith laughed, but the sound was anything but humorous. "Oh, there are plenty of suspects. Mr. Bergeron was not a popular fellow, it seems. It's the narrowing down of the suspects that's the problem."

Judith shifted in her chair, then began drumming her fingers against the tabletop. *She's nervous,* thought Charlotte, recognizing all too well the signs. Ever since Judith was a little girl, any time she was worried, or in an uncomfortable or a tense situation, she'd resorted to what Charlotte thought of as the nervous fidgets. The girl simply couldn't keep still.

"Which brings me to one of the reasons for my visit," Judith told her. Tilting her head, she pinned Charlotte with a look that Charlotte recognized all too well, and she grimaced, already suspicious of what was coming.

"Okay, hon, just spit it out and be done with it."

"Well, Auntie," she drawled. "Unfortunately, once again it seems that you know several of the suspects."

Charlotte's stomach turned queasy.

"I'm hoping that you can help me out," Judith added.

The very last thing Charlotte wanted was to be pulled into yet another murder investigation that involved clients. Once had been enough, thank you very much. And just the thought of it happening again made her feel ill.

"You've already questioned me and my employees. I don't know of anything else I can add."

"That was *before* we narrowed down the suspects, Auntie. You know I hate having to do this to you," Judith continued, "but to be honest, right now I can use all of the help I can get. I need to —"

"The coffee's ready," Charlotte interrupted, then busied herself with pouring it into the mugs she'd retrieved from the cabinet.

"Now, Aunt Charley, I know you don't want to talk about it, and I know all about your confidentiality policy concerning your clients, but this *is* a murder investigation. Whether you want to or not, I have to do this."

Gossiping or talking about her clients was prohibited. It had been a long-standing policy that Charlotte instilled in her employees the moment they were hired, one that she believed in so adamantly that any breach was grounds for immediate dismissal.

Charlotte brought the mugs of coffee over to the table and set one down in front of Judith. "I realize it's your job, hon, but that doesn't mean I have to like it." She seated herself across from her niece. Wrapping her hands around her mug and taking a deep breath, she asked, "So which of my clients are we talking about this time?"

Chapter Sixteen

"So far there's Katherine Bergeron, Vince Roussel, Marian Hebert, and a woman named Darla Shaw." Judith rattled off the names of the suspects as if she was reciting a grocery list.

All of them had been clients at one time or another, all except the last one. "Who's Darla Shaw?" Charlotte asked. It was a delaying tactic at best, and from the look on Judith's face, she knew her niece wasn't fooled one bit.

"Actually, she's the best possibility I've got so far. We've done a bit of backtracking and found out that after Bergeron faked his death —"

"You know that for sure?"

Judith shrugged, then laughed humorlessly. "As the old joke goes, nothing in this world is a sure thing, nothing but death and taxes."

Charlotte winced at her niece's cynicism. More often than not, being a police officer brought her in contact with humanity at its very worst. Add that to the background of being abandoned by her father, then having to grow up with a mother as unstable as Madeline had been after Johnny Monroe broke her heart, and it was no wonder the poor girl had such a jaded view of life.

Only the good Lord knew how hard she'd tried to make both Judith and Daniel feel secure and loved in spite of their parents. But one person could only do so much, and besides taking care of her sister's children, she'd had her own son to raise as well as a business to run so that she could feed all of them.

"Anyway —"

The sound of Judith's voice abruptly jerked Charlotte back from her brief mental journey into the past.

"Bergeron's been holing up on Key West for the past two years. But — as best we can determine — he'd been living with this woman named Darla Shaw for about a year. The theory is that he was just using her. After all, he needed somewhere to stay and probably needed money. Anyway, we figure that somehow she found out about his wife and little girl and followed him to New Orleans." Judith shrugged. "Maybe once she discovered for sure that he really had lied to her, she killed him in a fit of jealous rage. For now it's the best bet we've got, especially since no one has seen hide nor hair of Ms. Shaw since the murder."

Charlotte frowned. "But why would he come back to begin with?"

Judith shrugged again. "Who knows? Maybe he had unfinished business or maybe he got homesick." She shook her head. "It's just a theory. I didn't say it was a perfect one, but —" Judith narrowed her eyes. "Until we track down Darla Shaw, we have to explore all possibilities. Which brings me to Katherine Bergeron."

"I haven't worked for Katherine for several years," Charlotte quickly retorted. "But from what I remember about her, I can't imagine that she would be capable of committing murder."

"Oh, Aunt Charley, after what happened with the Dubuissons, you of all people should know better."

Charlotte flinched at the not-so-subtle reminder of how she'd been duped once before. Then, after a moment, she finally conceded. "You're right. Of course, you're right. I should know better."

Judith reached across the table and touched her arm. "I didn't say it to be mean or cruel, Auntie. It's just that . . ."

Her voice trailed away.

"Of course you didn't, hon," Charlotte reassured her. "I didn't think that for one minute. So — why Katherine? What motive could she have?"

After a moment, Judith nodded, then continued. "From what we've gathered, after Katherine's father died, Drew Bergeron began running things. After a few months, he conned his wife into signing over her shares of the company. Maybe she got suspicious and found out that he was ruining her real estate company and having an affair — who knows? Or maybe she figured he was getting ready to dump her, so she put out a hit on him. Thus, the reason he faked his *first* death."

Charlotte nodded in understanding. "But somehow she finds out he's still alive. And this time, she kills him herself?"

Judith nodded. "That about sums it up. Only one thing wrong with it, though. Vince Roussel is ready to swear that he and Katherine were together for most of the night that Drew was murdered. Which brings us to yet another suspect. Just how much do you know about Vince Roussel, Auntie?"

"I've actually only spoken to the man once, and that was when I signed the contract to do the Devilier house. All I know about him is what Louis told me — told us — on Sunday morning."

Judith nodded. "The real estate deal stuff. Yeah, I looked into that and it's certainly enough motivation, given Roussel's reputation. Louis was right about there being a deal between Roussel and Bergeron, a deal that went sour a year before Bergeron faked his first death. From everything I found out, Bergeron persuaded Roussel to back a real estate venture, an exclusive, gated neighborhood and country club along the shores of Lake Pontchartrain. Vince was supposed to double the return on his investment once the houses sold. No one really knows what happened. Maybe Bergeron blew the investment money or gambled it away. Whatever happened, it's possible that Roussel finally demanded his money or else, thus the reason Drew decided to fake his death.

"So — for whatever reason, Bergeron comes back, Roussel finds out, and this time Roussel makes sure Bergeron pays . . . with his life. Of course there's also the relationship between Katherine and Roussel to add fuel to the fire. Maybe Drew somehow found out about the affair, and maybe he came back to warn Katherine. Roussel got wind of it and killed him to get rid of him once and for all. But since Roussel is Katherine's alibi, that makes Katherine his alibi too."

"That's a lot of maybes, and a lot of conjecture."

Judith nodded. "I know that," she admitted. "That's why I'm hoping you can tell me something that might point me in the right direction . . . which brings me to Marian Hebert.

"Admittedly, she's the weakest suspect of all, but Ms. Hebert had plenty of reason to hate Drew Bergeron, the main reason being that he'd fired her husband. Though she didn't come right out and say it when we interviewed her, it was more than evident that she blamed Drew Bergeron for her husband's state of mind before his so-called accident. And I say so-called because there's been a lot of speculation about his death despite what our investigators found. Everyone we've talked to thinks he committed suicide."

In spite of what the police said, I don't think Bill's death was just an accident, and I still have nightmares. It haunts me, and now it's haunting my son too. Charlotte grimaced. And now Marian's words were haunting her.

"What is it, Auntie? Why the look?"

Charlotte shrugged. "Just remembering something Marian said. For what it's worth, she doesn't think her husband's death was an accident either. Like everyone else, she suspects he committed suicide. But unlike everyone else and for the sake of her children, she doesn't *want* to believe it. She's a very troubled lady."

Judith nodded. "Yes — yes, she is, but I strongly suspect she's got other problems as well." She shrugged. "It's either drugs or alcohol — I'm not sure which, and maybe it's both."

When Judith leveled a look that invited Charlotte to offer her own observations, Charlotte hesitated.

"Aw, come on, Auntie. You work for the woman three days a week. Surely you've noticed *something*."

As Charlotte battled with revealing what she suspected about Marian's abuse of alcohol, the perfect solution to the problem abruptly presented itself. "Marian couldn't have killed Drew, so none of this makes a difference anyway." She gave Judith a shrewd look. "As I recall, she had a dinner appointment with Jefferson Harper Friday evening. But then, you already know that, don't you?"

Judith sighed heavily. "Yes — unfortunately, that's true."

"Then why all the prying into her personal life?"

"There's an old saying, Aunt Charley. Knowledge is power."

"Yes, Judith," she retorted. "I'm very familiar with that saying."

"So — in keeping with that saying — is there anything else, anything at all that you can tell me further about Katherine Bergeron, Vince Roussel, or Marian Hebert that might help?"

"Judith, hon, please don't think I'm just being obstinate, but —" She held up her right hand, and, using the forefinger of her other hand, she emphasized each point by ticking off each of three fingers. "For one, I haven't worked for Katherine in over four years. Two, I only met Vince Roussel once, and three, there's no point in discussing Marian since she has an alibi."

Judith grunted in disappointment. "Humph! I should've known. Lou warned me I wouldn't get anything useful from you. But silly me, I thought that since you were my aunt . . ." She shrugged, leaving the sarcastic words hanging in the air.

"Judith Marie Monroe! Shame on you."

"Uh-oh, guess I'm in trouble now, huh?"

"If I knew anything helpful I'd tell you, young lady," Charlotte retorted. "And furthermore, I resent this — this attitude of yours and Louis'. Besides, we both know that Louis is more than a bit prejudiced when it comes to me. It still galls him that I was the one who solved the Dubuisson murder."

Judith held up her hands. "Okay, okay, Auntie, I surrender. And I'm sorry," she added meekly.

"As well you should be. And speaking of Louis — what's all this nonsense between him and your new partner, Will? What's he got against him?"

For long moments, Judith simply stared at her. Then, looking decidedly uncomfortable, she crossed, then uncrossed her legs, all the while drumming her fingers against the tabletop again.

"I'm not trying to pry," Charlotte assured her. "My main concern is your safety. Though Louis aggravates the tar out of me, I do respect his opinions, and it's very clear that he has a low opinion of your new partner."

"Ah — er, my safety isn't exactly the issue here, Auntie, so there's no need for you to worry about that."

"So — what is the issue, then?"

"Why don't we just say that Lou doesn't believe in mixing business and pleasure and leave it at that?"

Charlotte slowly shook her head. "Why don't we *not* leave it at that? Are you or are you not involved with this Will? And if you are, what's wrong with him that Louis would be so — so —"

"Oh, good grief!" Judith released a long-suffering sigh. "If you must know, yes — yes, we're involved. And the reason Lou is being such a stinker about the whole thing is because Will has a wife and kid."

"Oh, Judith, no . . ."

"It's not like that, Aunt Charley. Will is separated and getting a divorce. His wife's the bitch from hell, and he's trying to get custody of his little girl. Will doesn't want to do anything that would jeopardize his chances, so we have to be . . . careful right now."

"Like being seen in public with you? Oh, hon, don't you know, that's the oldest line in the world?"

Long after Judith left, a tumble of confused thoughts and feelings plagued Charlotte as she mulled over everything they'd discussed.

"So what do I do now?" she asked

Sweety Boy as she stood by his cage, her gaze fixed on nothing in particular outside the window. Within reason, she knew there was nothing to be done about Katherine or Marian, or even Vince Roussel being suspects in Drew Bergeron's murder investigation. They all had alibis. Besides, she'd learned her lesson once already, learned to mind her own business and leave police concerns to the experts, thanks to the Dubuisson family.

But Judith was another matter. Judith was family, and Charlotte loved her like a daughter, had, in fact, helped raise her and her brother.

More times than she cared to remember, while Madeline had been drowning in one of her depressive episodes, Charlotte had been the one who had nursed Judith and Daniel through chicken pox, measles, and stomach viruses. She'd been the one who had encouraged Judith to try out for high school cheerleader, and she, not Madeline, had been the one who had cheered Daniel on when he'd won the lead role in the school play.

"So how can I persuade her that this relationship is wrong, Sweety? How can I make her see that in the end, it's going to break her heart?"

Though the little bird chirped and squawked, it took Charlotte several moments before the sounds actually penetrated her self-absorption. Suddenly she grinned from ear to ear.

"Missed you. *Squawk*. Missed you, Charlotte. Squawk."

Charlotte felt like shouting. Sweety's words weren't exactly as clear as a bell, but they were clear enough for her to understand them. She wanted to jump up and down or dance a jig. For months she'd been trying to get the little stinker to say something besides "crazy" and had been just about ready to give up. And now . . .

Afraid to distract him, Charlotte tried not to move or even breathe heavily, for fear the little parakeet would stop.

But stop he did, and no matter how much she tried to coax him into repeating what he'd said, she finally had to give up.

Without the little bird for a distraction, her thoughts quickly returned to the conversation she'd had with Judith.

Over the years Charlotte had learned that the best therapy for worry and confusion was to either sleep on it or do something positive or productive instead of giving in to whatever was bothering her.

A nap was out of the question now, she

decided as she glanced at the cuckoo clock and saw that it was almost three o'clock. With the house clean and her bookkeeping done, she could either read, go shopping, weed the flower beds, or cook. Reading didn't appeal to her at the moment, and neither did shopping. And the last time she'd looked, there were relatively few weeds. That left cooking.

Maybe she'd cook something to take to Louis. After all, he was sick, and she owed him a meal anyway . . . sorta kinda. Something nourishing but not too spicy or rich, she decided. Comfort food, like chicken and dumplings, maybe.

After checking to make sure she had the necessary ingredients, Charlotte pulled out a package of chicken parts from the freezer. While the chicken boiled, she placed a call to Louis.

On the fourth ring, his answering machine picked up. Figuring he was probably asleep, she decided to leave a message.

"Louis, this is Charlotte. Judith told me you were ill, so I —"

"Yeah, Charlotte, I'm here," he interrupted, his deep voice a hoarse croak. "Hold on a sec while I turn off the machine."

"You sound terrible," she told him a moment later. "Judith told me you've been ill. Have you seen a doctor?"

"It's just the flu."

"So you haven't been to a doctor."

"I don't *need* to see a doctor, Charlotte. It's just a light case."

"Doesn't sound light to me —" Though she wanted to point out that someone his age could have all kinds of complications like pneumonia and dehydration, she thought better of it. No one liked to be reminded they were getting old. "Anyway," she continued. "I'm cooking supper for you. I should have it ready in about an hour and I'll bring it over then." Abruptly, Louis gave in to a fit of coughing, and Charlotte winced at the harsh, barking sound in her ear.

"Sorry about that," he finally choked out. "I appreciate the food." He cleared his throat. "But there's no use in you getting exposed and catching this stuff too, so just leave it outside the front door."

"Well . . ." Charlotte hesitated. "I guess you're right. When it's ready, I'll just knock on the door to let you know it's there. But Louis, if you're not better in a couple of days, you really should consider seeing a doctor." Before he could argue, she promptly hung up the receiver.

"Men!" she grumbled. As she glared at the phone, it abruptly rang, and Charlotte jumped at the sound. Taking a deep, calming breath, she finally answered it on the third ring.

"Maid-for-a-Day. Charlotte speaking."

"Aunt Charley, one thing I forgot to mention."

Charlotte frowned. What now?

"I'd just as soon my mother didn't know about my — er — relationship with Will right away — or anyone else, for that matter."

"Anyone meaning your brother, I assume."

"Daniel wouldn't understand either," was Judith's reply.

Charlotte wanted badly to point out that if Judith was ashamed of her relationship, maybe she should get out of it. But she didn't. "You're a grown woman, hon," she replied instead. "I don't approve, but what you do is your business."

The Friday morning sky was overcast and gray, and the air was heavy with humidity, all of which conspired to make Charlotte's already morose mood even worse as she climbed into her van.

260

One last day, she thought, her stomach tightening with dread as she backed out of the driveway. Only one day left to be fifty-nine, then she'd be sixty . . . a whole other decade.

So far, none of her family had mentioned any type of birthday celebration, and while she really didn't want a lot of fuss and bother, a part of her feared that no one would even remember . . . or care.

The short trip to Marian's house was uneventful. For once she didn't encounter delays due to the ongoing battle of maintaining the sinking streets and aging sewer system. Nor were there any problems because of the downed tree limbs that she'd had to contend with the week before.

By the time she pulled alongside the curb of Marian's house and parked, she'd decided that whether anyone in her family remembered her birthday or not, she certainly wasn't going to remind them. And if they didn't remember, then she'd just spend a quiet night at home with a good book. And maybe she'd have a good cry while she was at it.

When Marian answered the door, Charlotte was glad to see that once again she was dressed, and she was equally glad that there was no telltale smell of alcohol on the younger woman's breath.

"I've got a house I'm showing this morning," Marian told her at the door. "I should be back before noon." She motioned for Charlotte to come inside. "And this time I made sure the battery in my cell phone was charged, so you won't have to worry about answering the phone."

Charlotte stepped past her and set her supply carrier down on the floor in the foyer.

"Oh, and another thing —" Marian stopped a moment to search through her purse. Not finding whatever she was looking for, she refastened the clasp with a snap. "Just so that you'll know, if Sam finishes a job he's working on over on Napoleon in time, he might drop by to put a second coat of paint on the porch."

Marian turned, and with a harassed, worried look, muttering every step of the way, she hurried down the hall toward the kitchen. "Now, if only I could find my keys . . . But where did I put them . . ."

Shaking her head and wondering how anyone so unorganized could run a business, especially a real estate business, Charlotte picked up her supply carrier and followed.

"Here they are!" Marian triumphantly

scooped up the keys off the island countertop. "Right where I left them, of course." Just as Marian sauntered past her, Charlotte spied her cell phone on top of the counter near where Marian had found her keys. The phone was still sitting on the charger.

"Marian, wait up." She grabbed the cell phone and hurried after her. "Your phone — don't forget your cell phone."

With a groan, Marian stopped in her tracks. "What would I do without you, Charlotte? Thanks." She took the phone, then disappeared through the back door.

For a change, the kitchen was fairly clean. B.J.'s bedroom was a different matter. Charlotte wrinkled her nose the moment she entered the boy's room. What on earth was that awful smell? she wondered.

In addition to stinking to high heaven, dirty clothes were strewn from one end of the room to the other. Paper plates, with what looked like the remains of pizza on one and a hamburger on another, along with several empty drink cans, crowded the dresser top. A huge, open bag of chips lay beside the bed, and another bag peeked out from beneath the edge of the bed.

Some of the chips had spilled out of the open bag and were crushed and ground into the rug. Charlotte shuddered to think what else might be lurking beneath the bed besides the chips.

"Just do it," she muttered as she approached it and cautiously kneeled down to peer beneath the bed rail.

The moment she leaned down, she almost gagged. "Oh, gross," she grumbled as she got to her feet. "At least now I know where that smell is coming from." With one last disgusted shake of her head, she gathered up all of the dirty clothes, then left the room. Once she'd dumped the clothes in the laundry room and had put on a load to wash, she collected the cleaning supplies she would need to tackle B.J.'s room.

When she returned a few minutes later, she was armed with a broom, a dustpan, and her supply carrier. Using the broom, she began carefully raking out everything from beneath the double-wide bed. With the second pass of the broom, a small milk carton came tumbling out, the source, she strongly suspected, of the sour stench.

Sure enough, when she examined the carton, it was still about a quarter full of now curdled, sour milk. As she dropped the carton into a garbage bag, she supposed she should be thankful that it had curdled; otherwise, spoiled milk would have been strewn everywhere.

Two more passes of the broom beneath the bed yielded various dusty objects, some Charlotte recognized, like a shoe box and several socks. And others she didn't.

Charlotte bent down to pick up the shoe box to add it to the garbage bag too. Thinking it was probably empty, the weight of it surprised her and caused her to fumble and drop it. The top came off, and what looked like newspaper clippings, as well as several other items, scattered over the floor.

"Uh-oh." Now she'd done it, she thought, staring at the spilled contents. Besides her confidentiality policy, a client's privacy was of the utmost importance to Charlotte. Rummaging through a client's personal belongings was another of her big no-nos, and any time she hired a new employee, they got a full-blown lecture on the matter.

With a shrug and a muttered, "Oh, well," there was nothing to do but pick up the mess and explain the situation to Marian later. She only hoped that B.J. wouldn't think she'd been snooping through his stuff. Teenagers were especially touchy about their belongings.

Kneeling down, Charlotte reached for the clippings, then froze when the name in the headline jumped out at her. "What the —" She picked up the top article. "Murdered Man Found at Devilier House," she read aloud. With a deep frown etched across her forehead, she examined the other three articles. All were recent and all were also about Drew Bergeron's murder.

Still frowning, she stared with unseeing eyes at the remaining contents of the shoe box. Why would B.J. be collecting articles about Drew Bergeron's murder? What earthly reason would he have to do such a thing?

In hopes that the rest of the contents of the box would present some kind of explanation, she reached inside and pulled out one of the long, narrow tubes wedged into the bottom. "And what have we here?" she murmured, as she slid the tube apart.

Again Charlotte froze. But her heart began to pound like a jackhammer as scenes of the room where Drew Bergeron's body had been found flashed through her mind. The duffel bag . . . the scattered pictures . . . the ground-out cigar on the floor in front of the door leading into the closet, a cigar that looked exactly like the one she was holding in her hand.

Charlotte closed her eyes and slowly shook her head. "No," she whispered, recalling what Marian had told her. *He's failing in school, and just last week he got suspended two days for smoking.* "No!" Charlotte said louder, thinking about B.J.'s most recent suspension for fighting. "Not possible." There had to be another, more reasonable explanation, anything but what she was thinking.

Chapter Seventeen

Feeling a bit shaky, Charlotte sat on the bed. Staring at the suspect cigar and its case, still clasped in her fingers, she took a deep breath, then slowly released it.

Think, Charlotte . . . think.

She took another deep breath, and another.

While it was true that B.J. was a troubled teenager, there was no way that Charlotte could imagine him killing anyone. Fighting with boys his own age? Yes. But murder . . .

Charlotte shuddered, and instant shame washed through her for thinking such thoughts about the teenager. Still, the damning evidence was there, plain as day, and no matter what she wanted to believe to the contrary, she couldn't completely ignore the cigars and newspaper clippings.

B.J. had known how his mother felt about Drew Bergeron, had known that she also believed it was possible that his father's death had been a suicide. Even worse, he'd known that she held Drew accountable for his father's state of mind during the months before his death.

Had Marian's bitterness spread to her son, so much so that he would commit murder?

Ordinarily, Charlotte wouldn't have given much credence to the thought that a young teenager like B.J. from such a fine upstanding family could commit murder, but newspaper headlines in the past few years had proved different. The news had been full of young boys in different parts of the country who were committing mass murder, using guns to kill their teachers and classmates.

Guns.

Judith had said . . . or was it Louis? Charlotte couldn't recall which, but one of them had said that Drew Bergeron was killed by a single gunshot to the forehead with a twenty-two-caliber handgun. And if she remembered right, it was Louis who had said that the particular type of gun used could be bought anywhere and was almost impossible to trace.

Charlotte knew for a fact that there weren't any guns in the Hebert household. She'd cleaned that house from top to bottom and had never seen the first sign of a weapon. Would a boy like B.J. know where to get such a gun?

Even as she contemplated the issue of the gun, something kept nagging at the back of her mind, a loose end that didn't fit at all. But what?

When she finally realized just what it was that bothered her, she was even more confused than ever. For B.J. to have killed Drew Bergeron, first he would have to have known that Drew Bergeron was still alive, that he had faked his death two years ago. But how would B.J. have known such a thing when no one else knew? Everyone, including Drew's wife, had thought he was dead.

Clinging to that thought and feeling only marginally better because of it, Charlotte carefully slipped the cigar back into the tube. Then she placed it, along with the newspaper clippings, back where she found it inside the shoe box and shoved the box back beneath the bed.

Should she tell someone what she'd found? she worried as she busied herself with cleaning off the top of the dresser. Or should she keep quiet about it? She tossed the paper plates and empty cans into the garbage bag. If she did decide to tell someone, then who?

Not Louis, that was for sure. Besides,

though she wasn't certain, she didn't think he was officially on the case anyway. But maybe she should tell Marian, or possibly Judith.

Marian.

Whether she told Marian or didn't tell her, how on earth was she going to face the woman after what she'd discovered? But how could she tell her? Charlotte had been dusting the dresser, but she paused. How did you tell a mother that there was a possibility that her fifteen-year-old son had murdered someone?

Charlotte shook her head. She couldn't. She just couldn't do it. So that left Judith. But telling Judith wasn't the answer either, she decided as she plugged in the vacuum cleaner, turned it on, and began vacuuming the rug in B.J.'s room. Though she trusted her niece with her life, Judith was first and foremost an officer of the law.

In her mind's eye, Charlotte could already picture the whole scenario. B.J. being arrested. Marian going hysterical and having a nervous breakdown. Eight-year-old Aaron watching it all, having to be placed in a foster home because his mother was in a mental ward and his brother was in jail . . .

"No, no, no!" Charlotte muttered,

shaking her head again as she switched off the vacuum cleaner. The only thing to do was do nothing at all. For now, anyway. Besides, there was still the question of how B.J. could have known that Drew Bergeron was still alive in the first place.

Charlotte unplugged the vacuum cleaner, then dragged it into the hallway. The next room she tackled was the dining room.

When Marian hadn't returned by noon, Charlotte couldn't help feeling relieved. All morning she'd mentally debated the pros and cons of telling Marian what she'd found, but had yet to come up with a solution to the dilemma.

By the time Charlotte was ready to leave by two, Marian still hadn't returned. Charlotte figured that if she hurried, she just might be spared facing Marian at all.

She was rushing around, gathering up her supplies in the kitchen, when she heard a noise at the back door. When she whirled around, Sam was standing in the doorway.

"Sorry — didn't mean to startle you."

Despite his words of apology, the amused glint in his eyes said he'd known exactly what he was doing. It was hard, but Charlotte bit her tongue to keep from yelling at him for scaring the daylights out of her. He should have knocked first. And he knew that he should have. The fact that he knew galled her, but she was determined not to give him the satisfaction of getting a rise out of her, so she just continued staring at him.

After several moments of uncomfortable silence, he finally explained. "I just thought I'd better warn you against leaving through the front door. While I was at it, I went ahead and gave the whole front gallery a fresh coat of paint."

"Well, thanks for the warning," she retorted, forcing a brittle smile as she picked up her supply carrier with one hand, then hefted the vacuum with her other hand.

"Here —" Sam hurried toward her. "Let me help you."

"That's not necessary," she protested. "I can —"

He took the vacuum from her anyway. "It may not be necessary, but a lady like you shouldn't have to lug around this heavy thing. And by the way, I put up a 'wet paint' sign on the porch for when the boys come in from school."

Left with little choice, Charlotte followed him out the back door. Pausing only long enough to make sure the door was firmly locked once she'd closed it behind her, she then turned and followed him down the steps. But at the bottom step, she hesitated. "Marian and the boys usually come in through the back door, but maybe I should leave a note about the wet paint, just in case they don't notice the sign."

"Nah, that won't be necessary. I plan to hang around for a while until someone comes home. That little scamp, Aaron, would be just the one to ignore the sign on purpose."

Charlotte shrugged. "Well, if you're sure."

"There're a couple of shingles loose on the backside of the house that need fixing anyway. And I promised B.J. I'd help him with his science fair project."

As Charlotte followed the handyman around the side of the house to the front where her van was parked, the thought crossed her mind that maybe Sam would be the person to talk to about what she'd found in B.J.'s room. Marian trusted Sam and relied on him. Charlotte knew for a fact that B.J. spent a lot of time around Sam, and on more than one occasion, she'd seen the boy helping Sam with one of the many odd jobs he did around the house.

Just about the time she'd made up her mind to talk to Sam, though, she spotted Marian's black Mercedes turn the corner at the end of the block, and she immediately changed her mind. The moment Sam put the vacuum in the van, she slammed the back door and hurried around to the driver's side.

"Thanks for the help," she called out as she climbed inside.

"So when are you going to let me take you out to dinner?" she heard Sam say.

Marian's car was getting closer, so Charlotte pretended she didn't hear the question and firmly closed the door. Jamming the keys into the ignition, she switched on the engine.

Charlotte sent up a quick prayer of thanks that her van was parked in the opposite direction from the path of Marian's approaching car, and still ignoring Sam, she put the van in gear, then pulled away from the curb. Being rude to Sam didn't bother her. She figured he deserved it after he'd purposely scared the daylights out of her earlier.

But running away like a coward instead of facing Marian did bother her, and she was still berating herself when she turned into her driveway and spotted the small tray of dishes stacked by her front door.

Once on the porch, she recognized the bowls as the same ones she'd used to take Louis his dinner the day before. Since his car was gone, she figured either he was feeling well enough to go out or he'd gotten worse and finally decided to go to a doctor.

Charlotte unlocked the door, then picked up the tray and carried it inside. As usual, Sweety Boy began his routine of chirping and squawking as he pranced back and forth on his perch inside the cage.

"Hey, boy, did you miss me?" His only answer was a loud squawk followed by what sounded like several indignant chirps. "Come on, boy, say, 'Missed you, Charlotte . . . missed you, Charlotte.'"

Much to her frustration, the little bird kept squawking unintelligible gibberish, and after several minutes, she gave up.

There was only one message on her answering machine when Charlotte checked it. She pressed the play button and listened as she slipped off her shoes and slid her feet into her moccasins.

"Hey, Mom. I just have a minute, but I

wanted to invite you out to dinner tomorrow evening for your birthday — unless you have other plans, that is." He chuckled. "Thought I'd forgotten, didn't you?" He chuckled again. "If you do happen to have other plans though, cancel them. I'll pick you up around seven. Oh, yeah — I almost forgot. Dress up in something spiffy. I'm taking you to Commander's. See you tomorrow evening. Love you."

"I love you too, son," she whispered, a smile of delight on her lips as the machine beeped at the end of the message.

"Did you hear that, Sweety?" she told the little parakeet. "I have a date with my son, and he's taking me to Commander's Palace for my birthday." For an answer, Sweety Boy squawked and preened on his perch. But Charlotte's mind really wasn't on the little bird's antics.

Her smile grew wider. She couldn't remember the last time she and Hank had eaten out, just the two of them. And just the thought of dining out with her busy son at what she considered one of the finest, most prestigious restaurants in New Orleans gave her a warm feeling.

She'd eaten at the restaurant before, but not in a long, long time. Even now, her mouth watered, and she could almost taste the bread pudding soufflé. The dessert was famous, as was the landmark restaurant and the entire Brennan family, who owned Commander's as well as an array of other fine restaurants scattered over New Orleans.

During the remainder of the afternoon, Charlotte's emotions wavered between excitement about the dinner invitation from her son and dread because of the reason for his invitation in the first place. But underlying each of her thoughts and actions was the nagging worry about B.J. and what she'd found hidden beneath his bed.

Charlotte had just finished a light dinner of a broiled chicken breast and a green salad when she heard a car door slam in the driveway. Though she figured it was probably Louis, she went to the front window to check anyway.

Sure enough, Louis, toting a shopping bag emblazoned with a Macy's logo, was headed toward the porch. Even from a distance, she could tell he didn't feel well. His gait was slower than usual and his face was a pale contrast against the dark shirt he wore. Charlotte frowned. Since it was apparent that he was still ill, what on earth had possessed him to go to the mall?

Charlotte's lips thinned with irritation, and her temper flared. "Men!" she muttered. Most of them didn't have the sense God gave a goose when it came to being sick. Not only should he be in bed resting instead of traipsing all over creation, but now he'd gone out and carelessly spread his germs to other poor, unsuspecting victims.

Long after Louis disappeared inside his half of the double, Charlotte still fumed as she cleaned up the mess she'd made cooking her dinner. Just what *was* so all-fired important that he'd had to drag himself out of his sickbed to go out shopping? And why to Macy's of all places? Though Louis always looked neat, he never seemed overly concerned about what he wore and was the last person she'd expect to shop at Macy's.

Chapter Eighteen

If she discounted the hollow feeling in the pit of her stomach, being sixty didn't seem that much different, Charlotte decided as she climbed out of bed on Saturday morning. Maybe she ached a bit more than she used to, thanks to the touch of arthritis she occasionally suffered from, but a couple of aspirins now and then always took care of the minor aches and pains. From experience, she knew that it was usually a temporary inconvenience mainly occurring when the city was lucky enough to have a cold front push as far south as New Orleans.

Charlotte shivered. If the chill in the air and the cold floor were any gauge to measure by, the promised front had pushed through during the night. Though she always dreaded having to turn on the heat because it gave her a closed-in feeling and dried out her sinuses, she decided that maybe she should this morning, just long enough to take the chill off the house. That, along with a couple of aspirins and a hot shower should do the trick.

By the time she'd finished her shower and had her first cup of coffee, the house had warmed up enough that she felt safe to let Sweety Boy out of his cage for a few minutes. As usual, the little bird flew straight to his favorite perch, the top of the cuckoo clock.

Most of her life, Charlotte had countered her few bouts of self-pity with all the reasons she had to be thankful. But as she sat staring at the morning *Picayune* headlines with unseeing eyes, for once, she couldn't dredge up an ounce of thankfulness. All she could think about were the years stretching ahead of her, years with nothing to look forward to but a lonely retirement on a limited income and no one to share them with.

Sudden tears welled up in her eyes and her throat grew tight. If Hank's father had lived, things might have been different. Her whole life would have been different. Just how, she wasn't sure, but her imagination knew no bounds, and over the years she'd created many scenarios of how their life together might have been.

But he hadn't come home, not alive, and at times like now, when she allowed herself to indulge in the memory of him, she still felt the wrenching ache of her loss deep in her heart.

He'd been her first love, the love of a lifetime, and though she'd had a few meaningful relationships over the years after his death, she'd been too busy to concentrate on anything but raising a son and trying to make a living, not to mention that she'd never found anyone who could measure up to what she'd felt for Hank Senior . . .

Not until recently, a little voice whispered. Not until Louis Thibodeaux . . . A tear slid down her cheek, and she slowly shook her head. Too late, she thought. If only Louis had come along earlier, years earlier . . .

Just as well, she decided, especially since Louis hadn't given her any indication that he was interested in her as anything other than his landlady. Besides, what would a man his age want with a woman her age anyway? Men his age always went after much younger women, not some sixty-year-old, dried-up maid.

Charlotte was so caught up in the throes of her depression, it took a moment for her to realize that the ringing in her ears was the telephone.

With a sniff and swallowing hard, she pushed away from the table and answered it.

"Maid-for-a-Day, Charlotte speaking."

"Ms. LaRue, Ms. Charlotte LaRue?"

Charlotte frowned. "Yes."

"I'm Martin with Healthy Bodies. First, let me wish you a happy birthday, and second, I'm calling to let you know that you're in for a treat, a whole morning of luxurious pampering, compliments of your son. Included in this deluxe package is a full-body massage, a facial, and a complete make-over by our licensed cosmetologist, all designed for the ultimate experience in pampering, beautification, and relaxation. A taxi will pick you up at nine."

A bit dazed and feeling as if she were Cinderella and Alice in Wonderland rolled into one, Charlotte hung up the phone. She'd heard of the Healthy Bodies Spa, had often heard her clients rave about it. Once she'd even called to find out how much a session for herself would cost, but the price had been way out of her league and way more than she could justify spending.

"Now if only Prince Charming would come along," she muttered as she glanced up at the cuckoo clock and saw that it was almost eight-thirty already. Thirty minutes till blast-off and counting. Just thirty minutes to dress, eat breakfast, and coax Sweety Boy back inside his cage. But what did one wear to be pampered, beautified, and relaxed?

In the bedroom, Charlotte decided that she needed something warm and comfortable, something that she could easily slip in and out of. With the beginning of a smile at the corners of her lips, she chose her favorite sweat suit, a light gray one made of cotton that had worn soft from use.

At exactly seven o'clock that evening, Charlotte's doorbell rang. If nothing else, she could always depend on her son to be punctual, she thought, taking one last, satisfied look in the full-length mirror in her bedroom.

The spa had been wonderfully relaxing, so much so that at one point, she'd actually dozed off during the massage. But the facial and make-over were even better, and Charlotte was really pleased with the new look that the cosmetologist had talked her into. It was amazing what a new shade of makeup, along with a bit of blush could accomplish. "Yep." She nodded. "Ten years younger," she murmured, then laughed. "Yeah, right!"

Smoothing down the collar on her new, navy silk blouse, she turned away from the mirror and hurried to the front door. She'd enjoyed her experience at the spa so much that afterward, she'd treated herself to a rare bit of shopping. The blouse and matching skirt she'd splurged on were the results and made her feel oh-so-elegant.

When she opened the door, Hank's eyes lit up the moment he saw her. "Oh, wow! Just look at you!" he exclaimed. "Guess I made the right choice for a birthday treat, huh?"

Charlotte reached out and hugged her son tightly. "It was really, really wonderful, hon." She pulled back and smiled. "Just perfect. Thank you."

Hank grinned back at her. "Actually, I can't take all the credit. The spa thing was Carol's idea. But I thought it was a good idea too," he hastened to add. "We both thought you might enjoy a little pampering."

"Well, you were both right. And speaking of Carol, when are you going to make an honest woman out of her? I'm not getting any younger, you know, and I'd love to bounce a couple of grandchildren on my knees before I'm too old to enjoy them."

Hank laughed, then leaned down and whispered, "It's a secret, and besides, you'll never be too old. Now —" He made a sweeping gesture with his left arm toward his car. "If we're going to keep that reservation, we need to get going."

"Just let me cover Sweety Boy's cage, and I'm ready," she replied.

The perfect ending to a perfect day, thought Charlotte, moments later as she settled on the passenger side of Hank's BMW. Other than not being age sixty, what more could she ask for than to be pampered and beautified all day, then end it by having a cozy dinner with her son, just the two of them, at one of the best restaurants in the city?

As Hank backed the car out of the driveway, Charlotte turned her head and stared out the window into the night. Louis' car was gone, she noted with a frown. Funny, she didn't remember hearing him leave, so where could he have gone? Unless he was working, he rarely went out at night, especially on the weekends. It crossed her mind that he might be on a date, but she dismissed the idea as soon as she thought of it. More than likely, the detective was working overtime, probably on the Drew Bergeron murder.

Murder. B.J.

Charlotte's stomach tightened as thoughts of the troubled teenager returned again to plague her, just as they'd plagued her off and on all day.

When she'd first made her discovery beneath B.J.'s bed, she'd decided that ultimately the best thing to do was do nothing. But doing nothing had turned out to be the hardest thing she'd ever done. There just had to be another solution.

"Why so quiet, Mom?"

Charlotte glanced over at her son, and flashed him a quick smile. Maybe she should tell Hank about B.J., and for a moment she was truly tempted.

No, she decided. Telling Hank wasn't the answer. Her straight-arrow son only saw black and white, and never considered the gray areas. He would insist that she go to the police. If she refused, he'd take it upon himself to give Judith the information. Then, of course, there would be a lecture from him, all about her getting personally involved with her clients again. She could hear it now.

"Just woolgathering, son," she finally answered. "People my age tend to do that a lot, you know."

Traffic was moderate during the short drive until Hank turned onto Washington Avenue. Within a block of the restaurant, they slowed considerably. As with every-thing else about Commander's Palace, though, the valet service was quick and efficient, and the line of cars moved along in a timely manner.

In the distance, the restaurant was a sight to behold, and Charlotte smiled. Spotlighted by the surrounding street lamps and the soft glow of lights from within, it was a Victorian fantasy against the dark night, with its turrets, col-umns, gingerbread, and turquoise-and-white striped awnings.

Charlotte suddenly giggled.

"What's so funny?" Hank asked.

"Not exactly funny," she answered. "Just . . . well, kinda strange. Don't you find it a little odd how this wonderful, world-renowned restaurant sits directly across the street from one of the oldest cemeteries in the city? Sort of creepy, in a way. But what's funny is that no one seems to mind in the least or even care."

Hank chuckled. "You know, you're right. I never even think about it, but maybe that's because of the wall. With the wall surrounding it, you can't see the tombs that well, so no one really pays it any atten-tion."

Moments later, Hank pulled up beside

the restaurant's entrance. Immediately, two young valets dressed identically in black slacks and white polo shirts rushed over to open the doors on either side, and before Charlotte and Hank had taken more than a few steps, the BMW was whisked away to make room for the next vehicle.

The small restaurant entrance was crowded inside, but again, the line moved quickly, and within moments, Charlotte and Hank were greeted by one of the hosts behind the reservation desk.

"Ah, Dr. LaRue," the middle-aged man greeted them with a warm, welcoming smile. "So nice to see you again. I believe your reservation is for the Garden Room." He motioned toward the doorway. "This way, please."

The fact that the host knew her son by name came as no surprise to Charlotte as they wound their way through the busy downstairs dining area. Hank was a regular patron of the restaurant, and she was delighted that they would be eating in the Garden Room.

Commander's was divided into several different dining areas on two floor levels. Some were small, others large, some private, some open, but of all the rooms, the one on the second floor called the Garden Room was her favorite.

Once they had climbed the stairs to the second level, their host escorted them through yet another dining area, but when they got to the small anteroom that led to the entrance of their destination, the host abruptly stopped just short of entering the Garden Room, and Charlotte frowned as she peered past him. The room was dark, and the only thing visible at all were the twinkling lights that had been strung through the oaks just outside the windows.

"What happened?" Charlotte teased. "Did someone forget to pay the light bill, or are you just out of light bulbs?"

The moment the words were out of her mouth, the lights in the room suddenly flashed on, illuminating a crowd of laughing and smiling people near the center of the room.

"Surprise!" they shouted in unison. "Surprise! Surprise! Happy Birthday!"

Stunned, Charlotte froze. Next to her, Hank placed a steadying arm around her waist, and all she could do was stare wordlessly while every person in the room sang "Happy Birthday."

It took a moment for it to all sink in, and when it did, she had to lean heavily against her son. Sudden tears sprang to her eyes, and a self-conscious warmth spread over her face and burned her cheeks.

Through a blur, she saw Madeline, Judith, Daniel, and Carol, all front and center. Crowded on either side of them were her cleaning crew, including Nadia Wilson, standing next to Daniel. Little Davy was in her arms, his face all smiles. Louis was there too, and so was Bitsy Duhe, along with other faces of neighbors, friends, and clients.

Blinking away tears, Charlotte turned to Hank. Too choked up to utter a sound, all she could do was smile and mouth the words, "Thank you."

The second the song was over, Hank nudged her into the room, and she was immediately surrounded by a crush of family and employees, each greeting her with a hug or a kiss on the cheek.

Then others crowded around, and when Louis stepped up, Charlotte swallowed hard and her heart thudded like a drum. She'd never seen him in a suit before, and she couldn't help admiring how the dark gray color seemed the perfect foil for his steel-gray hair and dark eyes.

"I thought you were sick with the flu," she told him. Louis shrugged, and before she had time to realize his intentions, he leaned down and kissed her, full on the mouth.

He tasted of wine, and she felt the kiss all the way to her toes as she breathed in his unique scent, a clean smell of soap and the spicy cologne he always wore. All too soon, the kiss ended.

"Happy birthday, Charlotte," he whispered near her ear, his warm breath sending tiny shivers down her spine. "And by the way, you don't have to worry. I'm not contagious. I don't have the flu after all — just a bad sinus infection."

"Can you believe it?" Madeline said a few minutes later as they made their way to the dining table. "Hank reserved the entire room just for your party. Must have cost him a fortune — the music, the food, the cake and —" She shrugged. "Just everything."

Charlotte was every bit as overwhelmed by it all as Madeline to realize the expense that Hank had gone to in order to make her birthday so special.

The spacious Garden Room, with its walls of mirrors, white latticework, and huge windows had been designed to enhance the outdoor setting of oaks and palms visible through the windows, and had been decorated beautifully. Festive balloons in an array of colors hovered against the ceiling and baskets of flowers were scattered about.

Divided into two sections, a group of dining tables, covered with pristine white tablecloths and gleaming china, had been formed into a horseshoe shape in the center of the front section. Along the walls were more tables. A huge birthday cake sat on one while another one was stacked with gifts; the rest of the tables were filled with silver dome-shaped serving tureens and platters of food.

Except for the small string combo of musicians in one corner and a portable bar in the other one, the back section of the room had been left open for dancing.

Once everyone had finally settled at the tables, champagne was quickly served, and Hank stood up to offer a toast.

"Thank you all for joining us tonight to celebrate my mother's birthday," he said. "By the way, in case you're wondering, she's sixty going on twenty-nine and can still work circles around me." When the titter of laughter died, he continued. "Also, in case you don't know it, my mom is a very special lady. She's the kind of lady that any son or daughter would be proud to call mother." He turned to stare straight at Charlotte, and her already tight throat tightened even more as her eyes again filled with tears. "Every good quality that I possess," he continued, "and all that I've accomplished, I owe to you, Mom, to all the sacrifices you've made for me and to the wonderful example you set for me. So here's to you." He held out his glass. "To a wonderful woman who has not only enriched my life but has enriched the lives of everyone who's had the honor and privilege of knowing her."

"Hear, hear!" she heard Daniel and several others chime in. As glasses clinked and a round of applause ensued, the tears that filled her eyes overflowed.

"Speech!" someone called out. And that was all it took as a chant of "Speech! Speech!" was taken up by the others.

Grinning, Hank leaned over. "If you don't say *something*, we'll never get to eat."

Trembling with emotion, Charlotte dabbed at her eyes with the handkerchief that Hank had slipped her, and with his assistance, she stood. "Th-thank you," she said hoarsely, then had to clear her throat. "To say I'm overwhelmed is the understatement of the year. Here I was expecting a nice quiet evening with my son, and instead, I — I get this wonderful surprise." With a shaky smile and to more applause, she collapsed back onto her chair.

An hour later, Charlotte was so stuffed she could hardly breathe.

"Time to blow out the candles," Carol told her.

Charlotte made a face. "Do I have to?"

When both Hank and Carol nodded, she groaned. "Looks like the whole cake is on fire," she grumbled, warily eying the flaming confection in the center of the table along the wall. "Did they have to put all sixty on it?"

"Don't worry, Aunt Charley." Judith grinned. "We'll all help you."

"And don't forget to make a wish," Daniel called out.

"Make wish, make wish," Davy chanted.

To her relief, they were as good as their word, and once all the candles had been blown out, she was allowed to return to her seat of honor.

While several waiters cleared away the dishes from the dining tables to make way for cake and coffee, one began transferring the gifts from the gift table to where Charlotte had been sitting.

As Charlotte made her way back to her chair, she caught a glimpse of a well-dressed woman entering the room. Dread, like a deadly cancer, spread throughout Charlotte's very being, and as Hank seated her first, then sat down, thoughts of crawling beneath the table to hide came to mind.

Chapter Nineteen

Unfortunately for Charlotte, it was already too late to hide. Marian Hebert had spotted her and was heading straight for her. Even worse, Marian was bearing a gift, which made Charlotte feel ten times worse.

"Sorry I'm late," Marian told her breathlessly as she leaned down to give Charlotte a brief buss on the cheek. Hank stood up to greet Marian, allowing Charlotte a bit more time to compose herself.

Hank smiled politely. "Welcome. I'm Charlotte's son, Hank."

"Oh, my, so you're Dr. LaRue," Marian gushed and offered her hand. "It's so nice to finally meet you. I'm Marian Hebert." She held out her hand. "Charlotte has told me so much about you that I feel as if we've already met."

Hank briefly shook Marian's hand. "Nice to meet you too, Ms. Hebert. We're glad you could join us."

"Oh, thank you so much for inviting me, and I'm sorry I'm late. As I was about to tell Charlotte, I'm afraid I can't stay but a moment." She turned to Charlotte. "But the boys made me promise to bring you this." She set the gift, wrapped in gold foil paper and topped with a gold satin bow, down in front of Charlotte on the table.

"B.J. and Aaron helped me pick it out," she said. "Both of them really wanted to come, but there's a special post-homecoming activity at the school, and the boys were required to be there." She smiled at Hank. "My boys just love Charlotte."

Marian's words stabbed Charlotte right in the center of her guilt-ridden heart. Charlotte swallowed hard, and though she couldn't quite bring herself to look Marian straight in the eyes, she forced a smile. "Won't you at least stay and have a piece of cake and some coffee, Marian?" *Please don't stay . . . please don't stay . . .*

"I'd really love to, Charlotte — I really would — but I guess I'd better get back to the school myself."

Charlotte could only hope that the relief she felt didn't show on her face. "At least let me send the boys a couple of pieces of cake for later."

"I'll take care of it, Mom," Hank offered.

"Oh, no," Marian protested. "That's very kind of you, but I really must go now."

This time Charlotte's smile was genuine.

"Please tell the boys thank you for me."

Marian nodded. "Oh, I will, and again, happy birthday, Charlotte." Then, with a fluttery little wave, she rushed off toward the door.

The moment Marian disappeared through the doorway, Charlotte let out a relieved sigh and sagged against the back of her chair.

Tilting his head, Hank eyed her with a calculating expression. "Anything wrong, Mom?"

"Why, no," she lied, feeling even more guilty than she had felt before. "Of course not. What on earth could be wrong on such a lovely night?"

Her son knew her too well, and the look on his face said he didn't believe a word she was saying. "Are you sure? I got the distinct feeling that you really didn't want her to stay."

"Oh, Hank, don't be silly."

Since everyone had just about finished their cake, he didn't push it. "Time to open your gifts," he said.

The first gift that Charlotte opened was the one from B.J. and Aaron. It was a darling little jewel-encased music box. Perched on top of the lid was a tiny white dove. When she opened the box, the song

"Wind Beneath My Wings" played. Amid the ohs and ahs from her guests, Charlotte had to swallow several times to keep from sobbing out loud.

As if sensing how emotionally charged the moment was for her, Hank quickly handed her another gift to open.

Charlotte lost count of the number of lovely gifts she'd opened, and yet Hank kept placing more in front of her until finally there were only two packages left.

The smaller package of the two turned out to be a sweater set from Madeline.

"Oh, Maddie, it's beautiful, and so soft. Cashmere?"

Madeline nodded. "I thought that color blue would look good on you. And it will go nicely with those cream-colored slacks that Judith gave you."

"Thanks, Maddie. It's gorgeous."

The final and last gift was rather large, and the small gold tag on top of the ribbon indicated it was from Victoria's Secret.

Victoria's Secret! Who on earth would be giving her something from there?

She had yet to receive a gift from Louis, but surely he wouldn't . . . She lifted up the gift card, and her face grew hot with embarrassment. Whatever was in the box *was* from Louis.

Her instinct was to look at him, to see what kind of expression was on his face, knowing that she was about to open his gift. But Charlotte fought the urge and kept her eyes on the package instead. Just the thought of Louis shopping for her at all made her feel kind of funny, but only the good Lord knew what kind of gift the man had ended up with from Victoria's Secret.

Be nice, Charlotte. No matter what it is, be nice.

Charlotte tore off the wrapping paper, then lifted the lid off the box. There seemed to be layer upon layer of tissue paper that she had to go through before finally unearthing the gift itself. With a frown marring her forehead, all she could do was stare at the contents. Leopard print?

"What on earth?" she murmured, silently praying that it wasn't a nightgown. She'd never hear the end of it from her family if it was. Then, with trembling fingers, she lifted it out of the box. It wasn't a nightgown, but it might as well have been. The luxurious robe was made of satin on the outside and lined with a sumptuous soft terry. Beautiful . . . even sexy . . . but also practical.

"Oh, wow!" Madeline exclaimed. "Who

on earth is that from?" Before Charlotte realized her intention and could stop her, Madeline grabbed the gift card. "Louis? Louis gave you that?"

Judith leaned across in front of Madeline. "Uh-huh, now we know," she drawled. "And all this time you've been telling me that he was just a tenant and nothing else. Yeah, right, Aunt Charley."

Madeline nudged Charlotte with her elbow. "Come on, now, sister, dear. Do tell."

Rolling her eyes, and with as much dignity as she could muster, Charlotte ignored the teasing. All she could do now was hope that Louis hadn't heard the remarks.

Intending to thank him, she glanced over in the direction where he was seated. But his chair was empty, as empty as her insides suddenly felt.

While part of her was glad, relieved that he hadn't been around to hear Madeline's and Judith's teasing remarks, another part of her was truly disappointed . . . and puzzled. Where was he? she wondered, craning her neck to search for him. Had he left already, left without even saying good-bye?

Suddenly there was the piercing squeal of a microphone, and everyone at the table winced and groaned.

"Sorry about that," the leader of the string combo apologized. "But I have an announcement to make. We have the first request of the evening. So get your dancing shoes on and grab your partner. It's time to work off all that great food and birthday cake."

Charlotte immediately recognized the beginning, bittersweet strains of "Unchained Melody," and she recalled the last time she'd heard it, coming from Louis' half of the double. She closed her eyes for a moment. She was so caught up in the feelings the tune always evoked that when she felt the light tap on her shoulder, her eyes flew open and she jumped.

"Sorry. Didn't mean to startle you."

Charlotte jerked her head around and up.

Louis.

He hadn't left after all.

He made a little half bow, then held out his hand. "May I have the honor of this dance, milady?"

Charlotte swallowed hard. More pleased than she wanted to admit that he hadn't left, she gave him a warm smile. In keeping with his mock formality, she nodded once, placed her hand in his, and said, "But of course, kind sir."

The dance floor was only a few steps away, and as Louis pulled her firmly into his arms, Charlotte had the strangest feeling that she was exactly where she belonged, that in some odd way, she'd finally come home. Probably too much champagne, she thought, dismissing the sensation.

"So, did you like the robe?" he asked, his warm breath tickling her cheek as they swayed to the music. "I hope I didn't embarrass you, giving you something like that. The salesgirl assured me it would be appropriate enough, and to tell you the truth, I got tired of seeing you in that old ratty thing you wear around all the time."

"Ratty!" Charlotte pulled back just enough to look him in the eyes. "It's not that ratty, and I'll have you know I do not wear it *all the time.*"

"Aw, come on, Charlotte. Admit it. You needed a new one. Now didn't you?"

A grin tugged at her lips. "Well . . . I suppose so," she drawled. "I guess my old one *is* getting a bit worn looking — but not exactly ratty," she hastened to add.

"So you're not mad at me?"

Of all the men she'd ever met, she would never have dreamed that Louis Thibodeaux could be so insecure about something like a gift. "Louis, the housecoat is lovely, just perfect, and if you hadn't run off, I would have told you so right after I opened it."

"Humph! Well, that's a relief — and I didn't run off. Hank said it was time to get the dancing started, so I got the ball rolling."

"I should have known," she murmured. "So you're the one who made the song request?"

Louis shrugged. "Hey — I happen to like this song. It brings back a lot of memories of the good old days, if you know what I mean."

"For your information, I happen to like it too," she retorted. "For all the same reasons. And by the way —" With her hand that was resting on his shoulder, she smoothed the fabric of his suit. "I've been meaning to tell you all night that I really like your suit too. It looks very nice on you."

"Well, I hope so," he drawled. "It cost enough, but hey — I needed a new one anyway — or so that niece of yours keeps telling me."

"You just bought it?"

"Yeah, thanks to Judith. She's a lot like

you, you know — pretty stubborn at times. The other day when she came by, she wanted to see what I was planning on wearing to this shindig. Well, when I showed her my old suit, she snatched it right off the hanger and stuffed it in the trash can." He chuckled. "Just like a woman, throwing away a perfectly good suit just because the lapels aren't the right size or some such nonsense. Anyway — she called up this friend of hers who works at Macy's and —" He shrugged. "I ended up with this."

It was almost midnight before the last of the guests finally said good night. Since Davy had fallen asleep on Daniel's shoulder earlier, Daniel and Nadia had already left.

With only Louis and the rest of her family still remaining, Charlotte didn't feel like she was being rude when she announced, "I've had the most wonderful day that anyone could ever ask for, but this old birthday gal is tired and ready to call it a night."

She stepped over to where Hank and Carol were standing. "Thank you, son. And thank you, Carol." She gave Carol a quick hug. "Thank you both for everything. It's been a dream come true and a day I won't ever forget." She wrapped her arms around Hank's waist and hugged him tightly.

"You're very welcome, Mom," he said, hugging her back, then releasing her.

"We just wanted to make it special for you," Carol told her.

Louis walked over to join them. "I'm kinda pooped myself," he said, "and if you'd like, I can give Charlotte a ride home."

Hank glanced over at Charlotte. "Mom?"

"That would be just fine." She turned to Louis. "Thank you for offering."

"Well, let's get those gifts packed up and hit the road then."

Louis was quiet during the short drive home, and after all the noise and chatter of the party, the silence was a welcome relief for Charlotte.

Then, just as they turned down Milan Street, he cleared his throat, a gesture that Charlotte had learned usually indicated he was about to say something that he felt was important.

"You know, Charlotte, turning sixty is really not all that bad."

Of all the things Louis could have said,

that was the last thing she'd expected to hear from him.

He cleared his throat again. "I've been sixty now for a couple of years, and other than all the jokes about being an old man that I've had to put up with, not much else has changed."

"Easy for you to say," she muttered. "I think turning sixty's the pits. It just sounds so — so old. Besides, it's easier for men. Men only grow more distinguished looking the older they get, while women just grow older and more wrinkled."

"Now that's a bunch of hogwash if I ever heard it," he argued as he turned into the driveway. He shoved the gear into park, switched off the engine, then shifted in the seat to face her. "You'd easily pass for a woman ten years younger any day. Besides, it's what's in here —" With his forefinger, he tapped his head near the temple. "And in here —" With his fist he thumped the center of his chest. "That's all that really counts anyway."

Charlotte was speechless. Louis was lots of things, some of them she liked, some of them she didn't, but she'd never thought of him as a philosopher, and it wasn't that often that he handed out compliments so freely.

When she finally found her voice, all she could think to say was a simple "Thank you." And before the already awkward moment grew even more awkward, she gave him a quick smile. "And thanks for giving me a ride home." With that, she pulled on the door handle, pushed open the door, and climbed out of the car.

Following her lead, Louis got out too. "Why don't you unlock the front door, and I'll start unloading the gifts."

The moment Charlotte entered the living room, Sweety Boy chirped out a greeting from beneath the cage cover. Just to be safe, Charlotte decided to move him out of the room temporarily, at least until Louis left. "No use in you getting all upset this late at night," she crooned to him as she gently set his cage down on a chair in the bedroom.

Charlotte directed Louis to stack the gifts on the sofa in the living room for the time being. It took three trips back and forth before everything had been unloaded.

"That's the last of them," he told her, motioning toward the packages he'd just deposited onto the sofa, as he strolled to the front door.

"Thanks again," she said, following him.

At the door he paused, and when he turned to face her, suddenly she felt as if a thousand butterflies had taken wing inside her stomach. Would he kiss her again? But more to the point, did she want him to kiss her again?

"Charlotte, I —" He glanced down, then shifted from one foot to the other. "About last Friday night — when you came over to eat." He lifted his head and looked her straight in the eye. "I was pretty damn rude, and I never did apologize. Tonight — seeing how all those people showed up in your honor and listening to Hank's toast really made me stop and think. You're a nice lady, and you didn't deserve me taking my anger out on you."

The butterflies settled down, and compassion welled up within her. Charlotte reached out and squeezed his arm. "Was it anger or was it grief, Louis?"

He hesitated, then nodded. "A little of both I guess."

She smiled sympathetically. "The offer still stands, you know," she said softly. "Any time you want to talk about it, I'll be glad to listen."

"Yeah, I know. And I appreciate the offer — I really do." He shrugged. "Maybe one of these days . . ."

Then, once again, before Charlotte realized his intentions, he leaned over and kissed her, full on the lips. Almost before the kiss had begun, though, it was over and he pulled away.

"Good night, Charlotte, and happy birthday," he whispered.

Long after Louis had left and Charlotte had climbed into her bed, she could still taste his kiss. As she stared up at the dark ceiling in her bedroom, she couldn't stop thinking about him, his apology, or the dance they'd shared . . . or anything else about the Cinderella night she'd had, including the other kiss he had given her as well.

Even though she was tired, she kept reliving the entire evening over and over, from beginning to end . . . the sights and sounds, the food, all of the guests who had been there, the gifts . . . the music box from B.J. and Aaron . . .

Charlotte groaned. Turning over onto her side, she curled up in a fetal position.

B.J., again.

What was she going to do about that boy? Was he guilty of committing murder? Had he killed Drew Bergeron? *Guilty . . . innocent until proven guilty . . .*

Suddenly, she sat straight up in bed. "Shame on you, Charlotte LaRue," she muttered. All this time, all weekend long, despite her gut feelings to the contrary, she'd been condemning the teenager. Without even the benefit of a fair trial, she'd played prosecutor, judge, and jury and had condemned him, had spent hours worrying about who to tell or if she should tell anyone, and all without even giving the teenager a chance to defend himself or to explain.

Like a warm blanket on a cold winter's night, relief spread through her, and she snuggled back down beneath the covers.

"Monday," she whispered. On Monday, she would simply confront B.J. with what she'd found and see what he had to say for himself. Then she'd decide what to do about it.

Chapter Twenty

Charlotte hated confrontations of any kind, but she also hated the indecision that had plagued her over the past three days. Given a choice, she'd rather deal with neither, but Charlotte knew that there were some things in life, certain circumstances, where a person had no choice but to react.

A cold knot formed in her stomach as she glanced at the dashboard clock, then turned the van off of St. Charles onto Jefferson Avenue where B.J.'s school was located. Charlotte was well acquainted with the history of the private school B.J. attended, since Hank had also gone there during his high school days. Isodore Newman had been founded in 1903, and the exclusive school had been educating children for almost a century.

Normal time for dismissal was three-thirty, but Charlotte knew that once a week, on Mondays, B.J. stayed an extra hour for math tutoring. According to Marian, the teenager was highly intelligent and had always made top grades until recently. But since his father's death, his grades had taken a nosedive, enough so that she'd determined he needed the extra help.

After his tutoring session, if the weather was pleasant, he would walk the two blocks to St. Charles Avenue, catch a streetcar to the stop nearest his home, then walk the remaining distance.

Since it was only four-fifteen, Charlotte was a bit early, but she'd wanted to make sure she didn't miss B.J.

Jefferson Avenue wasn't a wide street, but not many were in New Orleans. Jefferson was a two-way street, though, divided by what natives of New Orleans referred to as the neutral ground. As in the Garden District, the Uptown area was shaded from the harsh glare of the afternoon sun by the many trees growing along the Avenue.

As Charlotte slowly approached the sprawling light-tan brick building trimmed in white, she spotted a perfect place to park, a place where she could remain in the van but still have a good view of the entrance to the school. Since the parking place was on the opposite side of the neutral ground, she had to continue past the school and make a U-turn farther up the street to get back to where she wanted to park.

Once she'd parked and switched off the engine, for a few moments, she sat and watched as small groups of laughing, loud-talking teenagers walked past the school.

Luckily for her, Marian had left that morning almost as soon as Charlotte had arrived to clean, saving Charlotte from having to wrestle with her conscience because she hadn't told Marian about B.J.

Charlotte suddenly sat up straight when she recognized B.J. emerging from the main entrance, a huge bulky knapsack strapped to his back. Unlike the other students who were paired off or part of a group, B.J. was all alone.

As she crossed the busy street, B.J. noticed her almost immediately, and the surprised look on his face would have been comical if not for the seriousness of the reason she was there.

"Hey, Ms. LaRue, what are you doing here?"

"Hey, yourself, B.J. Actually, I've been waiting for you."

The boy stared at her for several moments, then suddenly a cloud of worry tinged with fright came over his face. "Everyone's okay, aren't they? My mom, my little brother?"

"Oh, hon —" Charlotte reached out and squeezed his arm. "Of course they're okay. They're just fine. The reason I'm here has nothing to do with your family — not exactly, anyway." She motioned toward a concrete bench set against the backdrop of a row of hedges. "Let's sit over here."

The instant relief evident on his face gave Charlotte a pang of guilt. The last thing she wanted was to cause him more stress or pain than he'd already endured. But if her suspicions were right, and she prayed they weren't, then the teenager was in for more stress than he'd ever dreamed possible.

After they had settled on the bench, she turned toward him. "Thank you for my lovely birthday gift."

The teenager shrugged. "You're welcome." Then he frowned. "You came all the way over here just to thank me?"

Charlotte slowly shook her head. "No, hon. Not really." She swallowed hard. "B.J., you know I care about you, don't you — care about your welfare?" she qualified.

He shrugged. "Yeah — sure. So?"

"The first thing I want you to know is that I never snoop or pry into my client's personal belongings. But while I was cleaning your room last Friday, I found something that really disturbed me. Before I go to your mother or the authorities about what I found, I wanted to give you a chance to explain."

B.J. frowned. "Explain what?"

"Explain why you would have a shoe box full of cigars and clippings about Drew Bergeron's murder beneath your bed."

The boy's expression grew wary, then turned belligerent. He narrowed his eyes and glared at her. "You had no right to look through my stuff."

"Whoa, whoa." Charlotte held up a hand in a defensive gesture. "I didn't do it on purpose. I was cleaning out from beneath your bed and the box spilled open."

"Well you didn't have to look, and I don't have to tell you anything."

Charlotte sighed. "No — no you don't have to tell me anything, but I was at the Devilier house when Mr. Bergeron's body was discovered, and I saw a cigar ground out on the floor just outside the closet where he was found. And guess what? It looked just like the ones under your bed."

"So what! Could have been anyone's cigar," he retorted, his tone harsh and belligerent. "And why wouldn't I be interested in Mr. Drew's murder? He and my dad were friends, and my dad worked for him."

Charlotte nodded. "Yes, I suppose that sounds logical enough, but —" She crossed her arms, tilted up her chin, and peered down her nose at him. "You and I both know it's not the truth. So why don't you try again?"

His answer was an insolent glare.

After a moment, Charlotte simply shook her head. "Look, B.J.," she warned, "it's no secret that you've been in trouble lately. Failing grades, curfew violations, fighting at school, and getting suspended. With all of that, how do you think it's going to look to the police if they find out what's beneath your bed, especially given your family's connection to Drew Bergeron? Now, you can either tell me the truth or I'll have no choice but to go to your mom or to the police."

For what seemed like an eternity, the teenager simply glared at Charlotte, his jaw clenched while the muscles in his cheeks tightened, then loosened, then tightened again. The expression on his face was a picture of anguish, indecision, and something else that she could only guess was fear.

"I didn't do anything wrong," he suddenly blurted. His eyes filled with tears, and he blinked them back viciously. "The only reason I collected those newspaper articles was because I kept hoping the cops would find the killer. And I don't smoke! Not since I got suspended." He hesitated; then, in a choked voice, he said, "Those cigars belonged to my dad. When Mom cleaned out his stuff after he — he — after he was gone, I took some of his things to keep so I wouldn't forget him. I've got one of his T-shirts too, but Mom doesn't know and please don't tell her. She gets too upset, and when she gets all uptight, she drinks."

Charlotte had to fight against giving in to the sympathy tugging at her heart. "If you didn't do anything wrong, then why so defensive?"

With a shudder, B.J. dropped his head. "Okay, okay," he finally choked out. "I was there, but I —" He scrubbed his face with the back of his hand, then looked up. "I — I didn't do it, Ms. LaRue. I swear I didn't kill him. I've never even fired a gun."

And she believed him. "Why don't you start from the beginning, hon, and tell me what happened?"

Nodding slowly, he cleared his throat.

"Last Thursday, my mom needed me to deliver some papers to Ms. Bergeron, and when I was leaving her house, I noticed there was a man hanging around near the side fence. I thought it was kinda weird that he was taking pictures of Katie — that's Ms. Bergeron's little girl. You see, Katie was playing just on the other side of the fence."

Charlotte went still. *The photos.* Of course. That was why the pictures she'd seen scattered on top of the sleeping bag had looked so familiar. She hadn't recognized the little girl because she'd hadn't seen her since she was born, but her subconscious had recognized the place where the pictures had been taken, had recognized that the house and grounds belonged to Katherine Bergeron.

"Anyway," B.J. continued, "I had to walk past the man to get to the bus stop, and when I got closer, I realized that he looked just like Mr. Drew. I didn't believe it at first, and it really freaked me out. Mr. Drew was dead, but that man looked so much like him that I decided to hang around just to see what he was up to." B.J. paused, made a face, then shook his head. "You know — he never said a word to Katie. Just took the pictures and left."

"And you followed him," Charlotte offered.

"Yes, ma'am. It was just too weird, so I followed him down to that house."

"The Devilier house?"

He nodded. "That's when I figured out that maybe the man really was Mr. Drew and that he was hiding out there. You see, I'd heard my mom talk about the place, and I knew no one was renting it yet. So he had to be hiding out there."

Charlotte frowned. "But that was on Thursday, wasn't it? Why didn't you tell someone — tell your mom?"

"I was going to, but by the time I got home, Mom was in a hurry to leave to meet a client, and I didn't get the chance."

"What about Friday?" Charlotte asked him. "Why didn't you tell her then?"

B.J. gave her a sheepish look. "After what I pulled Thursday night, she wasn't in any mood to listen to anything from me."

"Oh, yeah." She nodded sagely. "That was the night you sneaked out after curfew, wasn't it?"

"Yes, ma'am."

"So what about Friday afternoon — after school?"

"She was gone to take Aaron to the

doctor." He hesitated. "But I almost told Ms. Bergeron," he added. "While Mom was gone, she came by to pick up a set of keys."

"But you didn't."

He shook his head.

"Why not?"

He shrugged. "I — I just couldn't — you know — find the right way to tell her. But after she left, I finally decided to call Sam. Since my dad died, Sam is the only one who really listens to me anyway, and I knew he'd know what to do."

"And what did Sam tell you?"

"Sam said that I'd better make sure that the man was Mr. Drew before I go around telling anyone. He said if I was wrong and told someone, and Ms. Bergeron or my mom got all upset, then I would be in big trouble for sure."

"So . . . Let me guess. You decided to go to the Devilier house that night and make sure."

"Well, how else was I gonna know?"

"Oh, B.J., B.J." She shook her head.

B.J. ignored her. "All I wanted was to find something that would prove the man really was Mr. Drew. I figured I could maybe sneak in and find something in his stuff — you know, like a driver's license or something."

"Did it ever once occur to you that who-ever the man was, he might be dangerous?"

"Oh, sure. That's why I waited till I saw him leave."

"And did you find anything?"

"Uh-uh. Just about the time I finally got inside, I heard someone else come in and I had to hide in a closet."

"Someone else?"

"Ms. Bergeron and some man I didn't know. They were looking at the apartments, I guess — you know, to rent?"

Charlotte nodded.

"Well, anyway, they finally left, and I had just started looking through the man's stuff when I heard someone else come in. So I hid again. I figured if he'd come back, then I could sneak out after he went to sleep, and if it was someone else —" He shrugged. "Then I would just wait until they left.

"I hid in a hallway closet just outside of the room where he had all his stuff and waited. It had to be him, though, because I heard him go straight to the room where his junk was and I could hear him fooling around in the bathroom — brushing his teeth and stuff.

"Just about the time that I thought he was settling down for the night, I heard the stairs creak, and then I heard voices. At first I couldn't hear what was being said 'cause they were talking kinda low. Then, the man — Mr. Drew — started yelling at whoever was there, and that's when I knew it really was him 'cause I recognized his voice. He kept saying 'Don't! Don't do it! No, please don't.'" B.J. abruptly paused and swallowed hard. "I heard it but didn't know what it was until later. All I could think about at the time was getting out of there as soon as I could."

"What did you hear?"

"A popping sound." He shuddered. "A gunshot." He heaved a sigh. "After that I heard footsteps. They sounded like who-ever was there was leaving, but I waited anyway — waited for what seemed like hours before I finally figured it was safe enough to come out. Then I hauled butt."

"Oh, B.J., why didn't you tell someone — your mom, maybe? Or better still, why didn't you go to the police?"

"Duh! My fingerprints are probably all over the place —"

"Ah, excuse me," she drawled, "but I really don't appreciate the sarcasm. I'm trying to help you, so show a little respect."

B.J. simply stared at her, then after several moments, he finally gave a grudging nod. "Yes, ma'am. Sorry. But like you said before, I've been in trouble a lot lately. The cops would think *I* killed him."

"What about your mom? Couldn't you tell her?"

B.J. rolled his eyes. "No way. She'd freak out for sure."

"So you've told no one."

"Well . . . not exactly. I did tell Sam."

"And?"

"Sam said to forget it and just keep my mouth shut. He said sooner or later the cops would find the real killer." He hesitated, then, "You believe me, don't you, Ms. LaRue?" He held up his hand as if taking an oath. "I swear it's the truth."

Charlotte managed a small, tentative smile. "I believe you, hon." And she did. But she also recalled what Judith had told her about Katherine and Vince supplying each other with alibis. What if Vince was the man Katherine was with, the one B.J. didn't recognize? And what if when they left the house, they saw Drew and decided to follow him? What if they confronted him, then killed him?

"I believe you," she murmured again. Then, carefully choosing her words, she said, "But I'm afraid I have to disagree with Sam. I think you need to go to the police and tell them exactly what you just told me." For reasons she couldn't explain, even to herself, the thought of how easily influenced B.J. was by Sam Roberts bothered her. There was just something about the man with his know-it-all attitude that set her teeth on edge.

B.J. cast his eyes downward and shuffled his feet against the concrete walk. "Hmm . . . maybe."

Charlotte placed her hand on his shoulder. "Look, hon, think of it this way. Something you say just might help the police find the real killer — or at least give them a clue to the identity of the person who killed Mr. Bergeron."

"Maybe I ought to talk to Sam about it first."

Charlotte grimaced. Sam again. Unease snaked through her. And what if Sam said no? Then what? she wondered. If she went to Judith and told her what B.J. had revealed, she'd be betraying his confidence. Once confronted with his story, B.J. might clam up or worse, he might even deny everything. It would be better for everyone concerned if she could somehow persuade him to cooperate.

Despite her own misgivings about Sam Roberts, Charlotte had to remind herself that he had been there for B.J. when the boy had needed someone. There was also the fact that Marian seemed to trust the handyman implicitly, and after all, Marian was B.J.'s mother. So who was she to question the man's integrity?

"Okay, B.J.," she finally relented. "Talk to Sam again if it will make you feel better. But make it soon, okay?"

The boy nodded.

"Now, you'd better run along before your mom begins to worry."

B.J. didn't need to be told twice. He grabbed up his knapsack, shrugged into it, and left. And as Charlotte watched him hurry down the sidewalk, an idea began to take shape. For B.J.'s sake, maybe it was time that *she* had a talk with Sam Roberts herself.

Almost immediately, Charlotte shied away from the idea. She was already involved more than she wanted to be, and approaching Sam Roberts was the last thing in the world she wanted to do.

With a sigh of frustration, she marched across the street to the van. But like a pesky mosquito, the idea simply wouldn't go away. If Sam knew that B.J. had confided in her, she might persuade him to rethink his advice to the boy and use his influence to urge B.J. to go to the police.

The more she thought about it on the drive home, the more it seemed like the only sensible thing to do. So if it was so sensible, why did she get the nervous heebie-jeebies just thinking about talking to Sam Roberts?

Chapter Twenty-one

The minute Charlotte got home, she grabbed the telephone directory to see if Sam Roberts was listed. She'd thought about simply calling Marian to get his phone number, but she really didn't want to do that unless she had no choice. Until she resolved her dilemma about B.J., the less contact she had with his mother, the better.

But finding Sam Roberts wasn't going to be that easy, she soon learned. There were six S. Roberts, but no Sam Roberts listed. Charlotte called all six of the numbers, but none turned out to be the Sam Roberts she was looking for.

Next she tried Directory Assistance, but again, she hit a brick wall when she was politely told that his number was unlisted.

"Now what?" she murmured, tapping out an impatient staccato rhythm with her fingers against the desktop and wondering why on earth someone in his line of business would have an unlisted number, of all things.

Suddenly, her fingers stilled. There was

no way around it, she finally decided. Whether she wanted to or not, she was going to have to call Marian.

Charlotte reached for the Rolodex. Marian would know his phone number and would probably know where he lived as well. Once she'd found Marian's number, she hesitated, her fingers hovering above the dial pad on the phone.

What excuse could she use for wanting to know Sam's phone number and address? She finally decided that she could always claim that she had another client who needed some repairs done, or better yet, she could say that she needed something repaired herself.

Marian answered Charlotte's call on the third ring. Charlotte crossed her fingers for luck. "I'm really sorry to bother you, Marian, but I need Sam Roberts' address. You see, the other day I asked him about repairing one of my kitchen chairs, and silly me — I forgot to get his address. I'd call him, but he's not listed in the phone directory, so I was wondering if you happen to know where he lives."

The excuse had holes in it as big as the Grand Canyon, and Charlotte held her breath.

Evidently, Marian didn't notice. When

she began rattling off the phone number and the address, Charlotte grabbed a pen and quickly scribbled down the information.

Though Charlotte had never believed in putting off till tomorrow what she could do today, after she'd hung up the phone she sat for several moments, staring into space. Once again she weighed the pros and cons of the decision she'd made to talk to Sam.

"Just do it," she finally muttered. Before she could change her mind, she shoved away from the desk, grabbed her purse, and marched out of the house.

The address Marian had given Charlotte was actually only a few blocks away. The house itself was also very similar in architecture to her own home and even included a small front porch and swing. The only difference was that Sam's house was in much better repair than her house; unlike hers, his had what looked to be a fresh coat of paint.

When Charlotte approached the address, she noted that there were no vehicles in either driveway, but she reasoned that his truck could be parked around back, since the driveways on either side went all the way to the back of the house.

Did he own the double? she wondered.

Or, like Louis, was he just renting one side of it?

Charlotte parked the van near the curb in front, got out, then walked slowly to the steps. Her misgivings about being there in the first place grew with each step she took as she climbed the stairs up to the porch. Reminding herself that she was doing this for B.J. was the only thing that kept her from running back to the van and driving away.

At the front door, she hesitated. Then, taking a deep breath for courage, she pushed the doorbell and waited. When several moments passed and nothing happened, she rang the doorbell again.

Hindsight was a wonderful thing, she thought sarcastically as she waited. Not only had she rushed out without going to the bathroom, a chore she always took care of before leaving the house, but she hadn't considered phoning ahead. If she'd phoned first, she could have saved herself the trouble and discomfort.

But she hadn't phoned ahead, and as she saw it, she now had two choices: She could hang around and wait until Sam showed up, or she could leave and come back again later.

Since there was no way of telling when

he might show up and she really needed a rest room anyway, Charlotte decided to leave. She also decided that before she went running off again, she'd call first next time. Turning away from the door, she crossed the porch and started back down the stairs.

While part of her was relieved that no one was home, another part of her felt the disappointment and frustration clear to her toes. Then, at the bottom of the steps, something in the grass caught her eye and Charlotte stopped dead in her tracks. Just to the left side of the bottom step was an object that looked suspiciously like a ground-out cigar butt.

Paranoid, she thought, with a shake of her head. She was becoming paranoid over cigar butts, for Pete's sake. Besides, as B.J. had so cleverly pointed out, just because it was the same brand didn't necessarily mean anything in and of itself; it could belong to anyone.

But even as she muttered, "You're being ridiculous," she grabbed hold of the stair rail for support and nudged the butt with the toe of her shoe. Though it was smashed flat, it did have the same odd shape as the ones beneath B.J.'s bed and the one at the Devilier house.

Charlotte was still staring at the cigar butt when the sound of a vehicle pulling into the driveway finally penetrated her concentration.

She glanced up and her heart began to thud when she saw Sam Roberts climb out of his battered truck. The man really needed a haircut, she thought. And he needed to trim that scraggly beard. He might not look half bad if he cleaned up a bit . . .

"Well, this is sure a surprise," he called out. "What do I owe this honor to — No, wait, let me guess. You've finally decided to give in and let me have my wicked way with you."

Charlotte swallowed hard and summoned up a polite little smile. "Not hardly," she told him with as much dignity as she could muster. "I'm here because I need to talk to you."

"Talking's a good beginning." He grinned and waggled his eyebrows. "A little talk. A little —"

"About B.J.," she hastened to add. "I'm here to talk to you about B.J.," she said with emphasis.

Sam's grin faded instantly, and for a moment, an odd expression flitted across his face. Was it hostility? Wariness? Charlotte couldn't be sure, but almost as soon as it appeared, it was gone, leaving her to wonder if once again her imagination was playing tricks on her.

"What's he done this time?" Sam asked her, his face now serious with worry.

"Nothing, I hope," she replied. "But that's what we need to discuss."

The line of his mouth tightened a fraction, but he motioned toward the front door. "Well, come on in and let's talk then."

Once again, misgivings about being there assailed her. Charlotte had been on her own for more years than she cared to count, and during that time, she'd learned to be cautious. There were just some things that a single woman didn't do, and one of them was getting caught all alone in a strange house with a man she barely knew and didn't really like in the first place.

She'd come too far to back down now, but for a moment she debated if it would be considered rude to suggest that they sit out on the porch instead. Then she thought of B.J. and the enormity of the problems facing the teenager. She finally decided that too much was at stake to quibble over *where* she talked to Sam. The boy's whole future could depend on this talk.

Gathering her courage, she took a deep breath and once again climbed the steps to the porch.

The inside of Sam's home wasn't what she'd expected at all. For one thing, it had been remodeled to include a small hallway. And like Louis' place, it looked nothing like she had imagined a bachelor's house would look like. No dirty clothes lying around. No unwashed dishes or scattered magazines or newspapers. It was tidy and extremely sparse. But unlike Louis' place, there was nothing at all in the way of personal effects. No paintings, no knickknacks or books, nothing to give her even a hint as to what type of man he might be.

He motioned toward the sofa. "Have a seat. Can I offer you something to drink? A Coke? Coffee? Or maybe something a little stronger?"

"No — no, thanks. Nothing for me." She stepped over to the sofa. "But you go ahead and get whatever you'd like."

He nodded, but as he turned and headed toward what she assumed was the kitchen, she called him back. "There is one thing, though," she said. "I do need to use your bathroom, if you don't mind."

In a matter-of-fact way that she truly appreciated, he pointed to another doorway. "Down the hall. Second door on your left."

Charlotte figured that the first door probably led to a bedroom, and wondering if it too was as sparse and devoid of personal effects as the living room, she slowed her steps as she approached it. Should she or shouldn't she? Surely just a quick peek couldn't hurt, could it?

From the doorway, Charlotte frowned as she gazed around the small room. Compared to the bedroom, the living room was cluttered, she thought, eying the even more barren, depressive room.

Like the living room, the bedroom was neat and tidy, but that was the only positive thing she could say about it.

The double-sized bed was covered with a plain cotton bedspread that had probably once been white, but now, due to either age or neglect, it had a yellowish cast to it. A little bleach and a good washing would do wonders for it, make it look almost new. Too bad she couldn't suggest it.

Next to the bed was a cheap, rickety-looking table, just large enough to hold an equally cheap-looking lamp and an alarm clock. The only other piece of furniture in the room was a small dresser, located against the wall at the foot of the bed. Except for one lone framed photograph, the dresser top was completely bare.

From where she was standing and because of the angle of the frame, she couldn't see the photo. Again, she had to ask herself, should she or shouldn't she?

Knowledge is power if you know it about the right person. And right now, she needed to know all she could about Sam.

Charlotte could faintly hear the sound of an ice tray being emptied, and with one ear tuned to the noises in the kitchen, she eased farther inside the bedroom. As she approached the dresser, out of the corner of her eye, she saw several packing boxes. Because the boxes were stacked on the floor along the wall that the bedroom shared with the hallway, they hadn't been visible before. But it was the photo on the dresser, not the boxes, that interested her at the moment.

The photo was a family portrait of a man, a woman, and two little boys. From the style of the clothes they were wearing, she figured the photo was at least twenty years old. But as she examined each family member, her gaze kept returning to the man.

Charlotte narrowed her eyes and pursed her lips. She'd seen him before . . . somewhere. But where?

Despite the fact that the man in the photo was twenty years younger and that he was trim, clean-shaven, and had dark hair, logic dictated that the man had to be Sam, and that the woman and boys had to be his family. Even so, the vast differences between the appearance of the man in the photo and the man she knew as Sam weren't what made her question the logic of the two being the same person. Age and looks could easily alter the appearance of a person. Impossible as it seemed, what made her question the logic of the two men being the same was that she was sure she'd seen the man in the picture somewhere before, seen him looking exactly the way he appeared in the photograph. But where? And when?

Suddenly conscious of the time that had passed, Charlotte turned to leave. But as she passed the row of packing boxes, the one nearest the door caught her attention. It was packed with what looked like a lot of books, but what caught her eye was the framed certificate lying faceup on top of the stack.

Charlotte bent closer. Just as she'd

thought, the certificate was a university degree, a degree from Tulane University made out to someone named Arthur Samuel. So who the devil was Arthur Samuel? The name was familiar, though she hadn't the foggiest why at the moment. But more to the point, why would Sam have someone else's degree?

Time . . . hurry . . .

Charlotte quickly made use of the bathroom facilities, and by the time she returned to the living room, Sam was waiting for her.

He stood up when she entered the room. "I was beginning to wonder if you fell in," he teased. "Either that or had a heart attack and croaked on my bathroom floor. But what I was really hoping for was that you decided to give me a freebie and clean it."

Charlotte didn't really appreciate his brand of humor, and just the thought of the filthy bathroom made her shudder. Unlike the other two rooms in the house, the bathroom was really gross. The shower was caked over with soap scum and body hair, the sink was smeared with toothpaste, and the inside of the toilet bowl was the stuff nightmares were made of.

"As you can see," she retorted, "I didn't

fall in or die of a heart attack."

"Guess you didn't clean the bathroom either, huh?"

Charlotte grimaced, but chose to ignore his comment. "Now, about B.J."

Sam shrugged and motioned toward the lone chair in the room. "Well, why don't you have a seat and let's talk?"

Once they were both seated, Charlotte began by explaining about finding the box beneath B.J.'s bed, and she ended with what B.J. had revealed after she'd tracked him down at school.

"So you see," she said. "For his own good, B.J. really needs to go to the police and tell them what happened, what he saw. And I was hoping that I could persuade you to talk to him, to convince him that's the best thing to do."

For several long moments, Sam stared at her, but nothing about the expression on his face gave her a clue as to what he was thinking.

Then, abruptly, he stood. Pushing his hands deep into his pockets, he walked over to the window and gazed out into the front yard.

"B.J.'s a good kid," he finally said. "Just mixed up. I should have encouraged him from the beginning to go to the police.

Guess I didn't because I know how brutal the police can be, especially with a boy like B.J. who's been in so much trouble lately."

He turned to face her. "But I see your point, and I will talk to him."

Relief washed through Charlotte, and since she'd accomplished what she'd set out to accomplish, she stood, indicating she was ready to leave. "I appreciate it and it's the right thing to do. When he's ready to tell the police his story, let me know. My niece is a police detective, and contrary to your opinion of the police, she isn't the brutal type. I'll make sure she's the one he talks to."

Though Charlotte was relieved that Sam had agreed to talk to B.J. and she was confident that the teenager would listen to his friend and do the right thing, it wasn't B.J. that filled her thoughts on the drive home.

For reasons she couldn't begin to fathom, she found herself preoccupied with what she'd discovered in Sam's bedroom . . . the family portrait . . . the Tulane University degree . . . the strange name on the degree . . .

But why? Why did those things bother

her, but more to the point, except for Sam's influence on B.J., why should she even care about anything to do with Sam Roberts or his bedroom?

Chapter Twenty-two

On Tuesday morning, Charlotte felt grumpy and out of sorts as she drove to Bitsy Duhe's house. Not only had she slept badly, but she'd made the mistake of letting Sweety Boy out of his cage while she showered and dressed. She'd almost finished her shower when the silly parakeet had scared the daylights out of her by dive-bombing straight into the shower spray. The force of the spray had knocked him against the shower door, stunning the little bird senseless. He'd finally revived, but she was still worried about leaving him.

To make matters worse, traffic was moving slowly, and when she turned onto Magazine Street, it came to a complete standstill. Even now, as she parked in front of Bitsy's house, she still hadn't figured out what the holdup had been.

Most days when Charlotte cleaned Bitsy's house, the old lady was waiting for her at the door. The fact that Bitsy wasn't waiting didn't concern Charlotte at first. But when she rang the doorbell and no one answered, she began to worry. Bitsy had seemed fine at the party Saturday night, but a lot could happen to an elderly lady living alone in two days. What if she'd fallen and broken a hip, or worse, what if she'd had a heart attack and died in her sleep?

Charlotte decided to knock instead of ringing the bell again, just in case the bell was on the blink. She rapped loudly. "Miss Bitsy, it's Charlotte. Are you in there?"

Several more agonizing minutes passed; then, though faintly, Charlotte detected a noise on the other side of the door. When she recognized the sound of the security chain being unlatched, relief washed through her. When the door finally opened, her short-lived relief vanished.

"Oh, Miss Bitsy. What on earth?"

For as long as Charlotte had worked for Bitsy, the elderly lady had always taken pride in her appearance and was always dressed, complete with makeup, by the crack of dawn each morning. The fact that she was still in her gown and robe would have been disturbing enough, but Charlotte could never recall seeing her look so pale and drawn.

With the limp wave of a hand, Bitsy dismissed Charlotte's concern. "Just a bit under the weather this morning." Her normally shrill voice was barely more than a breathless whisper and sounded far too weak to Charlotte's ears. "Probably just a cold," Bitsy continued. "Thanks to that awful Mrs. Jenkins. She sat behind me in church on Sunday, and if that woman sneezed once, she must have sneezed a hundred times during the service."

Charlotte stepped through the doorway and placed an arm around the old lady's waist. "Well, here, let's get you back inside, out of the draft." She nudged her back into the foyer, away from the door. "Judith told me there's a lot of flu going around right now." She released her hold long enough to close and lock the front door. "Did you have your flu shot yet?"

Bitsy looked at her with soulful eyes. "I kept meaning to, but what with Jenny's visit and everything, I just never got around to it."

Charlotte set down her supply carrier. "Well, first things first. Let's get you back to bed, then I'll call and see if we can get you an appointment with your doctor."

Bitsy shook her head. "Oh, Charlotte, I'm really not up to driving to the doctor's office and then having to sit there all morning."

Charlotte gently ushered the old lady back toward her bedroom. "Don't worry about that for now. Just leave it to me, okay?"

When Bitsy finally nodded, Charlotte smiled. "Now, off to bed with you."

Once she'd made sure that Bitsy was tucked back into bed, she asked, "Have you had anything to eat this morning?"

Bitsy had already closed her eyes. "Nothing yet," she mumbled. "Not hungry."

"Well, you just rest for right now, and in a few minutes, I'll bring you in a nice bowl of oatmeal and some juice."

It was midmorning before Charlotte was finally able to speak with Bitsy's doctor. Other than a prescription for a medication that would make her rest a bit more comfortably, he told her that essentially all that could be done was have Bitsy drink lots of liquids and get plenty of rest.

After determining which pharmacy Bitsy used, Charlotte left only long enough to pick up the prescription the doctor had called in. Once the old lady was resting more easily, she continued the chore of cleaning the house. But while she cleaned and alternately checked on Bitsy, Charlotte worried. In her opinion the old lady was much too ill to be left all alone.

It was almost lunchtime when Charlotte came to a decision. Whether Bitsy liked it or not, Charlotte decided that she would insist that Bitsy call her son or one of her granddaughters. She was sure they'd want to know and take steps to make sure the old lady was cared for.

Bitsy didn't like it.

"There's no use in calling Bradley," the elderly lady argued. "He'd just worry and there's nothing he can do anyway. I'll be just fine."

"If you don't call him, I will," Charlotte argued back. "As his mother, you would want to know if he was ill, wouldn't you?"

Bitsy nodded slowly.

"Well, why wouldn't he want to know that you're ill?"

"That's different," Bitsy quickly retorted.

"If you don't call him, I will," Charlotte repeated.

"You don't understand, Charlotte. If Bradley thinks I can't take care of myself, he might try to force me to move out to California or even put me in one of those awful homes for old people."

Sudden tears sprang into the old lady's

eyes, and Charlotte wanted to cry herself. "Oh, no, Miss Bitsy. He wouldn't do that, not just because you're temporarily sick." But even as she spoke the words, she knew that the old lady was probably right. That was exactly what her own son might do in a similar situation. Why, he was already nagging her to retire, wasn't he? Retire and let him take care of her. And she wasn't nearly as old as Bitsy.

More tears ran down the old lady's wrinkled cheeks. "Please don't call him, Charlotte. Please," she whispered.

Feeling more ashamed of herself with each passing moment for upsetting the old lady, Charlotte rushed over to Bitsy, and placing her arm around her shoulders, she gently hugged her. "I'm so, so sorry. I didn't mean to get you all upset. I'm just worried about leaving you here by yourself with you being so sick. Please don't cry."

After a moment, Bitsy sniffed, then nodded. "I'm okay." Then with a spunk that Charlotte had to admire, she pulled away from Charlotte and said in a shaky voice, "Tell you what. There's an agency that provides nursing care for us old folks at home, if we need it. I think they call themselves the Special Care Agency. If you promise not to call Bradley, I promise to call Special Care and see if they can send someone out for a couple of days."

Charlotte smiled. "I think that's a perfect solution. And again, I apologize. It's just that I care about you and was worried about leaving you."

The agency Bitsy called phoned back after lunch to inform Bitsy that yes, they could send someone out right away. Even though Charlotte had almost finished cleaning the elderly lady's house, she decided that she would wait around until the nurse arrived, just to make sure whoever the agency sent was suitable.

She had just put away the last of the dishes from the dishwasher when, out of the clear blue, like the flash of a lightbulb in a dark room, she remembered where she'd heard the name Arthur Samuel before.

Arthur Samuel was the professor Bitsy had told her about, the one who had been convicted of vehicular homicide so many years ago. Bitsy had even showed her a picture of him in her granddaughter's yearbook.

Hoping against hope that Bitsy hadn't got around to mailing the yearbook back to her granddaughter yet, Charlotte hurried into the living room.

The moment she entered the room she spied the book still lying on the table in front of the sofa, just where Bitsy had left it a week ago. Charlotte picked up the book, and seating herself on the sofa, she quickly thumbed through the pages until she found the particular picture she was searching for.

At first she couldn't believe her eyes, but the more she stared at the man in the picture, the more she became convinced that Arthur Samuel, a former professor of chemistry at Tulane University, and Sam Roberts, the scruffy handyman, were one and the same person.

Charlotte was still staring at the picture when the doorbell chimed. "Probably the nurse," she murmured.

Closing the yearbook, she stood and placed the book back on top of the table. But as she rushed off toward the foyer, a myriad of questions whirled through her mind.

Was Sam Roberts really Professor Arthur Samuel? They could be brothers instead, or even distant cousins, which would account for the remarkable resemblance. Still, if Sam Roberts and Arthur Samuel were the same person, it made sense that the professor would have changed his name because of his past. His looks would have changed too. After all, he was twenty years older now. But why on earth would he want to return to New Orleans in the first place?

. . . she divorced him, took the kids, and moved back to Kansas where she was from. If what Bitsy had said was true, why wouldn't he have moved to Kansas to be closer to his children?

Charlotte shook her head and unlatched the security chain at the front door. Lots of reasons, she decided. His children would be grown now and might not even live in Kansas. Besides, why would he want to live near his ex-wife? She was probably married again with a completely different life.

When Charlotte opened the door and saw the person standing on the other side, she was suddenly struck speechless. All she could do was stare up at the towering giant of a man.

"Hi, there. I'm René with the Special Care Agency."

Despite his size, he wasn't fat. Just huge. He was probably in his early thirties, she figured, and though he was dressed in typical nurse scrubs, he didn't look like any nurse she'd ever seen. His wealth of dark hair was long, but he'd pulled it back and secured it with a rubber band at the nape of his neck. On the lobe of one ear a small diamond stud twinkled back at her, and lodged in the side of his nose was a tiny gold hoop.

Charlotte swallowed hard. "May I see some identification please?" she finally asked.

"Sure thing." With a quick and easy grin that showed a row of even white teeth, he pulled out a billfold and produced a picture I.D. card. The card, emblazoned with the Special Care Agency logo, identified him as René Lewis, RN.

Satisfied, but still a bit leery, Charlotte nodded, then motioned for him to come inside.

"So where's Miss Bitsy?" he asked, glancing around.

Charlotte closed the door, but something about the way he'd asked about Bitsy gave her pause. "She's in bed. Do you know Mrs. Duhe?"

Again he produced that easy grin. "Oh, sure. She and I are old friends, and I have to tell you, I jumped at the chance to take care of her. She's a real sweetheart and such a feisty little thing to boot."

Though Charlotte still wasn't completely

comfortable with the young man, she couldn't easily ignore the obvious respect and affection in his voice.

Any doubts she might have had disappeared the moment Bitsy saw René walk into the room.

"Oh, René," she cried. "I thought that's who I heard." Her pale, faded face absolutely beamed with delight.

René grinned. "Now, what's all this about, young lady? What on earth is my best girl doing all laid up in the bed sick?"

A gentle giant, Charlotte decided as she watched René bend over and plant a kiss on the top of Bitsy's head.

"Let's get some vital signs on you, sweetheart," he told Bitsy. "Then you can tell me what sort of mischief you've been up to lately."

By the time Charlotte was ready to leave, she was more than confident that Bitsy would be well taken care of. But just in case the old lady took a turn for the worse, Charlotte left her own name and phone number with René.

Just goes to show, you shouldn't judge a book by its cover. The old adage was so true, Charlotte decided as she pulled away from the curb in front of Bitsy's house. But did the same principle apply to Sam Roberts? Was she misjudging him without really looking beneath the surface?

"Only one way to find out," she murmured. And she knew just the person to ask.

Chapter Twenty-three

As soon as she got home, Charlotte slipped off her shoes and pulled on her moccasins. She immediately headed for the telephone, then abruptly stopped and did an about-face.

"First things first," she murmured, eying Sweety Boy's cage. "Hey, there, Boy." She approached the little bird's cage. "You took quite a spill this morning." She poked her forefinger through the wires to gently stroke his head. "Guess that'll teach you that little birds don't belong in big, bad showers, huh? You feeling better? Huh, fellow? You look a bit perkier."

Though the little bird rubbed against her finger and seemed alert enough, the fact that he'd yet to utter a sound since she'd come through the door was worrisome.

"Aren't you going to talk to me? Say, 'Missed you, Charlotte. Missed you.' "

The little bird continued staring at her but remained silent. Not even a tiny chirp.

After weighing the pros and cons of letting him out of the cage, she decided that maybe it would be best for the remainder of the day if she continued to keep him confined, just until she was sure that he had fully recovered.

Had the shower incident traumatized him more than she'd thought? With a deep frown of concern and one last glance at him, she finally turned away and walked over to her desk. If he still wasn't talking by tomorrow, she supposed she'd have to consider taking him in to the vet.

At her desk, Charlotte flipped through her Rolodex until she found the name and phone number she was looking for; then she placed her call.

Mary Johnson was the daughter of a couple whom Charlotte had once worked for over the period of several years. But Mary just happened to be a managing editor for the *Times-Picayune* as well. If anyone knew where she could get more information on Professor Arthur Samuel, Charlotte figured that Mary would know.

When Mary answered the call on the fourth ring, Charlotte sat down at the desk and reached for a pen and notepad.

"Hi, Mary. This is Charlotte LaRue."

"Oh, hey there, Charlotte. It's good to hear from you." Then she laughed. "Please don't tell me you're calling to complain about another one of our reporters. And speaking of that particular rude and pesky man, you'll be happy to know that he's gone — moved to Houston last I heard."

"No, hon, I'm not calling to complain. But I can't say I'm sorry that awful man moved on." Charlotte shuddered, remembering how the freelance reporter had tried to chase her down after he'd found out that she worked for the Dubuissons. "So how are your folks? Still enjoying their retirement?"

"Your guess is as good as mine," Mary told her. "What with me working all hours here at the paper and them traveling all over the country, I hardly ever see them anymore."

"So what happened to the flea marketing and junk sales hobby they were into?"

"Well, to quote Dad, 'It got to be too much like work.'"

Charlotte laughed. "Sounds like something he would say — but listen, I don't want to interfere with *your* work, but I was hoping you could help me out with something."

"Now, Charlotte, you know I will if I can. So — what's up?"

Charlotte rolled the pen between her fingers. "I need to track down some background information on a man — something that happened, hmm — probably a good twenty years ago. This particular incident would have been written up in the newspaper."

After several moments of silence, Mary answered. "Twenty years is a long time, certainly before I hired on. I'd say your best bet would be the public library. They keep stuff like past issues of newspapers on microfilm, but you need to narrow it down to a particular month or else you'll end up wasting a whole lot of time searching through old issues."

Charlotte frowned. "There's no faster way?"

"Afraid not. Like I said, twenty years is a long time ago."

Because it was fairly close to where she lived and because she really loved the historical significance of the old building, Charlotte decided to go to the Latter Library on St. Charles Avenue. During the short drive, she racked her brain, trying to think of some significant incident that might have happened around the time that the hit-and-run had occurred.

If only she could pinpoint the month . . . Maybe October, she finally decided, vaguely remembering something about a costume party she'd worked that particular night.

Luckily, Charlotte was able to find a parking spot on St. Charles Avenue in front of the library.

Each time she visited the Latter Library, she was conscious of its history. The turn-of-the-century house had once been the home of a wealthy New Orleans merchant, then later the home of a celebrated millionaire aviator as well as a retreat for the millionaire's wife, a famous silent screen star. But ultimately, the final owners were a couple who'd had a son die in Okinawa during World War II. As a memorial to their son, they had presented the old house to the New Orleans Public Library.

As Charlotte hurried to the entrance, she glanced at her watch. At best, she figured she only had a couple of hours before the library closed.

Once inside, she quickly explained to the librarian what she needed. To her disappointment, she was told that she would have to go to the main library headquarters located on Loyola Avenue to do research dating back twenty years.

Though not near as old or historic as the Latter Library, the main library had its own claim to fame and had once been presented the Design Award for Public Buildings in *Progressive Architecture* magazine.

Once again Charlotte explained what she needed.

The librarian she spoke to, a perky young woman, directed Charlotte to go to the Louisiana Division.

"You're in luck," she told Charlotte with a smile. "If I'm not mistaken, we have copies of the *Times-Picayune* that date back as far as 1837 — all on microfilm."

After more than an hour of scanning files, Charlotte finally located the articles about the professor's arrest and trial. One of the articles included a head shot, and again, Charlotte was struck by the resemblance between the professor and Sam Roberts.

As she scanned through the articles, she began to notice a pattern. Time after time, during his arrest, and later, during his trial, the professor was persistent in proclaiming his innocence. But other than his avowal of innocence, Charlotte didn't learn anything that proved to be of much help.

By the time she left the library, most of the work traffic had thinned out. Her drive home was uneventful, but like a persistent itch that refused to be soothed, thoughts about the professor and Sam plagued her.

Were they the same man? Even if they were, what difference did it make in the grand scheme of things anyway? And why in the devil did the whole affair bother her so much?

B.J., she decided as she turned into her driveway. The only reason she cared at all was the friendship between Sam and the boy, and the influence that Sam seemed to wield over the teenager at such a vulnerable time in the boy's life. To Charlotte's way of thinking, that was more than enough reason to check up on Sam Roberts' background.

Even after Charlotte switched off the engine, she sat staring at the garage wall. Who else could she ask? she wondered, or where else could she find out information on Sam Roberts?

Under other circumstances, she could have asked Louis or Judith. Either of them could easily check into Sam's background. But then she'd have to tell them why she was asking, and that was something she couldn't do . . . not yet.

That left only one other person who might know something about Sam, hopefully something that would put her mind at rest. Unfortunately, that person was

Marian Hebert.

Since Sam had worked for Marian's husband and now worked for Marian, Charlotte was sure that Marian would have to know something about Sam's background . . . where he came from, his marital status, all the things people normally made small talk about.

With a frustrated sigh, Charlotte gathered her keys and purse and headed inside. Brick wall time, she decided as she unlocked her front door. There was just no way of asking Marian about Sam Roberts' background without betraying B.J.'s confidence . . . Or was there?

On Wednesday morning, Charlotte awakened to the sounds of Sweety Boy chirping away in his cage. Though she was relieved to know that the little bird had found his voice again and a trip to the vet wouldn't be necessary after all, not even his squawks and chirps could cheer her up after the agonizing night she'd spent tossing and turning.

Off and on, during the seemingly endless night, she'd come up with, and discarded, several ideas on how to approach Marian about Sam Roberts without betraying B.J. The most obvious way was to pretend a personal, romantic interest in Sam. But the possibility that Marian might decide to play matchmaker and tell Sam that she'd been asking about him made Charlotte discard the idea immediately.

Then, just before dawn, Charlotte had finally settled on something that she felt might work.

The scheme she'd decided on was really pretty simplistic. What she needed was an innocuous way of introducing Sam into a conversation with Marian. Since Marian had attended Tulane University, Charlotte figured she'd simply mention the fact that Bitsy's granddaughter had just been in town for the Tulane homecoming. Then she could casually bring up the subject of the yearbook and the remarkable resemblance between Sam and the professor; thus Sam would be introduced into the conversation.

But plotting a scheme and actually implementing it were two different animals altogether. Charlotte never had been good at deception, and in fact, abhorred anything that even resembled it. She figured that just this one time, though, she had no choice. B.J. was in trouble, and his whole future might depend on what she could find out.

With a herculean effort, Charlotte finally forced herself to climb out of bed when all she wanted to do was burrow back beneath the covers and forget everything. When she reached for her housecoat, she hesitated before pulling it on. With a sigh, her gaze strayed to the closet, where she'd hung up the new one.

Fingering the worn cotton terry of the old housecoat, she frowned. Except when she'd tried on the new robe to see if it fit on the morning after her birthday party, she had yet to begin wearing it. But why?

"You know why," she grumbled as she jerked on the old one. Silly as the notion seemed, just knowing that Louis had picked out the new one smacked of an intimacy that she wasn't yet comfortable with, nor sure she was ready for. Never mind that each time she looked at it, she was reminded of the two kisses they'd shared . . . well, not exactly shared.

Rolling her eyes toward the ceiling, and with a shake of her head, she stomped off toward the living room.

Most mornings, Charlotte made a point of letting Sweety Boy out of his cage for a few minutes while she dressed. Though he appeared to be back to normal, she decided that keeping him confined a little longer would be best, just until she was sure he was okay.

"If you're still doing okay, I promise I'll let you out when I get home this afternoon," she told him as she refilled his feeder with birdseed.

But Sweety Boy wanted out now, and he quickly scooted toward the cage door when she opened it to replace his cuttlebone. "Oh, no, you don't." She blocked the opening with her hand. "Not this morning, fellow." Using her forefinger, she nudged him back toward the far end of the cage. "Be a good little bird now, and I'll clean out that yucky cage Saturday."

By the time Charlotte left for work, the sky had clouded over and a fine drizzle had set in, making the air chilly and dreary. As she backed her van out of the driveway, she glanced toward the other driveway and frowned. Louis' car was gone.

Thinking back, she didn't remember seeing it last night either. Nor did she remember hearing him come home during the night. So where was he? Had he come home?

Unease crept through her veins as she drove down Milan Street. Within reason, she knew there was probably a perfectly logical explanation for why he hadn't come home. After all, he hadn't retired yet. He still had two months left, and in his line of work, it seemed that the criminals never slept. But logic aside, she also knew that in his line of work, there was always the possibility of danger as well. Maybe she should call Judith, just to make sure he was okay, to make sure he hadn't been hurt or . . .

"And maybe you should mind your own business," she muttered as she slowed for a traffic light. Louis was a grown man and could take care of himself just fine, thank you very much.

Most of the morning, Marian was in and out of the house on business, but when she'd come home after lunch, she'd told Charlotte, "Enough is enough for one day."

Charlotte couldn't agree more, she finally decided an hour later as she finished up in the boys' bathroom. *Enough was enough.* No more procrastination.

Except for cleaning Marian's office, she'd almost finished for the day, and like it or not, she was running out of time. *So just do it and get it over with.*

Inside Marian's office, she set her supply carrier down by the desk. Then, with deliberate steps, she marched out of the room. Once in the hallway, she paused and tilted her head, her ears tuned to any noise that might tell her in which room she'd find Marian.

The clinking of dishes led her to the kitchen, and when she entered, Marian was at the stove, pouring a jar of spaghetti sauce into a small saucepan to heat.

Marian glanced up and gave Charlotte a quick smile. "Finished already?"

Charlotte shook her head. "Almost. I still have your office to clean." She walked to the cabinet. "I just need a drink of water." She removed a glass from the bottom shelf. "I swear, it's like I've been thirsty all day long." She shook her head. "It was like that yesterday too, at Miss Bitsy's house. I just couldn't seem to get enough to drink." She walked over to the Kentwood water dispenser stand by the cabinet and filled her glass.

"Maybe you ought to go in for a good checkup," Marian suggested.

Charlotte took a long drink of the water, then rolled her eyes. "Been there, done that — just last week — and I'm waiting for the test results."

Since her health was the last thing Charlotte wanted to discuss, before Marian could ask any more questions, she said, "And speaking of Miss Bitsy. You know her granddaughter — the one who lives in New York?"

"Jenny?" Marian offered.

Charlotte nodded. "That's the one. Well, a week or so ago she was in town for the Tulane homecoming reunion."

Though Marian looked at her a bit strangely, Charlotte plowed right on ahead. "Miss Bitsy was so excited about the visit and was brimming over with all kinds of information about all the festivities. Jenny had even brought her yearbook with her." Feigning excitement, Charlotte widened her eyes and smiled. "And guess who I saw in it?"

When Marian raised a skeptical eyebrow, Charlotte grinned. "There you were — all of you at some party! Until I saw that picture, I had no idea that you and your husband and Drew Bergeron had all gone to Tulane together."

Marian gave Charlotte a tiny, nervous smile. "That was a long time ago."

Charlotte nodded. "Over twenty years, according to the date on the yearbook." She paused a moment; then, swallowing hard, she continued. "Such a shame about what happened with that professor that year though. You know — the one who was arrested for that hit-and-run." She frowned. "I think his name was Arthur something." She nodded. "Oh, yeah — now I remember. His name was Arthur Samuel. He was a chemistry professor, I believe."

Marian grimaced, and though she tried to hide her reaction by turning back to the stove to stir the spaghetti sauce, all the color had suddenly drained from her face.

Puzzled by Marian's response, Charlotte took another quick drink of water to give herself a moment to regroup. *In for a penny, in for a pound.* Lifting her chin, she pressed on. "I'd completely forgotten all about it until Miss Bitsy pointed him out. But you want to know something funny? If he'd had a beard and longer hair, and if he was twenty years older, he'd look just like Sam Roberts."

Though Charlotte wouldn't have believed it, Marian's face grew even more pale, and her hand began to shake. To cover the trembling, she rapped the spoon she'd been stirring with sharply against the saucepan, then laid it on the stovetop. "I need a drink," she muttered.

"Of course they say that everyone has a double somewhere in the world," Charlotte persisted as Marian headed straight for the bar that separated the kitchen from the living area. Then, affecting a nonchalance that she didn't feel, she said, "Probably just coincidence that they look alike, and B.J. seems to think the world of Sam."

Marian opened the bar cabinet and took out a decanter of what looked like bourbon.

"But that's good, don't you think?" Charlotte continued as she watched Marian pour a healthy amount into a glass. "Good that he has a male figure he can relate to . . ." Charlotte's voice trailed away as Marian downed the drink within seconds, then poured herself another one. "Marian?"

Marian shook her head. "He's found out," she mumbled, downing the second drink. "Oh, dear God, somehow he's found out."

Charlotte frowned. Marian wasn't making sense. Of all the reactions she'd anticipated, she hadn't expected her to fall to pieces right before her very eyes. "Marian — What on earth? What are you talking about? Found out what?"

As if she'd just remembered that Charlotte was in the room, Marian jerked around to face her, her eyes wild with terror. "He's

371

found out, I tell you. He's —"

The sudden peal of the doorbell seemed to make Marian even more frantic. "No," she cried. "Please —" She waved toward the general direction of the front door. "See who that is and make them go away."

Charlotte held up her hands, palms out, in a placating gesture. "Sure — okay — no problem." With one last worried look at the younger woman and a frown of concern, she headed for the hallway.

Marian's reaction was way over the top, but why?

He's found out.

What on earth had she meant and why had it made her so nervous?

Just as Charlotte reached for the doorknob, she froze.

. . . I know how brutal the police can be . . .

She hadn't thought much about Sam's remark at the time, but suddenly his words took on a whole new meaning. "Of course," she whispered. Why else would he make such a statement unless he'd experienced it firsthand? And if he'd experienced it firsthand, then . . . *If it looks like a shoe and wears like a shoe, then it must be a shoe.*

The doorbell chimed again, and Charlotte jumped. Later . . . She'd have to think about it later.

Taking a deep breath, she pasted on a polite smile and opened the door. But Charlotte's smile faltered when she saw the bedraggled woman standing on the porch.

The woman looked to be in her mid-thirties, and she was soaked through and through from the top of her stringy bleached hair down to her mud-caked loafers. Because she was wet, at first Charlotte figured her for a homeless person. But after a quick perusal of the woman's clothes, she changed her mind. Despite the fact that the woman's jacket, blouse, and slacks were soaked, her clothes were quality.

Suddenly the woman pulled her hand out of her jacket pocket. At the sight of the handgun, a whisper of terror twisted Charlotte's insides, and her legs went weak.

But when the woman shoved the gun against her stomach, Charlotte gasped from the sharp pain, and the whisper of terror became a deafening roar in her ears.

Chapter Twenty-four

"My name is Darla Shaw," the woman snarled.

Darla Shaw. A memory clicked in Charlotte's mind. Darla Shaw was the woman Drew Bergeron had been living with in Key West, but worse, Darla Shaw was also Judith's number-one suspect.

"I think we have some unfinished business," the woman spat. Using the pressure of the gun, she forced Charlotte backward, into the foyer. Once they were both inside, she used the heel of her muddy shoe and kicked the door shut.

The sound of the door slamming was like the crack of a whip, and Charlotte jumped. *Think, Charlotte! Think!* But Charlotte's heart was hammering against her rib cage so hard that she could hardly catch her breath, never mind think.

The woman's dark eyes flashed contempt as her gaze slid over Charlotte from head to toe. "You're a lot older than I thought you'd be," she sneered.

Older?

"What gets me, though, is why he'd want some old broad like you when he had me?" Punctuating each word with a jab of the gun, she added, "Of course, all he wanted from you was money."

Marian! She thinks I'm Marian. Charlotte opened her mouth in denial, but nothing came out but a squeak.

"All I've heard for weeks was Marian this and Marian that," the woman ranted, confirming Charlotte's suspicions. "Oh, yeah —" the woman gave an exaggerated nod. "I know all about you and what you did. And I know all about your little arrangement with Drew." She shook her head, then moaned, "I told him not to come — the idiot! I begged him." Then she shouted, "But would he listen? Oh, no — not him, not Mr. High and Mighty Know-it-all. Not Mr. Stud," she spat.

The woman's lower lip curled into a snarl. "And I was right, wasn't I? He shouldn't 'ave come 'cause you killed him — killed him deader than a doorknob." Spittle flew out of her mouth. She licked her lips, then narrowed her eyes. "But I got news for you, sister. You're gonna pay and pay big. Only this time —" She thumped herself on the chest. "This time you're gonna pay *me*."

The woman was convinced that she was Marian, and though Charlotte wanted to deny it, wanted to tell her she had the wrong person, every instinct she had warned against it.

Charlotte swallowed hard, and praying that Marian had overheard the woman ranting and raving and wasn't too far gone to have sense enough to call the police, she decided that the only way to stay alive was to play along . . . or play dumb.

Gathering every ounce of courage she had within her, she decided to play dumb. She slowly shook her head. "There's been a mistake of some kind. I don't know any Drew, and I don't know what or who you're talking —"

"Liar!" the woman screamed. "You're a damned liar. This is the right address, and you're Marian Hebert! I know 'cause Drew told me all about your fancy house in the uppity Garden District. And I know all about you and what y'all did — you and Drew and that husband of yours — how you all got drunk as skunks that night and stole that professor's car, and how *you* were the one driving."

He's found out . . . somehow he's found out.

If Charlotte hadn't already been scared speechless, she would have been shocked speechless as well, and if she'd had any doubts about Sam Roberts and Arthur Samuel being the same man, those doubts had been put to rest, once and for all.

Even as Darla continued ranting, everything she'd said began to make a weird kind of sense. They were all connected: Drew, Bill, Marian, and Sam aka Professor Arthur Samuel. And if what Darla was saying was true, then it was no wonder that Marian suffered from emotional problems, along with alcohol abuse, and it was no wonder that Sam had changed his name and attempted to change his looks. Sam didn't want to be recognized.

If Marian, Drew, and Bill had stolen the professor's car that night, then they had let an innocent man pay for their crime. Even worse, though, somehow, some way, Sam had figured out that the three had stolen his car and that one of them had been responsible for the murder he'd been accused of.

A cold chill ran through Charlotte. Two of the three, Bill and Drew, were dead.

Sam had worked for Bill, and Bill had been killed in a suspicious explosion.

Then there was Drew. Charlotte had no doubt that Sam had also killed Drew as well . . . the cigar butt outside the closet, just like the one at Sam's house, and just like the one she'd seen outside the closet at the Devilier house . . . the purple Mardi Gras mask on Drew's face. Purple, green, and gold, all traditional Mardi Gras colors: purple for justice, green for faith, and gold for power. Sam Roberts aka Professor Arthur Samuel was out for justice, and in his own macabre way, he was letting the world know that he was finally getting it.

But how? How had Sam even known that Drew was still alive to begin with? He must have, though, and now, out of the three, only Marian was left.

Darla suddenly poked Charlotte hard with the gun. "*You* did it. You were the one who killed that man, and you let that professor take the rap." Her breath was coming in short gasps. Then an evil looking smile pulled her lips into a parody of the emotion, and she whispered loudly, "And I know something else too. I know exactly how much you were paying Drew to keep his mouth shut, so don't go trying to weasel out of it. But now you can pay me instead. Last I heard, there's no statue of limitation on murder, so if you don't pay, I'll go to the cops."

Call her bluff. It was a desperate ploy, one that could easily push the woman over the edge, but Charlotte figured she didn't have a lot of choices. In what she hoped looked like a defiant gesture, she lifted her chin and glared down her nose at the woman. "I think that's the best idea yet," she told her. "Go ahead. Go to the cops. Better yet, use my phone and call them right now."

For what seemed like an eternity, the woman stared at Charlotte. Then sudden anger flashed in her eyes and her face turned beet red. "I don't think so," she said, her voice harsh and chilling. "You think you're so smart, but I've got news for you. I'm smarter. Those two brats of yours are due home any minute now, aren't they? Either give me the money or I'll kill them both." She leaned closer to Charlotte's face, then screamed, "I mean it! I'll kill the little brats, so give it to me now!"

Out of the corner of her eye, Charlotte caught a glimpse of movement from the front porch through the side window. *The boys!* Were they home already?

"Okay, okay!" Charlotte threw up her hands and tried desperately to think of some way to distract the dangerous woman. Time. She needed to buy time. Praying that Marian would hear her and keep the boys out of the house, she raised the pitch of her voice. "I'll get you your money!" she told her. "Anything — but please don't hurt my boys." She motioned toward the end of the hallway. "I keep money in my office back there."

Darla poked Charlotte with the gun. "That's much better. Now let's go get it. Turn around —" Charlotte turned. "Slowly now," the woman warned. "And you'd better not try anything."

All the way down the hallway, Charlotte felt the pressure of the gun in the small of her back as she forced her trembling legs to move toward Marian's office.

Once inside the room, Charlotte motioned toward the desk. "The money's in the desk."

When they reached the desk, Darla snapped at her, "Get it, but you'd better not try anything."

"H-how much do you want?" Charlotte asked as she eased slowly to the other side of the desk.

"All of it," Darla snapped. "I want all that you've got."

Now what? Not knowing what else to do, Charlotte leaned down, pulled open a drawer, and began riffling through it. Since Darla was on the other side, Charlotte was pretty sure she couldn't see what she was doing. The drawer she'd pulled out was full of folders that contained what looked like invoices. But there was also a box of envelopes as well. She pulled out an envelope, and in hopes of making it look as if it were full of money, she began slowly stuffing it with the invoices. What she needed was to buy time.

She had almost stuffed it full when she suddenly noticed that her supply carrier was within reach. As she eyed the contents of the carrier, an idea began to slowly take shape. Could she do it? Did she have enough courage to even try?

Charlotte had noticed that Darla was nervous and kept glancing around the room, especially toward the doorway. Still pretending to stuff the envelope with money, out of the corner of her eye, Charlotte watched and waited, hoping for just the right opportunity. The moment Darla glanced away, she grabbed one of the spray bottles that she was sure contained ammonia.

With her finger on the trigger, she hid the bottle behind her back. Holding out the envelope in her other hand, she sent up a short prayer for courage, then slowly stood. She thrust the envelope toward Darla. "Here's your money," she told her. "Take it and get out."

Just as Charlotte had hoped, Darla had eyes only for the envelope. And just as she'd hoped, the greedy woman had to lean across the desk to get it. Leaning across the desk would throw her a bit off balance. The second she leaned forward, Charlotte whipped the bottle of ammonia from behind her back, aimed it directly at Darla's eyes, and pumped the trigger.

Ammonia spewed out, coating Darla's face. Darla screamed, dropped the gun, and began clawing at her eyes. The gun fell with a heavy thud on top of the desk.

Charlotte dropped the ammonia bottle, and keeping a wary eye on Darla, she immediately scooped up the gun. Once she had it, she ran for the door.

The sound of police car sirens reached her ears, and Charlotte sprinted down the hallway toward the foyer. The moment she jerked open the front door, she froze.

For the second time in the course of an hour, she found herself facing the wrong end of a gun.

Two policemen were already on the porch, their guns drawn, and more were spilling out of patrol cars.

"Put it down, lady," the taller of the two policemen shouted. "Put the gun down now!"

"Okay, okay!" she shouted back. "See —"
She bent down and placed the gun on the
porch. "I'm putting it down."

"Easy, lady. Now kick it this way."

"Gladly," she muttered, as she kicked
the gun toward the two policemen.

The moment the gun slid away, the
shorter policeman approached her. "Hands
above your head."

"Officer, if you'd just let me explain —"

"Do it, lady! Hands above your head."

Charlotte raised her hands. "Please, sir,
I'm just the maid. My name is Charlotte
LaRue and my niece is Detective Judith
Monroe. The woman you want is inside,
and that's *her* gun."

"Hey, Joe," a familiar voice shouted.
"She's telling the truth. She's okay."

Charlotte sent up a prayer of thanks as
Billy Wilson bounded up the steps. "Oh,
Billy, am I ever glad to see you."

After Charlotte gave an abbreviated version of what had happened, Billy sent two
of the other officers inside the house after
Darla Shaw.

Within minutes, Darla was in custody
and an ambulance had been called to
transport her to the nearest hospital.

With Darla subdued, Charlotte explained that her employer was still inside

the house somewhere. Accompanied by Billy, she went back inside to look for Marian.

"That ammonia trick was some smart thinking on your part, Ms. LaRue," Billy told her at the doorway to the kitchen. "That took a lot of guts. Just one thing, though. It sure seems strange how you're always around when this stuff happens."

Charlotte shuddered. "Not my choice, I assure you. Just lucky, I guess," she mumbled sarcastically. "Seriously though, I am lucky that you were here and vouched for me . . . again. Thanks, Billy."

Billy shrugged. "No big deal."

When they entered the kitchen, it was empty. Charlotte shook her head. "I don't understand where she could be. I —"

Billy heard the noise at the same time that Charlotte heard it. He pointed to the pantry, and Charlotte nodded.

"Marian, it's Charlotte." She walked to the pantry. "You can come out now. The police are here." She opened the door, and her face fell. "Oh, Marian . . ."

The pantry was the walk-in type, but there was barely room to turn around inside. Marian was scrunched up, sitting on the floor, her whole body shaking. In one hand was a butcher knife, and in the other hand she was clutching an empty liquor bottle.

She glanced up at Charlotte. "Oh, Ch-Charlotte! I — I was s-so scared." When she stumbled to her feet, the knife and bottle clattered to the floor, and Charlotte had to grab her to keep her from falling. "Is — is she gone?" she stammered, her words slurred. "Is that awful woman gone?" Her breath reeked of liquor and Charlotte frowned.

"Not yet," Charlotte told her. "But it's safe. The police have her now."

Marian was deathly pale and continued to shake. "I don't feel so good." Then she suddenly groaned. "Oh, noooo — I — I think I — I'm going to be sick." She crossed her arms, hugging her stomach, and doubled over.

"Okay, okay — just hold on!" Charlotte told her.

"Here, let me help you," Billy offered.

Between them, they got her to the bathroom just in time before Marian threw up. Knowing how embarrassed Marian would be later, Charlotte assured Billy that she could handle things, then shooed him out of the bathroom. Once she'd firmly shut the door, she wet a washcloth and wrung it out, then waited. When it seemed that nothing else could possibly come out of the poor woman, Charlotte flushed the toilet, then kneeled down beside Marian and began blotting her forehead with the wet washcloth.

"Thanks, Charlotte," she whispered, still pale and shaky a few minutes later. "I — I was so scared and I just couldn't seem to stop drinking, especially after I heard what that woman said." She stared at Charlotte with miserable eyes. "I — I guess I owe you an explanation."

Charlotte shook her head. "You don't owe me anything, Marian, but I'm afraid the police are going to have a lot of questions. And — I have to confess — I am curious. But I'm more concerned than curious. About you," she added, "and about B.J."

Marian suddenly grabbed Charlotte by the arm. "Please, Charlotte — please don't tell them all that stuff that woman said."

Charlotte covered Marian's hand with her own. "I'm not the one you have to worry about. Who you have to worry about is Darla Shaw and what *she* tells them."

"Well, she can tell them anything she damn well pleases, but it's not true — not about me driving the professor's car that night. Oh, I thought it was. For almost

386

twenty years I thought it was my fault — that I was the one driving when that poor man was killed." She shook her head. "We were all so drunk that night, but I was the worst of the lot. I was so spaced out that I don't even remember what happened. But one thing I know now — it wasn't my fault. I didn't steal the professor's car, and I swear to you, I didn't run over that man. I wasn't the one who was driving that night. I didn't kill him."

Given Marian's inebriated state, Charlotte decided that she was telling the truth. And because she was a bit less inhibited than she might have been sober, Charlotte pressed her advantage. "And what about Drew Bergeron?" she asked softly. "Did you kill him?"

"I wish I had. I've wished it a thousand times. If anybody had reason to" — She thumped herself on the chest — "it was me. For the past two years, ever since his so-called first death, Drew's been soaking me dry — blackmailing me. And this whole mess — everything — is all his fault. His and Bill's," she murmured, casting her eyes downward to stare at the floor.

After a moment, she sighed. "Poor Bill. He was so angry when he found out. It was only then that he finally told me the truth, only after he realized that Drew was still alive and had been blackmailing me. That was the day before Bill — before he died."

Her expression grew hard. "You see," she said bitterly, "it was Drew all along. Drew was the one driving that night, and he'd persuaded Bill to let me think that I'd been at the wheel. Then they both persuaded me to let the professor take the blame."

Charlotte frowned. "All those years, your own husband let you think that you'd killed a man?"

Marian shook her head. "We weren't married then."

"So why didn't he tell you later, after you were married?"

"Guilt," she answered. "Plain and simple — he felt too guilty about everything, and by that time, things had gone too far. After the professor was convicted, I — I had a nervous breakdown and tried to — to commit suicide — too much booze and drugs, and too much of my own guilt, thinking that I had not only killed a man, but had let an innocent man go to prison.

"It was after my suicide attempt that Bill told me he hadn't realized how much he loved me until then. But seeing me like that —" She shrugged. "He blamed himself and said that was when he decided to spend the rest of his life trying to make it all up to me.

"At that time I was a basket case, and so needy —" She shook her head. "I'd always loved Bill anyway, so it was easy just to give in and let him take over, let him take care of me. And you know how those things go. Time passes and it gets harder and harder to tell the truth."

Unfortunately, Charlotte did know. She'd spent years living her own lie, pretending that she had married her son's father before he left for Vietnam when she hadn't. Only after Hank was almost a grown man and had begun asking questions had she found the courage to tell him the truth.

Marian sighed. "Once Bill told me the truth, I was furious — so angry, so hurt, and —" She swallowed hard. "All those years —" She bowed her head and rubbed her forehead. "Anyway —" She dropped her hand and raised her head. "We had a huge fight — lots of yelling and screaming — and I threatened to take the boys and leave him, divorce him. Then, the next day —" Her eyes suddenly filled with tears. "The next day he was gone — killed in that explosion.

"Oh, Charlotte —" Tears spilled down her cheeks. "It was all my fault. In spite of his lies and deceptions, Bill really loved me and the boys. We were his world, and when he thought I was taking them away, he —" She covered her face with her hands and sobbed softly.

Several moments passed before Marian spoke again. "I didn't kill Drew," she finally whispered. "But he deserved to die."

Though Charlotte was relieved and satisfied that Marian was telling the truth, she had still needed to ask, had still needed to hear Marian deny it.

"Marian —" She reached up and squeezed Marian's shoulder. "About your husband. If it's any consolation, I don't believe that he killed himself. In fact, I don't think his death was an accident either. I'm convinced that Mr. Hebert was murdered. I'm also convinced that you need to tell the police exactly what you've just told me."

Marian suddenly jerked away. "No!" Her eyes were wild with panic as she glared at Charlotte. "Don't you see? If I tell the police, they're going to think *I* killed Drew. Then, who's going to take care of my boys?" She shook her head. "No way —

and if you tell them, I'll deny it — deny it all."

"Whoa — just calm down," Charlotte soothed. "In the first place, *I'm* not telling anybody anything. But just listen to me for a minute. If I'm right, Sam Roberts is really Professor Arthur Samuel, and he's seeking retribution and revenge for his life being ruined. He wants justice.

"I don't know how he did it, but somehow he found out about that night. Somehow he found out that the three of you stole his car and killed that pedestrian, then set him up to take the blame. He's already murdered Drew, and I believe he also murdered Mr. Hebert. Two out of the three of you are dead. . . ." Charlotte's voice trailed away, and she gave Marian a moment to mull over what she'd said.

Then, softly, she continued. "Don't you get it? If you don't go to the police, he'll eventually kill you too, just like he killed Mr. Bergeron and your husband."

Marian's face was a kaleidoscope of conflicting emotions, and Charlotte pressed her advantage. "One other thing you need to consider. Sam has already befriended B.J. and Aaron. They both trust him. What if he decides to take his revenge out on them?"

Chapter Twenty-five

"No!" Marian moaned. "Not my boys! He — he couldn't. He really cares about B.J. and Aaron." She shuddered. "He wouldn't do that."

"Are you sure?" Charlotte grabbed Marian by both shoulders and shook her once, hard. "Are you willing to bet your sons' lives on it?"

For long seconds Marian stared at her, her eyes wide and uncomprehending.

"Don't be naive, Marian. We're talking about a man who lost everything because of what the three of you did to him — his family, his job, his reputation — everything! I was there when they found Drew Bergeron. I saw his body. Sam shot him at close range in the head, execution style. This is a man who has already systematically killed off two of the three people he blames for ruining his life. And if you don't stop him, he'll kill you too. Even worse, what better way to get his revenge on you than to first take away everything that means anything to you? And even if he doesn't kill your sons, what will happen to them if he kills you?"

Once again, Marian's eyes filled with tears that spilled over onto her cheeks, and finally she nodded. "Okay," she whispered. "I'll do it."

Relief flooded through Charlotte. "Good!" She released her hold on Marian. "The first thing we need is a sympathetic ally. I'm going to call my niece, Judith. If you remember, she's one of the detectives that questioned you after Drew's body was found."

"That's why she looked so familiar that day."

Charlotte nodded. "After I phone Judith, you need to call your attorney. For now, though, just let me do all the talking out there until Judith gets here. Okay?"

"Okay," Marian whispered.

"Now —" Charlotte pushed herself up off the floor and stood. "Let's get out of here. No — wait! On second thought, maybe we should just stay in here as long as we can. That way, we won't have to answer so many questions until Judith comes."

"Sounds good to me," Marian agreed. "Believe me, I'm not in any hurry."

Charlotte nodded, then pulled her cell

phone out of her apron pocket. She'd just dialed Judith's number when Marian suddenly lurched to her feet. "The boys!" she sputtered. "What time is it?"

The number was ringing, but Charlotte quickly glanced at her watch. "It's a little past three, but I thought I —"

Marian closed her eyes and sighed. "Oh, good." She closed the lid of the toilet and sat down. "It's still a while before they get home from school."

Then who was on the porch? Charlotte didn't have time to think about it. At that moment, Judith answered her call.

"Judith, hon, it's me. I'm at Marian Hebert's house, and I need you to get over here as soon as possible."

"What's wrong, Aunt Charley?"

"I'll explain when you get here — and Judith, it's urgent, so please hurry." Charlotte ended the call, then handed the phone to Marian. "Call your attorney."

While Marian was on the phone, Charlotte put her ear to the bathroom door and listened. Was Billy still out there, waiting for them to come out, or had he posted another officer at the door to wait for them?

She didn't hear any movement or voices, but there was only one way to find out for sure, she decided. Easing the door open, she peeked out into the hallway. *So far, so good.* No one was standing guard at the door, and from the sounds she was hearing, no one was even in the house. They were all out front or on the porch.

Now if they could only keep stalling until Judith got there. She eased the door shut again. Marian was still talking on the phone, and though the bathroom was adequate, it was small.

Charlotte had never been claustrophobic before, but the small confines of the bathroom, along with the lingering smell from Marian being sick, was starting to get to her.

Delayed shock, she decided as she gripped the edge of the countertop. But who wouldn't feel weak and queasy after what she'd just been through? Or at least that's what she kept telling herself.

Suddenly, there was a sharp rap on the bathroom door. The noise reverberated and echoed in the small tiled room, and Charlotte almost jumped out of her skin.

"Ms. LaRue! Everything all right in there?"

"Ah — yes, Billy," Charlotte answered. "Everything's fine."

"Ma'am, we need to ask a few more questions."

"Okay," she told him. "Just give us a couple more minutes." To Marian she whispered, "Is your attorney coming?"

Marian nodded and handed Charlotte the phone. "He's on his way."

"Good. Now remember — let me do all the talking." She helped Marian to her feet. "Ready?"

Marian shrugged. "Not really, but I guess I don't have any choice." She glanced in the mirror, then made a face. "At least I won't have to lie about not feeling well. All they have to do is look at me."

Charlotte gave her a quick smile for courage. Then, ever conscious that she needed to buy time until Judith got there, she took a deep breath and opened the door.

"Billy, why don't we all go into the family room? I'm sure Ms. Hebert would be much more comfortable in there than standing around on the porch. She's still feeling a bit weak," she added for good measure.

Billy took one look at Marian and nodded his agreement. A few minutes later, he and another officer joined Charlotte and Marian in the family room. Marian was sitting in one of the two chairs that faced the sofa, and Charlotte chose to remain standing nearby, in hopes that the attention would be on her instead of Marian.

"This is Officer Hardy," Billy told Charlotte.

Charlotte nodded, recognizing the policeman as one of the officers who had held a gun on her earlier on the porch.

"We've talked briefly to Ms. Shaw, ma'am, but we'd like to hear your version of what happened."

Carefully choosing her words to avoid any references to Darla's real motivation for showing up on Marian's doorstep, Charlotte kept her explanation as simple as possible, starting with Darla mistaking her for Marian.

"That poor woman," she said when she'd finished. "Evidently she was just crazy with grief over the death of Mr. Bergeron and, for whatever reason, she got it in her head that Marian had killed him. Of course, that's ridiculous. Marian wasn't anywhere near the Devilier house on the night that he was murdered." She shrugged. "Like I said, I figure she was just crazy with grief, and because Mr. Bergeron and Marian had once been friends, she got confused. I'm just grateful that Marian had the good sense to phone you guys and that you showed up so quickly."

The explanation she'd given had holes in it big enough to drive an eighteen-wheeler through, and she prepared herself, fully expecting to be interrogated further.

Footsteps coming down the hallway momentarily distracted the officers, and when Judith marched into the room, Charlotte sagged from relief.

After giving a nod of greeting to the two officers and to Marian, Judith directed her attention to Charlotte. "You okay, Aunt Charley?" When Charlotte nodded, Judith turned to the two officers. "Could you guys give me a few minutes alone with my aunt?"

Once the two officers had left the room, Judith approached Charlotte. "Are you sure you're okay, Auntie? You look a little pale to me." She motioned toward the sofa. "Why don't you sit down over here?"

Charlotte nodded. "I'll sit down, but I'm okay, hon. Just still a bit shaky. It's not every day I get guns pointed at me," she added.

Judith seated herself beside Charlotte. "Now, what's this all about, Auntie?"

Charlotte took a deep breath. "I know who killed Drew Bergeron."

Judith threw a suspicious look at Marian, then turned her attention back to her aunt. "I'm listening."

"Before you jump to any conclusions —" Charlotte tilted her head toward Marian. "Let me explain. There are still some missing pieces to the puzzle, but it all started over twenty years ago. Marian, her husband, and Drew Bergeron were all friends at Tulane. As college kids do sometimes, they all got drunk one night."

As quickly as she could, Charlotte recounted the story about the three stealing the professor's car for a joyride and about Drew and Bill letting Marian believe that she had been responsible for the death of the man that Drew had run over during their escapade.

"According to the news articles I read," Charlotte continued, "the man who was run over gave a description and part of the license number of the car that hit him before he died. The professor — Professor Arthur Samuel — had already been given several tickets for drunk driving, and of course the police arrested him. The professor was tried and convicted, and served a ten-year sentence for a crime he didn't commit. I don't know how he did it, but I believe that the professor somehow found out the truth and is now getting his revenge."

Judith held up a hand. "That's a pretty tall tale, Aunt Charley. In the first place, it's kind of hard to buy that they were able to convince Mrs. Hebert that she was driving."

"Ah, excuse me," Marian interrupted. "As embarrassed as I am to admit it, it wasn't hard at all. You see, I was so out of it that I really didn't remember any of what happened that night after a certain point. As they say, drugs and alcohol don't mix."

Judith nodded slowly. "Hmm, yes — well, I guess it's possible, but —" She turned back to Charlotte. "How do you know so much about this professor, Auntie, and what does this have to do with Drew Bergeron's murder or Darla Shaw, for that matter? And where is this professor now?"

Charlotte sighed. "It's a bit complicated," she finally answered. "Just bear with me while I try to explain."

Beginning with the day Bitsy had showed her the Tulane yearbook, Charlotte told her niece about the events that had transpired. Since she was now sure that Sam Roberts had murdered Drew Bergeron and possibly Bill Hebert too, she saw no reason to reveal B.J.'s presence in the Devilier house when Drew Bergeron was murdered. At least not yet.

"You see," she continued, "Marian employs a handyman named Sam Roberts. Since I had seen Sam around here quite a bit, it struck me that there was a marked resemblance between Sam and the professor." Then she explained about the cigars beneath B.J.'s bed, and leaving out the reason she'd been at Sam's house, she told Judith about seeing similar ones there as well as at the Devilier house. "B.J. had kept some of his dad's things, and that included the cigars. I guess since he and Sam had struck up a friendship of sorts, B.J. had given him some of the cigars. Of course there's also the purple Mardi Gras mask thing. I've been thinking about it a lot, and the only thing I can come up with is that the color purple stands for justice. The professor is finally getting justice for what was done to him.

"When Darla Shaw showed up at the door today and began ranting and raving, it all began to make a weird sort of sense." Charlotte's gaze slid to Marian, and Marian, understanding that it was her turn to talk, nodded.

"You see," Marian began, "for the past

two years Drew Bergeron has been black-mailing me. I guess Darla Shaw knew about it and when Drew was murdered, she went a little crazy and got it in her head that I had killed Drew. Lord knows, I had enough reason to, but I didn't," she quickly added. "Anyway — this Darla Shaw woman decided to take up where Drew left off with the blackmailing thing."

"But there's more, Judith," Charlotte added. "I also believe that Sam Roberts killed Marian's husband as well. If you check into it, I think you'll find that Bill Hebert's death was under suspicious cir-cumstances — and did I mention that Sam Roberts worked for Marian's husband first, before he worked for Marian?"

For long moments Judith simply sat there, silently staring first at Charlotte, then at Marian, and Charlotte held her breath.

Judith abruptly stood. "You know what, ladies?" She gave each of them a pointed look. "I think I believe you — at least enough to bring Sam Roberts in for ques-tioning."

Charlotte released her breath in a huge sigh, and Marian dropped her head as if offering up a silent prayer of thanks-giving.

Judith cleared her throat. "But Mrs. Hebert —"

Marian raised her head and looked at Judith.

"Don't plan on leaving town any time soon."

Charlotte stayed with Marian until the police had cleared out. "Why don't I fix you a fresh cup of coffee?" she offered, when the last police car drove away.

"Oh, Charlotte, I'm sure you have other things to do besides wait on me."

What Charlotte really wanted was to stay a bit longer, mostly to satisfy herself that Marian was going to be okay. "Well, I was hoping to wait around for the boys to get home anyway. I've been meaning to thank them for that lovely music box they gave me."

"Thanks, Charlotte. Thanks for everything." Marian closed the front door. "The boys should be home any minute now, and I could sure use a cup of something." Then she gave a nervous laugh. "I'd say I could use a drink, but that's what got me into this whole mess to begin with."

Charlotte nodded, and knowing she could be jeopardizing her job to even suggest what was on her mind, she decided that she had to try, job or no job, for Marian's sake as well as the welfare of Marian's sons. "Marian, I know it's none of my business, but have you ever considered AA?"

Marian shrugged and began walking slowly toward the kitchen. "I used to go, but I quit. Now, though — after all that's happened — who knows, maybe now would be a good time to start up again."

In the kitchen, while Charlotte prepared the coffeemaker, she decided she might as well broach another touchy subject while she was at it.

Marian had seated herself at the kitchen table, and Charlotte turned to face her. "Ah — Marian, I was just wondering about something. I was just wondering if there's some way we can get around B.J. knowing that I blew the whistle on Sam. I don't want B.J. to think that I betrayed him — you know, about the cigars," she added, still uncomfortable about the secret she was keeping about B.J. being present on the night that Drew Bergeron was murdered.

Marian smiled. "Well, he won't hear it from me." She shook her head. "Poor B.J. No wonder he's been so moody lately. I had no idea that he'd kept some of Bill's things. That's how out of it I've been since Bill died."

Charlotte had to bite her tongue to keep from telling Marian that she'd been more out of it than she could dream when it came to B.J.

"But not anymore," Marian added firmly. "Life's too uncertain and too short. Bill loved our sons with all of his heart, but Bill's gone. And I owe it to him and the boys — and myself — to get on with my life and to take care of our boys."

"Yes," Charlotte murmured. "Yes, you do."

Charlotte and Marian had just taken their first sips of coffee when they heard the clatter of the boys on the back porch. Within seconds, like a whirlwind, Aaron and B.J. burst through the kitchen door.

"Did not!" Aaron yelled at his brother.

"You little brat!" B.J. yelled back. "You did too."

"Mom! B.J. said I —"

"Zip it!" Marian ordered.

"But Mom," Aaron whined.

Marian shook her finger at him. "I said zip it. Right now! I'm tired of this bickering and it's going to stop."

The astounded look on both boys' faces

was priceless, and Charlotte had to bite her lower lip to keep from grinning.

"There's going to be some changes around here," Marian told them in a stern, no-nonsense voice. "Some new rules, starting today, and the first rule is no more fighting. Now, both of you, show some manners and say hello to Ms. LaRue."

When Charlotte finally decided it was time to go home a few minutes later, Marian walked her to the van. "I just wanted to thank you again for all you've done today," she told Charlotte. "I don't know what would have happened if you hadn't been here."

Charlotte smiled. "No thanks needed. Besides, you're the one who called the police."

A puzzled frown shadowed Marian's face. "That's just it. I didn't — didn't call the police, that is."

Charlotte went stone still. "You didn't?"

Marian shook her head. "No."

It was Charlotte's turn to frown. "Then how — who —"

After a moment, Marian gestured toward the house next door. "Maybe one of the neighbors?" she suggested.

Charlotte sighed, still a bit confused.

"Maybe." She paused, then finally shrugged. "Oh, well, guess it doesn't really matter who called in the long run. The point is that *someone* called them and they came."

Later that evening, Charlotte had just loaded the dirty dishes from her supper into the dishwasher when she heard a car door slam out front. Within minutes, there was a knock at the door.

"I was just thinking about calling you," Charlotte told Judith when she opened the door. Judith came inside, and Charlotte closed the door. "Have you eaten supper yet, hon?"

Judith shook her head. "Not yet, Auntie. I just stopped by for a moment, though. I have a dinner date at seven."

Charlotte narrowed her eyes. "With Will?"

"No, Auntie, not with Will. That's over."

"Over as in you're not partners anymore?"

Judith rolled her eyes toward the ceiling. "Over as in we're not lovers anymore," she said bluntly. "And I've put in a request for a new partner."

Though it was difficult, Charlotte was able to maintain a neutral expression instead of grinning from ear to ear with relief.

"Actually, I'm meeting Billy Wilson," Judith told her.

This time Charlotte did grin. "I think that's just wonderful. He seems like such a nice young man."

"Yeah, right! That's not what you said a few months ago. As I recall, I think what you said was something like, 'Someone needs to teach him some manners.'"

"Humph, that was different," Charlotte retorted. "That was before I got to know him a little better." She paused. "You know, it just now occurred to me that Billy and one of my employees have the same last name. Wonder if they're related?"

Judith shrugged. "Could be distant cousins."

Charlotte nodded. "I'll have to ask Nadia. Anyway —" She dismissed the subject with a wave of her hand. "If I can't feed you, would you like something to drink? Some iced tea or coffee?"

"No, thanks, Auntie. I just came by to check on you and to let you know that we've arrested Sam Roberts."

"Arrested him?"

Judith nodded. "One thing led to another, and he ended up confessing to murdering Drew Bergeron. I have to tell you, though, that was the strangest interrogation I've ever conducted. It was almost as if he'd been waiting for us and was relieved when we finally showed up. In fact, even more strange, he seemed more concerned about Marian Hebert than his own arrest. He kept asking was she okay and were her boys okay. He even asked about Darla Shaw — asked if we'd caught her. And that was way before anyone even mentioned anything about her." Judith shook her head. "Like I said, though, I just dropped by to tell you he's been arrested and to make sure you're okay."

"Well, it's a relief that he's been arrested, and I'm just fine, hon. Now stop being such a worrywart, and get on out of here." Charlotte nudged her toward the door. "Go get something to eat and —" Charlotte gave her an exaggerated wink. "Tell that nice Billy Wilson hello for me."

Judith burst out laughing. "Okay — okay, I can take a hint."

As Charlotte stood at the door and watched her niece drive away a few minutes later, she couldn't stop thinking about what Judith had said in regard to Sam Roberts' concern for Marian and the boys. And what of Darla Shaw? How had he

even known that Darla Shaw was there . . .
unless . . .

Just as Charlotte closed the door, she
froze, her hand still on the doorknob. "Of
course," she murmured. The reason Sam
knew about Darla Shaw was because he'd
been there, on the porch. The movement
she'd seen through the window had been
Sam, not the boys. Could he also have
been the person who had called the police
as well? But why? If he'd been out for
revenge, then why would he want to help
Marian?

Charlotte locked her front door and
walked over to stare out the window into
the dark night. She would probably never
know for sure who had called the police,
but in spite of everything, she'd like to
think that Sam had been the one. She'd
like to think that there was some part of
him able to recognize that, like him,
Marian had also been an innocent victim.

Charlotte turned away from the window
and stepped over to Sweety Boy's cage.
"People sure do get themselves in a mess,
don't they, Boy?"

The little parakeet pranced back and
forth on his perch. "Crazy," he chirped.
"Crazy, crazy."

"Yeah, and birds too, huh, Boy? Even

little birds get themselves in a pickle some-times."

Judging by his looks and actions, the little bird had completely recovered from his mishap in the shower. Even so, Charlotte was still nervous and a bit gun-shy about letting him out of his cage again.

"So tell me. What do you think about Judith and Billy? Any possibilities there?"

For an answer, Sweety Boy squawked and fluffed his wings.

"Well, if you want my opinion," Charlotte told him, "going out with Billy Wilson sure beats the heck out of having an affair with a married man." She shook her head. "The very nerve of that — that Will Richeaux person. And him with a wife and a child."

Charlotte turned away from Sweety Boy's cage and walked over to the coffee table in front of the sofa. On the table was a small spray of silk flowers and the special candle that she intended placing on Hank Senior's tomb.

She smoothed a finger over one of the red roses in the spray. All Saints' Day was on Saturday, so on her way home from Marian's earlier, she'd stopped off at a flo-rist on Magazine Street.

"I should have bought candy too," she

murmured. Though there didn't seem to be as many trick-or-treaters as there used to be in her neighborhood, she figured it was better to be prepared, just in case. Besides, she was sure that Nadia and Daniel would bring Davy by. Charlotte smiled. She'd have to pick up an extra-special treat for the little boy.

Still staring at the flowers, she thought of Hank's offer to take her to the cemetery. Would he remember?

Chapter Twenty-six

Charlotte's doctor appointment was scheduled for ten o'clock on Thursday morning. With dread heavily weighing down every footstep, she walked up to the front desk to let the receptionist know she was there.

The waiting room was full, with few available empty chairs. Charlotte had just seated herself and picked up a three-month-old issue of *Good Housekeeping* magazine when, to her surprise, her name was called.

Even more surprising, a nurse led her back to a small, well-appointed office instead of an examination room.

"The doctor should be in momentarily," the nurse told her.

Charlotte barely had time to look around the office before the outer door opened, and the doctor walked in.

"Good morning."

Charlotte acknowledged his greeting with a nod and a tentative smile.

After seating himself behind the desk, he opened a folder and studied it for several minutes. Then he glanced up.

"Everything looks good, Ms. LaRue. Since you don't have a history of fainting and, according to the test results so far, you appear to be healthy for a woman your age, I really think your fainting spell was probably due more to the stress of the situation."

"Well, that's a relief," Charlotte muttered.

The doctor held up his hand. "But there is one more test I'd like to run."

"What kind of test, and for what?"

"It's a glucose tolerance test."

Charlotte's stomach tightened. "Isn't that a test for diabetes?"

The doctor nodded. "Make an appointment to come in as soon as you can." He stood. "The nurse will give you instructions."

Diabetes. Charlotte shuddered. "Ah — excuse me, but is that really necessary?"

He shrugged. "Mostly precautionary, but the sooner you take the test, the sooner we can rule out the possibility of you having diabetes."

The minute the doctor disappeared through the doorway, Charlotte pulled out her cell phone and placed a call to Marian Hebert. He'd said "as soon as you can," and Charlotte figured she might as well get it over with and be done with it.

Marian's answering machine picked up the call.

"Marian, this is Charlotte. Something's come up, and I'll either need to reschedule to come in on Saturday instead of tomorrow or I can send someone else out tomorrow. Just give me a call and let me know which you'd prefer."

Charlotte disconnected the call and stood just as the nurse came in. She handed Charlotte a paper. "These are your instructions, Ms. LaRue, and an explanation of the procedure. You will need to fast — nothing to eat or drink after midnight on the night before you come in for the test."

Charlotte nodded that she understood, and slipping the paper and her cell phone back inside her purse, she followed the nurse out of the office.

Once back out into the front office, she headed straight for the receptionist's desk and scheduled an appointment for the next day.

It was almost noon by the time Charlotte finished running her errands and pulled into her driveway. One of her errands had been to purchase candy for Friday night. Besides a couple of bags of assorted candy, she'd bought an especially huge lollipop shaped like a pumpkin as a special treat for Davy. While picking out the candy, she'd noticed that all of the Halloween decorations had been marked down to half price. Not since Hank was a boy had she bothered decorating her porch for Halloween, so with thoughts of Davy, on a whim, she'd bought a ceramic pumpkin, a fake spider's web, and other various creepy items to put out.

The first thing she did once she was inside was check her answering machine. There were two messages. Charlotte tapped the play button.

"Mom, about Saturday. It looks like the best time for me to take you to the cemetery is around ten. Let me know if that's okay with you. Love you."

The machine beeped and the second message played.

"Charlotte, this is Marian, returning your call. Don't worry about coming in tomorrow, and I'd just as soon you wouldn't send anyone else. Everything here is still in pretty good shape from Wednesday's cleaning. And it's about time those boys of mine learned how to do a few chores anyway. Just make sure you come on Monday, okay?" There was a pause, then, "Another thing, Charlotte. I went to an AA meeting last night. Just thought you might want to know. Oh, and one more thing. My attorney doesn't seem to think I'll have any legal problems because of everything that happened, but we'll talk more later. Bye now."

And the truth shall make you free. Charlotte smiled as she headed for the kitchen. It was a start. A good, positive start. Maybe now Marian could finally get on with her life and be the kind of mother her boys so desperately needed her to be.

After a quick lunch, Charlotte set about decorating the porch. The few things she'd bought didn't take long to put out. Once she'd finished, she walked to the curb, turned, and with her hands on her hips, she stared back at the porch with a critical eye. Satisfied, she was walking back to the steps when Louis pulled into the driveway and parked.

Charlotte frowned. "Hi there, Louis. What are you doing home this time of day?"

Louis shrugged as he approached the porch. "I had some time coming, and I have some thinking to do."

417

Charlotte's frown deepened. "Sounds serious."

"Yeah, I'd say it was pretty serious." He seated himself on the top step and motioned for Charlotte to sit beside him. Once she was seated, for several moments he simply stared out into the street.

Finally, he cleared his throat, and still staring out into the street, he said, "I spent a good part of this morning interrogating Sam Roberts." He shook his head. "Questioning him was a really strange experience. He cooperated fully, even seemed to be relieved that he'd been found out."

Recalling that Judith had said the same thing, Charlotte nodded when Louis shifted his gaze to stare at her.

"He also admitted that he killed Bill Hebert," Louis told her.

"I suspected as much."

Louis shrugged. "Even if he hadn't confessed, we could have still tied him to Drew Bergeron's murder. Just this morning we finished tracing the Mardi Gras mask back to him. With DNA testing, we can also link him to the cigar found at the crime scene."

Charlotte tilted her head. "So what's still bothering you about it?"

Louis shoved his fingers through his hair

and heaved a heavy sigh. "He had it all — reputation, a family, a position in the community — and he lost it. Lost everything. That man has spent most of his life either paying for a crime he didn't commit or searching for a way to clear himself. According to what he said, once he got out of prison, he spent almost every penny he earned on private detectives to find out the truth about what really happened that night.

"He started out simply trying to clear his name because he didn't want his children to think their father was a killer. But somewhere along the way, he snapped, and the lines got crossed. Almost like a self-fulfilling prophecy, he became the very thing he'd been accused of — a killer. Now he has nothing but more prison and probably a death sentence to look forward to." Louis paused, then muttered, "Such a waste of a life — of three lives if you count Drew Bergeron and Bill Hebert."

Along with Marian Hebert, Charlotte silently added as she narrowed her eyes shrewdly. It was obvious that Sam's fate wasn't the only thing on Louis' mind. Something was still bothering him. "You do think Sam's guilty, don't you?"

"Oh, yeah. He's guilty all right. Tell you

one thing, though, the whole thing really made me stop and think, made me realize that life's too short to waste. When you're young, you think you have all the time in the world to do whatever. But if you're lucky enough to grow older, you begin to realize just how little time you really have."

He cleared his throat, and when he leveled a look at Charlotte that was tight with strain, she held her breath, wondering what was really on his mind.

"When Stephen — that's my son — was about twelve, my wife left us," he finally said. "She just packed a bag and walked out one day. Said she couldn't take it anymore, what with the long hours I was keeping and all the trouble Steve kept getting into. The next thing I knew I was being served divorce papers."

Charlotte inwardly winced. Louis' admission explained a lot, and though she didn't agree with his chauvinistic attitude toward women in general, at least she understood it better.

"I tried my best to raise Steve by myself after that," he continued, "but guess I didn't do such a bang-up job. After she left us, he went from bad to worse and was always in some kind of trouble. For the most part, since I was a cop, I was able to bail him out each time. But when he was seventeen, he and the bunch of no-good hoodlums he hung around with got all drugged up one night while I was working and robbed a liquor store. The owner of the store was killed, and though Steve swore that he didn't pull the trigger . . ." Louis' voice trailed away.

After a moment, he continued. "That was one time I couldn't bail him out. He and his buddies were tried as adults and convicted of manslaughter. He served twenty years in Angola." Louis shrugged. "He's been out of prison now for about seven years. According to what I hear, he's doing okay for himself. It was while he was in prison that he began painting, and after he got out, he married a woman who owned the art gallery that had been displaying his paintings. And they had a little girl. He now makes a living down in the Quarter with his paintings.

"That painting I have — the one of the young girl. She's my granddaughter," he confessed. "He sent it to me along with the others."

"How old is your granddaughter?"

Louis shrugged. "I guess about six."

"And you haven't seen or spoken to your son since he got out?"

With a look of pure abject misery on his face, Louis slowly shook his head. "It's worse than that. I — I was so angry with him when he got mixed up in that killing, so humiliated — being a cop and all — that I disowned him — cut off all relationship with him. Then, the longer it went, the harder it became to swallow my pride. I haven't seen or spoken to him since he was sent to prison twenty-seven years ago."

"Oh, Louis." Charlotte was horrified. She couldn't begin to imagine such a thing, couldn't imagine having no contact with her son for that long a time.

Judge not, lest ye be judged.

The words from the Bible verse she'd once memorized popped into her head and tugged at her conscience. While it was true that she couldn't imagine such an estrangement, to be fair, she'd never had to deal with a son convicted of murder either, she reminded herself.

"All my fault," he continued. "All those years wasted, and even if I try to fix it now, he probably doesn't want to have anything to do with me. I'm just afraid it's too late."

Charlotte reached out and squeezed his arm in a gesture of sympathy. "Maybe not. Didn't you say that your son *sent* those paintings to you?"

"Yeah, about a month ago."

"Then stop being so dense, for Pete's sake. Can't you see? That's his way of reaching out to you, of trying to make amends."

"Maybe," he said with a shrug.

"So what's the problem?"

Louis' Adam's apple bobbed as he swallowed hard. "Would — would you go with me — I mean, if he'll agree to seeing me, would you go along?"

"Oh, Louis, I don't know. It's not really my place."

"Well, it is if I say it is," he retorted indignantly.

On Saturday, All Saints' Day turned out to be a warm seventy degrees with plenty of sunshine. With Hank beside her and her arms full of the flowers she'd purchased, Charlotte and her son entered Lafayette Cemetery Number One through the Washington Street entrance.

Cemeteries in New Orleans were unique. Elaborate above-ground tombs and mini-mausoleums had been erected out of necessity due to the high water table of the city.

Charlotte paused by the bronze plaque near the entrance. "I'm amazed each time

I come here," she told Hank. "It's hard to believe this place has been in existence since 1833."

Hank simply smiled at her and waited until she was ready to walk on.

Families were already crowded around the freshly whitewashed tombs that were adorned with beautiful sprays of flowers. Though respectful, an almost festive reunion-type atmosphere prevailed among the many visitors.

Hank's father's tomb was located not far from the entrance, down the second pathway. Charlotte knelt beside it and reverently placed the spray of flowers at the front of the tomb.

"I wish I could have known him," Hank told her as he stared at the tomb. When he added, "Known all of them," Charlotte realized he was referring to his father's family as well. As was customary, Hank had been buried in the same tomb as his parents and grandparents.

Charlotte stood, then reached out and squeezed her son's hand. "Me too, hon. Me too."

"Tell me about him again, Mom — about all of them — like you used to when I was a little boy."

It had been many many years since her

son had asked about his father, and Charlotte's throat was thick with emotion as she began to talk. "Your father was a lot like you — in looks and personality. He was about your height and build, with the same sandy-colored hair and sky-blue eyes." She swallowed hard. "Each time I look at you, I see him, especially around the eyes.

"He was a kind man," she continued, "a man who truly cared about people." She paused for a moment, then said, "I think I must have told you that he had also wanted to be a doctor. That's the reason he went ahead and joined the Army, even before the government began drafting for Vietnam. You see, after his parents' deaths — your grandparents' — it took most of their assets to settle their debts. Unfortunately for your father, your grandfather didn't believe in life insurance either, so, like you, he had to make his own way in the world."

"Not totally like me," Hank pointed out. "I had you helping me every step of the way."

Charlotte smiled. "Yes, you did. Me, student loans, and that job you had as a bouncer for a while. But anyway, back when your father was in the Army, once soldiers had finished their enlistment requirements, they could go to college and the government would help pay for it. He had it all planned. He —"

"Charlotte! Charlotte LaRue!"

Recognizing Bitsy Duhe's squeaky voice, Charlotte turned to see the older lady headed straight for them.

Hank leaned down and whispered, "Isn't that Mrs. Duhe, one of your clients?"

Charlotte had to smile, but she nodded. "Yep, that's her — Ms. Bitsy Duhe, in all her glory." Charlotte was truly relieved to see that the old lady was up and about again. And what a sight to behold she was with her flowery dress billowing around her and her hat that looked like an umbrella.

"It *is* an umbrella," Charlotte murmured with a giggle.

"Did you say something?" Hank asked with a frown.

Charlotte motioned toward Bitsy. "Her hat. Miss Bitsy's hat is a miniumbrella on a headband."

Epilogue

On days like Thanksgiving, Charlotte wished for a bigger house. This particular year she was hosting the celebration for family and friends, and her small half of the double was bursting with people. She and Madeline had been cooking and baking for days, and food covered every inch of available counter space in the kitchen along with several card tables that had been temporarily set up for the occasion. She could barely move without bumping into someone, since everyone seemed bent on congregating in the kitchen. But then, that was what Thanksgiving was for, wasn't it?

As Charlotte looked around, trying to count heads, she sighed. Why had she invited everyone and his brother this year? *Because you're a sucker for happy endings.* Not only was her family there, but Louis' son and family were joining them too.

Someone tapped her on the shoulder, and as if just thinking about him had conjured him up, Charlotte glanced back to see Louis right behind her.

"You feeling okay today?" he asked.

Counting to ten, Charlotte prayed for patience before she answered. Ever since Louis had heard the results of the glucose tolerance test she'd taken, he'd turned into a regular worrywart and a nag . . . along with her son and the rest of her family.

"I'm feeling just fine," she finally said. "Remember? I'm just a borderline diabetic. And as long as I watch what I eat and take that little pill every day, I should continue to be just fine." She forced a polite smile. "But thank you for your concern."

"It's me who should be thanking you. I really do appreciate you inviting my son and his family over today, so just in case I haven't done so already, thanks."

Charlotte shook her head. "You did thank me, Louis, about ten times and counting."

Louis grinned. "Well, let's make it eleven, then. Thanks. Thanks a bunch."

"That's twelve," she retorted.

"Can't be too many. I would have never got up the courage to make contact with him if it hadn't been for you."

"Aunt Charley?"

At the sound of her niece's voice, Charlotte turned toward the doorway.

Louis waved his hand. "She's over here, Judith," he called out. When Judith came closer, he teasingly told Charlotte, "Between you and me, I think things are getting serious with her and Billy. He —"

Judith playfully hit him on the arm with her fist. "Talking about me behind my back again, Lou?"

"Oops! Caught red-handed," he replied with a wink at Charlotte. To Judith he said, "I think that's my cue to mosey out into the backyard and rescue your brother. Last time I checked, my granddaughter and that little kid, Davy, were trying to see which one could wear out Daniel first with the airplane rides."

Leaving Charlotte and Judith laughing, Louis slipped out the back door. Charlotte turned to Judith. "Was there something you needed, hon?"

"No — not really, but I did want to tell you the latest on Sam — I mean Arthur Samuel."

"Latest?"

Judith nodded. "Why don't we go into the hall or the bedroom? I'd just as soon not broadcast it to everyone." With a jerk of her head, she indicated the people surrounding them.

"You lead the way and I'll follow,"

Charlotte told her.

Once they had maneuvered their way through the crowded kitchen and closed the door to the bedroom, both women sighed dramatically, then laughed.

"I can't believe how many people we have this year," Judith commented. "And all that food is unreal."

"The more the merrier?" Charlotte quipped, tongue in cheek.

"Humph! If you say so, Auntie. And don't look at me like that. Contrary to what you think, I am not antisocial. I just like my own space." She waved a dismissing hand. "What I wanted to tell you though was that it looks like Sam — Arthur — will never make it to trial."

Charlotte was so stunned, it took a moment for her to digest Judith's words. "Why on earth not?" she finally asked.

"He's got cancer of the liver and the prognosis isn't good at all. According to the doctor who was called in, even if he should make it to trial, he'll never live long enough to see the inside of a prison."

For a moment, Charlotte was thoughtfully silent. "Justice," she finally whispered.

"What was that, Auntie?"

Charlotte shook her head. "I was just

thinking out loud how ironic it is that Sam — Arthur, that is — was the one who was seeking justice and now it's come full circle. And speaking of justice, what's happened to Darla Shaw?"

Judith sighed. "Well, she's in a lot of trouble — blackmail, attempted armed robbery — take your pick. But since she doesn't have any priors, and with a decent attorney, who knows?"

"And B.J.?"

"What about B.J.?" Judith smiled slyly and winked at her aunt.

"Nothing," Charlotte answered with an understanding grin. "Why, nothing at all. But enough of all of that. For today I don't want to think about Sam or Darla or Drew Bergeron or the Heberts. For today, I just want to enjoy my friends and family." She hesitated for a moment. Then, with a teasing grin, she asked, "So how's that nice Billy Wilson these days?"

Judith rolled her eyes toward the ceiling. "You can ask him yourself in a little while, since I took the liberty of inviting him over for dinner. Although now," she quickly added, "I'm having second thoughts. Billy grew up an only child from a very small family. Poor man won't know what to think about this bunch."

Charlotte cleared her throat. "Er — ah, rumor has it that things are, shall we say, getting serious between you two."

Judith rolled her eyes toward the ceiling. "Well, don't believe everything you hear, Auntie, especially if it comes from Lou."

It was about an hour later when Charlotte asked Hank to gather everyone in the kitchen.

"Can I have everyone's attention, please?" he called out. "Attention, please!" When, after a few moments, the talking and laughter died down, he said, "My mother wants to thank you all for coming and sharing in this day of Thanksgiving with her. We'll have the blessing, then everyone can dig in."

As prearranged, Hank said the blessing, and while Charlotte listened to her son's deep, soothing voice give thanks for their family, their friends, and being able to live in a free country, in spite of her resolve concerning Arthur Samuel, her thoughts drifted back to what Louis had once said about him and to what Judith had just told her.

Arthur Samuel had once had everything important in life: a family, a career, his health, and respectability. Now he had nothing. Such a needless tragedy, she thought sadly. And all because somewhere, somehow, he'd lost his way. In the beginning, he'd been a victim, but in the end, seeking revenge had cost him everything. Now he would die all alone in prison, without the benefits of the love of friends or family or respectability.

Sudden shame washed through Charlotte. Considering Arthur Samuel's fate, her own problems seemed petty by comparison, and turning sixty was just a small grain of sand on the seashore of life.

Charlotte cringed just thinking about how selfish she'd been over the past month, moaning and groaning and sitting on her pity pot about something so insignificant as another birthday, when she should have been down on her knees, giving thanks. Yes, she had a health problem, but at least she could continue to live a normal life. But even more, she had a wonderful family who loved and supported her, and friends who respected her.

". . . and thank you, Lord, for this food we're about to receive, and we ask your blessings upon it. In Jesus' name we pray. Amen."

Adding her own personal prayer for forgiveness and thanks, Charlotte whispered an affirming "Amen."

A Cleaning Tip from Charlotte

To prevent grimy buildup and to clean stained grout in a ceramic tile floor, add a small amount of chlorine bleach to warm soapy water each time you mop. Be sure and rinse well afterwards. A word of caution: never mix bleach with products that contain ammonia.

About the Author

Barbara Colley is an award-winning author whose books have been published in sixteen foreign languages. A native of Louisiana, she lives with her family in a suburb of New Orleans. Besides writing and sharing her stories, she loves strolling through the historic New Orleans French Quarter and Garden District, which inspired the setting for her Charlotte LaRue mystery series. Readers can write to Barbara at P.O. Box 290, Boutte, LA 70039 or visit her web site at http://www.eclectics.com/barbaracolley-annelogan.

The employees of Thorndike Press hope you have enjoyed this Large Print book. All our Thorndike and Wheeler Large Print titles are designed for easy reading, and all our books are made to last. Other Thorndike Press Large Print books are available at your library, through selected bookstores, or directly from us.

For information about titles, please call:

(800) 223-1244

or visit our Web site at:

www.gale.com/thorndike
www.gale.com/wheeler

To share your comments, please write:

Publisher
Thorndike Press
295 Kennedy Memorial Drive
Waterville, ME 04901